PRIMAL ICE

PARANORMAL FANTASY

ANN GIMPEL

CONTENTS

PRIMAL ICE

ICE DRAGON SERIES, BOOK THREE

Paranormal Fantasy

By
Ann Gimpel

Tumble off reality's edge into myth, magic, ice, and dragons

Copyright Page

Edited by: Kate Richards

ISBN: 978-1-948871-53-2 I

BOOK DESCRIPTION, PRIMAL ICE

Renegade dragons. A dying Earth. The magic powering all worlds is fading, and no one knows why.

As the life he's known for millennia hovers on the brink of ruin, the dragon prince, Konstantin, gathers allies. He would have liked to be better prepared for all-out war, but time grows short. Waiting is no longer an option. Working with his twin sister, a seer, he unearths a shocking sequence of prophecies. Visions that shake the foundations of everything he believed was true.

Newly created dragon shifters, Johan and Erin, are on a supernatural fast-track. No longer human, they have yet to fully embrace their magical sides. Knowledge can only be gained so fast, but if they don't ditch their reservations, they'll be swallowed by darkness.

Seduced by a madman, driven by greed, wicked creatures have become bold. Shifters, Sidhe, and land-linked magic are determined to crush the threat eager to steal their power, but even their combined forces might not be enough to bail them out.

****Primal Ice is book three of the Ice Dragon trilogy. For the very best reading experience, please start at the beginning with Feral Ice and Cursed Ice.****

BOOKS IN THE ICE DRAGON SERIES

Feral Ice, Book One

Cursed Ice, Book Two

Primal Ice, Book Three

AUTHOR'S NOTE

Ice Dragon is a trilogy, so a long tale split into three books that need to be read in order. I was fascinated by Antarctica long before I visited there, and my two trips were so incredible, I still stumble over words to describe the awe I felt at the vista of ice-crusted ocean, hardy mosses and lichens, and the proliferation of wildlife. Tame critters who are as likely to peck at you or sit on your lap as they are to put on an amazing show—as if you weren't even there.

A story about ice dragons has been percolating for a few years now. It was time to breathe life into it.

DRAGON TIME

Konstantin's dragon here, folks. We're two-thirds of the way through what is, essentially, my story. Yet none of you know me at all. I'm about to correct that. Not to be outdone, Katya's dragon wants a voice as well.

"What about us?" Johan and Erin's dragons bugled from where they'd just broken through into the dragons' borderworld.

The "us" took on echoes as dragons appeared from every quadrant and moved closer. Worse than a pack of hyenas scenting a feast, everyone wanted a piece of the action, but it was impossible.

For a whole lot of very good reasons.

"Are any of you part of the serpent battle?" I demanded, blowing fire. I swear, these insurrections can spiral out of hand if you don't get a jump on them right away. Dragons are born warriors, though, so the possibility of battle has more allure than a fresh, bloody carcass.

"We could be part of it." A beefy dark-red male lumbered closer, his golden eyes spinning like pinwheels.

"Seems to me, you'd welcome more help," a white dragon bugled. White is rare among our kind. This particular female is only the third white dragon I've seen during my rather lengthy life.

I stood taller and asked her, "How do you envision that working?"

She shrugged amid the rattling of scales. "We show up and fight."

If I'd been in Konstantin's body, I'd have dipped my head into my hands. All we needed were a bunch of mateless dragons steeped in bloodlust. Lacking a human bondmate's cooler head, they'd become impossible to control in short order.

Katya's dragon nudged me. *"Maybe it's not such a bad idea as all that,"* she hissed in shielded mind speech.

I chose to ignore her. Turns out it was a mistake because she fanned her golden wings and clacked her double rows of teeth together to get everyone's attention. "The thing about battles," she said, punctuating her words with ash and smoke, "is there are always leaders. When Y Ddraigh Goch gathers his minions for an undertaking, they do as he orders them."

"Aye, but he's a god," a blue dragon pointed out dryly. "The rest of us have equal standing."

Cries of, "We are dragonkind. We answer to no one," filled the air.

I wondered if our god, Y Ddraigh Goch, was listening. If not, he ought to be. He'd swoop down and disabuse this crowd of their notions of independence damned fast.

I bumped Katya's dragon to make certain she heeded my words. "Good place to stop," I muttered, not bothering with telepathy.

"But I never even got to the part about asking them if they could see their way clear to following you." She turned her whirling gaze my way but not for long.

Facing the growing crowd of dragons again, she said, "This is precisely why those of you who are not bonded with humans cannot help us fight the serpents. Battles are choreographed, planned ahead of time. Yet they oftentimes slew sideways. Whoever commands the action must make decisions that impact everyone. You would be expected—nay, required—to do precisely as you were ordered."

Grumbling and fire filled the air, along with more, "We answer to no ones."

I stared at the assemblage, willing them to disperse. I knew better than to try for an out-and-out command. Me telling them to find something else to do would make things worse. They'd never leave then.

Done glaring at my brethren, I scanned rock-studded sand. Our borderworld is a barren place, marked by a string of active volcanoes. At any given time, one or more are erupting. They keep the place hot and ashy, but it's our home, and we love it. Several subterranean caverns house underground springs. Water makes it possible for us to raise game animals, but most of us prefer to travel to neighboring worlds where there's always been exceptional hunting.

Magical creatures enjoy eating, but we can go for long periods without food. Unless we select a human to bond with. Dragon shifters require a lot of calories, so it gives us an excuse to hunt.

Dragon ire was increasing. The smoke eddying about me thickened. I felt like thumping Katya's dragon soundly. She'd made it appear the topic of the upcoming war was up for discussion. It wasn't.

"Silence!" I bellowed and followed the single word with judiciously applied shots of magic into the center of the crowd.

Once the dragons had quieted some, I said, "I appreciate your warriors' hearts, but shy of talking Y Ddraigh Goch into leading a troop of dragons against the serpents, you'd be more trouble than help. Each dragon would have its own plan, and many of them would run counter to the common good."

"We'd all be there killing serpents," the red explained. "How could that not shorten the—"

"How would we kill them? They're immortal. You know, like us," another dragon, this one green, spoke over him.

Eyes whirled faster. Scales rattled. Bugles and trumpets nearly deafened me. The crux of the problem with the serpent war had hit home. We couldn't kill them. Worse, a few renegade dragons had jumped ship and now worked alongside the serpents.

It made them ridiculously strong since they could blend serpent power with our own brand of magic. From what we'd seen so far, it also allowed them to hide themselves behind powerful illusion.

"Sorry I got them stirred up," Katya's dragon mumbled.

I didn't answer. Dragons are hotheaded by nature. Nothing I could say would alter that tendency to shoot from the hip and think about it later. As quickly as they'd formed a crowd, the dragons drifted away.

Soon only the four of us remained.

Good.

Perhaps we can get through introductions—which should have happened far earlier in this tale. The only reason I have a spot of time on my hands is because Konstantin is in wait mode. The shifters who volunteered to help quell the serpents are maximizing their magic, so when we launch our first strike it gives our enemy something to think about.

I chafed at any delays at all. They offered the serpents time to shore up their own magic, but I could see Kon's side of things too. If we lost too badly during the initial skirmish, it would be all that much harder to recapture lost ground. Beyond that, none of us has any true idea how many dragons are part of the serpents' cadre.

Konstantin and I made certain Y Ddraigh Goch knew we harbored turncoats in our midst. While we can't kill serpents or dragons, our god is capable of doing away with them. If we only had serpents to deal with—and not our own kind—we might have a chance. I'm off on a bit of a tangent here, but if I were running the show, I'd leave the serpents to do whatever with Earth. Once they'd killed off everyone, we could appeal to other gods—the ones who manage all universes—to ensure Earth met the same fate as Mu.

Blown up, and then sucked into magnetic holes deep in space.

But it's not my call. Konstantin rarely explains himself to me. He doesn't have to because I can read his mind. Not that he harbors any fondness for Earth, but Erin, the dragon shifter he's almost, almost mated to, used to be human. Earth is her home, and she would be sad to leave it.

I believe he's taking on the serpents to protect Erin's home, but that might only be part of it. He's never been one to walk away from a challenge, or to allow evil free rein. It's one of the reasons I bonded with him before he was born. I saw his strength, his potential. And I knew he would be a solid bondmate for me.

Sometimes, a mateless dragon will ask why I shackled myself to a human. There are downsides, but my human half exerts a modulating effect. My life is far richer for sharing it with Konstantin. I had no idea he would grow to be the dragons' princeling, but even if that hadn't happened, I would still be satisfied with my choice.

Those days—when dragons eagerly chose human bondmates—are long behind us. Not many new dragon shifters are born anymore. I'm not certain why that is, but I bet it has something to do with men no longer believing in magic. Science has displaced it, and not to anyone's betterment.

When you stop believing in the impossible, your world grows far smaller, duller, less exciting. People's days are filled with drudgery rather than possibilities. I have no clue why they settle for so little, but that's another story, and truly a digression. Not at all what I planned for my special time with you, our readers.

"I want to talk about Katya," her dragon spoke up.

"Yes, and I can tell them about Erin," the red dragon offered. "Not that I know her well, but they should understand why I agreed to bond with her."

"Same for Johan." The green dragon bobbed his head.

"Lead out," I invited. Saving Konstantin for last was a good idea. He was the closest thing dragon shifters had to royalty, mostly because of his link to the land, but more about that neat piece of magic later.

Katya's golden dragon flared her wings. Tongues of flame shot from her nostrils. "Katya is unique among women," the dragon began. "Of course, I may be prejudiced because she is mine, but I fell in love with her when she was but a seedling in her mother's womb. A space she and Konstantin shared, although not without the occasional squabble.

"I used to worry we would never have a mate of our own, but we do now." Smoke curled from her nostrils and open mouth. "My only two complaints were no mate and our long tenure on Earth. From what I've seen, it's not a good place for dragons or anything magical. Men are steeped in phony science. Phony because they dredge up arguments to line their pockets with worthless money. No one cares about learning anything.

"I left Katya for a while because I couldn't pry her away from Earth. Luckily, we got past that. She has no idea why I returned. The bare truth is Konstantin's dragon rounded me up. We exchanged a few harsh words, but he was right that my place was with Katya."

She turned toward the green dragon, newly bonded to Johan. "Your turn. As our new mate, your tale should dovetail with mine."

The green stood taller. His gaze slid across our small group. "I never thought to bond with anyone, but one day our god showed up. He didn't force me by any means. Merely told me he thought I would make a good bondmate for a worthy human."

The dragon shook his head until his scales rattled. "I tell you, if I'd had any idea how horrible Johan's first shift would be—how little he knew—I'd not have been so quick to agree. Katya showed up in the nick of time. Without her and her dragon, Johan would have died. And left me feeling like a miserable failure. I admit, I was angry with him even after he finessed that first shift.

"It made no sense, and it was unconscionable of me to blame him for being what he was—human. It took us a while to find common ground after that little incident." He puffed smoke and ash. "I readily acknowledge I am young for a dragon, but it doesn't excuse my behavior. After my faux pas with Johan, I made an unforgivable error—defied a direct command from Konstantin—and nearly ended both myself and Johan."

"Humility is the beginning of wisdom," I muttered, wincing as I remembered that incident. We'd nearly lost Johan. It had taken all Konstantin's skill to bring him back.

Johan's dragon blatted laughter, laced with smoke. "Humility and dragon don't belong in the same bunch of words."

I chuckled and then laughed. "Right you are." I clapped

him on the back and looked at the red dragon bonded with Erin.

"One more thing." Johan's dragon aimed his next words at Katya's dragon. "I am very much anticipating our mating flight."

She puffed steam until it billowed around both her and Johan's green. He added more to the mix. Before they decided on their own mating flight, absent their human counterparts, I pushed my body between them, murmuring, "I'm certain it will happen soon."

"Not until we have a better handle on the serpent problem," Katya's dragon said resolutely.

"That could take a while." Johan's dragon sounded resigned, and not especially pleased about his mate's position.

I understood the unhappy part. While Erin was almost promised to us, she and Konstantin had yet to make love in either form. Until that happened, she could still change her mind. "Your turn." I nodded toward Erin's dragon. I longed to tell her how beautiful she was, but perhaps she'd be as skittish as her bondmate.

She tilted her head. "I'm not certain what I can add. Erin had just as hard a time with her first shift as Johan. I feared she wouldn't survive, yet I wouldn't have blamed myself."

"Why not?" I was curious after what Johan's dragon had disclosed.

"Y Ddraigh Goch was there. I assumed if the human woman died, it was his will."

I recalled the scene on the borderworld all too well. Konstantin's desolation and his certainty it would be his fault if Erin perished. Yet she'd figured things out, and I'd been relieved and grateful—two very undragonlike emotions. Kon would have ripped the world apart if Erin died, and I'd have been there every step of the way trying to mitigate his grief and guilt.

Getting back on an even keel would have taken centuries. Our opportunity to take on the serpents would have gone by the wayside.

"Anyway," the red dragon went on, "I like Erin Ryan. She has pluck, grit, and a spark that shines from within. No one takes advantage of her, not without her dressing them down. She and I are well mated." Lashes brushed her scaled cheeks. "It is my hope one day you and I will be mates as well," she told me.

Surprise ratcheted through me. I hadn't expected her to acknowledge the almost-complete mating ritual. I bowed before her and took care to puff steam. "Such is my hope as well." I sounded horribly formal, but tucked away where no one could see it, my cock swelled and curved against my scaled belly.

To divert my attention away from jumping skyward and dragging Erin's dragon with me—a forbidden act since our humans had yet to formalize their troth—I let a purifying blast of fire escape my jaws. Unbonded dragons could have all the sex they wished, but once we joined our lives with a dragon shifter, that aspect of our free will dissolved.

"I would tell you of my bondmate, Konstantin," I began. "His link to the land is poorly understood, so I will start there. All worlds hold untold power within their core. Many of them began as flaming balls of heat that turned to primal ice as they cooled. Over eons the ice ceded to a rich diversity of living creatures. From time to time, ice returned. It is a world's way of cleansing itself of taint."

I blew out more fire. "Konstantin can merge his mind with the land's deep knowledge. Watching him work his land-linked magic is fascinating—and humbling. He has infinite patience. Many a time, we have sat for months waiting for a stubborn world to notice us. Mu was like that. It did not reveal its secrets easily, nor did it trust Kon's intent. Probably because he did not truly believe he possessed land-linked power."

"He doubted himself," Katya's dragon concurred. "It was us—me and my bondmate—who convinced him to keep trying."

I scowled, but she spoke true. Dragons could lie, but it wasn't easy. "A needed boost," I murmured. "And one we are forever grateful for."

"Pfft." Katya's dragon puffed smoke and ash and fire. "Dragons are rarely grateful. It's not part of who we are."

I kept my mouth shut. It might not be part of who we claimed to be, or the image we projected, but I'd experienced my share of gratitude. Like when Erin hadn't died on the borderworld where she met her dragon.

"Konstantin should be establishing a link with Earth," I went on. "By the time we return, it may well be intact. It is one element that could work in our favor—"

"We need you back here now!" Kon's voice blasted into my mind.

The other dragons' heads snapped up. Clearly, they'd heard the summons too.

"Did we accomplish enough?" Katya's dragon asked me.

"I believe so," I replied and shaped magic to return us to the grotto deep beneath the ice sheet covering the southern end of Earth. As I worked, I thought about humans. And dragons. We're good for one another. Dragons encourage their humans to reach for the stars. Humans are good for selecting which stars are most likely to yield fruit.

On that whimsical note, I shall cede my centerstage spot to Konstantin. If I can finagle my way back to talk with you again, I shall. Dragons do like to have the last word. And now, I have battles to plan, enemies to slay, and a world to conquer.

Draping the edges of my spell around the other dragons, I headed all of us toward our bondmates. I can't speak for my companions but merging with Konstantin fills me with joy. Every single time. No matter how bad a mood he's in or how out of sorts. I love him. He is mine, and I am his.

It's the miracle of the shifter mate bond.

KONSTANTIN

"Stop protecting me!" Erin Ryan screeched. Luxuriant blonde hair fluffed around her tall, thin frame, and her blue eyes with their thick golden rims, bled fury. Dragon shifter eyes were usually pure gold, but hers had retained some blue since her transition hadn't occurred until she was well into her adult years.

"What would you have me do?" Konstantin took a step back from where he'd indeed been sheltering Erin from blasts of magic. They were in a workshop dedicated to honing fighting skills. Built by a dragon who'd long since departed, it held holographic simulacrums of various battle scenarios. A cunning magical vortex fired the holograph's light field.

Erin shot an annoyed glance his way. "Let me figure this out on my own. How else will I learn? When I was a surgical resident, I made mistakes. Lots of them. Luckily, the human body is quite resilient. It's possible a few people died sooner than they would have anyway, but those patients taught me a lot." Breath steamed through her clenched teeth. Her dragon must still be gone—along with his and the others. If it were present, she'd have showered him with smoke and ash.

"As you wish." He should take a few more steps away, but his feet weren't in a cooperative mood.

"How about if we move outside?" Katya, his twin sister, suggested. "We can leave Erin and Johan here to work on shaping magic into strong defensive maneuvers." Katya's copper hair was caught up into two thick braids that fell down her back to waist level. Like him, she had the golden eyes with deep green centers typical of dragon shifters while in their human bodies.

Protectiveness surged. He was not about to leave Erin, his almost-mate, to fend for herself, but then he rethought things. He was acting as if he didn't have any faith in her, which wasn't true.

Well, maybe it was a little bit true. He had plenty of faith in her as a human and a healer, her previous vocation. But magic and being a dragon shifter were brand new. It was hard to watch her make mistakes when he could shield her from them.

"She'll do better if you're not breathing down her back," Katya said in their private mind speech. Hooking a hand beneath his arm, his twin smiled brightly at Johan, her brand-new mate, and Erin. "We'll be outside by the lake."

Konstantin cleared his throat. He'd been out maneuvered, but he'd be damned if he'd slink away. "I'll round up the other shifters, and we'll determine preliminary assignments."

Johan cut the flow of magic he'd been coaxing into submission and ran lightly to Katya, giving her a hug. "So long as those assignments ensure we fight side by side, I will not contest them."

Konstantin bit back a spate of harsh words. He was the commander of this endeavor. Not Johan. They had enough trouble facing them; he did not need to deal with shifters who complained about how their skills had been delegated.

Katya hugged her mate back before letting go. "You can express opinions," she reminded him.

He made a sour face. "Damn. I am doing it again." He trotted to Konstantin and extended a hand. "Sorry, man."

"It's fine." It wasn't, not really, but his tone said more than the words themselves. He shelved the lecture about hierarchies and allegiance and respect and teleported one floor up to where the great room and library spread around him.

Katya shimmered into being next to him. "He means well," she murmured.

"I can't have him second-guessing me in the middle of a battle."

"He'll be too busy then." She loped into the library and tidied up stacks of books and scrolls Erin and Johan had been using to learn about magic and magical lore.

"Maybe so. Should you be rearranging those? What if our mates had them open to a particular spot?"

Katya tilted her head to one side. "These source materials respond to magic. All Johan and Erin need to do is open their minds to the knowledge they seek."

"Do they know how?" He was certain he hadn't taught them that particular skill.

"No, but one of us can make certain they possess that piece of information. Speaking of coaching, I'd like to take a brief peek into my glass and see if my previous interrogation about the future repeats itself on a second look."

Sensing more lay behind her request, he asked, "Would you like me there?"

"I would. No water to rear back and slap me this time, but the way my last spell imploded was disquieting."

"Of course. Where do you wish to work?"

Katya pursed her mouth into a thoughtful line. "Not my sleeping chamber. I've had so many failures there, it seems like it's cursed. If we go outside, the other shifters will want to craft battle strategy. It's our nature."

He thought about all the empty structures he and his dragon kin had built deep beneath Antarctica. He'd offered many of them to their shifter allies, but some remained unoccupied.

"How about the primary house on Level C?"

She nodded. "It would be perfect. Let me grab a couple of mirrors, and I'll meet you there."

"Sure you don't want to use water again? Another lake is near that building."

A muffled snort was followed by, "No."

"See you soon, Sister." He visualized the deserted house, constructed similarly to this one in that much of it was sunk into the earth. The walls of its great room formed around him, and he ran up one flight to the kitchen where he tapped into rich ore veins in the dirt walls to provide light. Once the room brightened, he was sorry he hadn't left it dark. A thick layer of dust covered everything. He blew the top layer off and used his bare arms to do a somewhat better job.

As usual, he was naked. It was his fallback garb when human. He had garments, and he'd even dressed a time or two because Johan and Erin weren't used to running about unclothed. Thanks to the gods, they'd mostly gotten over their false modesty. He and Katya had taught them to draw heat from the earth to warm themselves.

How was Erin doing? Would his absence truly enable her to learn faster? The thought bothered him, and he gave himself a brisk mental shake. For one thing, they weren't yet mated.

Not because of him.

The reason they hadn't consummated their mating bond was because she wasn't 100 percent certain. If he was too heavy-handed, too much of a possessive bastard, she probably never would say yes. The commitment was permanent, a daunting concept to someone who'd spent her entire life in a culture steeped in walking away when the going got tough.

Humans didn't use to be like that. Something about the longer, easier lives they lived had made them less willing to work through hard times. A hundred years earlier, no one expected sunshine and roses and perpetual happiness.

He snorted and cut the flow of his mental meanderings. What he thought about modern humans didn't matter a whit. He and Katya had argued about revealing themselves to Johan and Erin. He'd prevailed, and they'd broken a cardinal rule.

For a host of excellent reasons, magic was to remain hidden from humans. That was true even when mortals still believed in occult phenomena.

The path he'd insisted they tread hadn't been without significant problems, but two new dragon shifters were the result. If they still thought more like humans than dragons, it was understandable.

Erin flashed through his mind. She was never far from the surface, but she had to understand who he was, how he operated. If he soft-pedaled aspects of himself to lure her into saying yes to mating with him, that wasn't right, either. Hell, she wasn't perfect—not by a long shot. But he accepted all of her.

Or did he?

When he jumped in, prevented her from figuring out magic on her own, he was scarcely accepting her. No. He was trying to shape her into someone different. In this instance, he wanted her to be more competent magically.

Yeah. So she doesn't end up kidnapped by a sea-serpent. His inner voice held a caustic edge.

A blast of familiar magic presaged Katya's arrival. "Here I am." She glanced around the kitchen that looked a lot like theirs. "Dusty in here."

"You should have seen it before I cleaned up. Inside or out?"

She creased her forehead in thought and moved a sizeable oblong mirror in a golden frame to her other hand. "Maybe down one level to the great room? It will give us space to work."

"Us?" He angled a sharp look at his twin.

"Yes. I thought about this and want to include you in my casting."

He motioned her through the door and followed her down a flight of stairs. "Are you going to tell me why?"

Katya was silent until she'd placed her palms across ore veins running through the walls. Much as he'd done upstairs, she coaxed light from the minerals until the cavernous space glowed a soft bluish-white.

Turning to face him, she said, "Our magic is complementary. When I returned from a skirmish with the serpents with a serious wound in my side, Johan poured some of the mildly alcoholic elixir we both make over it to clean it. He had no way of knowing it would help, but an infusion of your magic was just the thing. It chased out the taint and allowed my own power to kick in and heal me."

Konstantin raised his eyebrows. "Lucky for you it was one of my batches. It could just as easily have been one of yours."

"Oh, I know. Regardless, I believe my scrying spell will be stronger for including your ability."

"It's not one of my magics," he reminded his twin. "This could boomerang on us. Badly."

She nodded. "Yes. I thought about that before I asked. If things seem to be going badly, cut the flow of your power."

He blew out a tense breath, not liking the direction this was headed. "And leave you alone?"

Katya regarded him from under hooded lids. "Stand down, Brother. I said I wished to include you, but you're free to decline. Make a choice. You're building arguments on both sides."

As usual, his sister had his number. So far, he'd forwarded arguments about why it was a questionable idea, and followed them with irritation when she'd told him to withdraw his magic if the spell went awry.

"Happy to help," he said and left it at that.

She settled cross-legged on the inlaid stone floor and patted the spot in front of her. He understood and sat across from her so their knees almost touched. She moved the mirror until she held it in both hands and began to chant softly.

He opened a channel to his magical center and felt her latch onto his power, weaving it in with her own. They'd shared magic many times, and she was correct in her belief their ability was synergistic.

Almost as if someone had planned things out while they were still sharing their mother's womb. They'd had a few mishaps as children where they'd underestimated the reach of their combined magic and brought a few buildings tumbling down.

Their dragons had rebuked them so harshly, their mother hadn't had to say a word.

He couldn't see the glass part of Katya's mirror because it was tilted away from him, but the golden frame took on a glowing aspect, turning the air around it iridescent. Katya's voice rose and fell, and he shut his eyes, hoping to encourage whatever vision was forming behind the glass to show itself.

Her tug on his magic intensified; he gave her what she needed. The canvas behind his closed lids began to swirl. As he'd hoped, blackness ceded to a collage of colors that finally formed recognizable objects. He altered position so he had a view of the mirror.

It should match the images in his mind. So far, it did.

A ship, the *Darya*, bobbed in the restless Southern Ocean. It was nighttime, though far from totally dark. People hurried to and fro on the ship's broad quarterdeck. Konstantin wanted to look within, but scrying didn't work that way. As he understood it, visions showed themselves, and you interpreted them later.

The sea became choppier. With a sinking feeling, he switched his focus from the deck to the sea, not surprised when a dark, triangular sea-serpent head broke through between wave crests. Where there was one, there had to be more. Had the serpents targeted the *Darya* and somehow leveraged magic to further corrupt the men who had boarded her?

He was still turning that idea over—except he couldn't figure out what would have been so attractive about the small research vessel—when the vision disintegrated. The one replacing it looked like a European city, but several hundred years earlier. The streets were cobblestones. Rather than cars, horses and carriages were in evidence. Gutters on both sides of the street ran sour with human waste.

A closer look convinced him the city was Heidelberg, a place he and Katya had visited a time or two. The vision shifted slightly to a spot near where a bridge spanned the Neckar River. Konstantin blinked, certain it had to be a trick of the odd lighting in the vision, but the serpents he thought he'd seen were still swimming lazily in the river. They'd cloaked themselves in illusion so they'd look like logs or rocks, but he recognized them.

Dragons' balls! He'd assumed the serpents' escape from their banishment was recent, but the scene spread before him had occurred hundreds of years earlier. Before he had a chance to dissect it further, Heidelberg shattered and was replaced by the headlands above their lair beneath Antarctica.

The sun shone down on a rocky shoreline. No ice. No serpents. The last time he'd looked, ice was at least a foot thick, and the place had been crawling with sea-serpents. Was the empty headland a promise of victory? Or merely a snapshot from the past?

A thought rocked him. The land might know. He'd been working on getting Earth to talk with him through his land-linked magic, but she didn't trust him and hadn't responded. At least not so far. He understood her heavy silence. She'd been sorely used by mankind, raped and pillaged and sacked as thoroughly as the Visigoths had plundered early trade routes.

The headlands vanished, replaced by another desolate vista, this one populated by a group of naked men and women sitting around a roaring fire. Hair in many colors shrouded them thickly, and they were laughing and singing and drinking from animal skins. Who were they? Early humans? Or did they possess magic.

This was Katya's spell. Did he dare shoot a thread of seeking magic into the middle of it? Would he disrupt her scrying? Worse, might he end up doing what he'd feared: forcing the spell to blow up in both their faces?

As he watched, one of the men leapt to his feet. The air around him developed a reddish hue, and he changed into a dragon. Konstantin blinked harder. What he'd just seen wasn't possible. Dragon shifters had never sat around bonfires. No need since they tapped warmth from whatever land they stood upon. He forced back the seeking magic that wanted out and took a good hard look at the man.

Breath rattled from him. Not a dragon. A sea-serpent, but before the dragon god, Y Ddraigh Goch, stripped them of their wings. So this scene was from antiquity.

Fascinating. Even then, serpents hadn't spent much time with their dragon kin. There were no dragons in this group. He'd assumed the seeds of rebellion began when a few serpents plotted against the dragon god's children, but maybe its roots reached far earlier.

Katya's breathing was ragged. Her knuckles were white where she gripped the glass. The dark-haired man, who'd shifted into a gray sea-serpent, had turned and faced squarely into the mirror. His eyes whirled hypnotically, just like dragon eyes, except they were dark.

"I see you spying on us," he sneered. "Dragons always were dim-witted, but thanks for the channel through time." Around him, the others jumped up. Teleport magic glistened around them.

"Katya. End the spell," Kon managed despite a tongue that wasn't overly cooperative.

"Can't." Her mind voice was shockingly weak.

He tried to pry the mirror out of her hands, but she held it in a death grip. Blood flowed where the frame cut into her hands. Damn! Her blood would grease the skids, make it even easier for the serpents to jump through time.

The last thing they needed was more serpents, especially the original variety before Y Ddraigh Goch had divested them of wings and some of their magic.

Kon struggled to cut off her access to his magic. It should have been immediate, but precious seconds ticked by before he untangled his magic from hers. An abrupt surge in his ability told him she couldn't have been the only magical entity bleeding him.

His twin was crying silently. Tears formed gemstones as they hit the stone floor, pattering around her. In full command of his power again, he wrenched the glass from Katya's hands. A quick glance told him the serpents were crafting travel spells.

Why the hell hadn't the vision abated. His twin would probably have his head, but he crashed the mirror down on the stone floor. It took three tries, and a hefty shot of magic, before it shattered. With its demise, he felt Katya's spell curl into itself and die. Outraged shrieks battered him, but they perished damned fast.

At first, he assumed Katya was giving him hell, but when he looked at her, she was staring at her lacerated hands and still crying. They'd had an incredibly close call since the serpents had been near enough for him to hear them. He hoped he'd stranded them in some in-between spot, one with no air where they'd drift forever.

He scooted nearer his twin and grasped her hands in his, sending healing magic into the torn places. "It's all right. They're gone."

She regarded him through eyes swimming with unshed tears. "Because of you. I waited too long. If my dragon had been here, she'd never have let me make that mistake."

"I'm not sure about too long. I didn't know what they were."

"Me, either. By the time I figured out they weren't dragons, they had me. I have no idea how they reached through my casting. It's not supposed to work that way." She shook her head and extracted a hand to brush tears from her cheeks.

"Once we all had the same magic," Konstantin reminded her. "It's why they were so quick to recognize you, and why it was so easy for them to..." He stopped, not wanting to criticize Katya. Not now when she was so distraught. She recognized she'd made a mistake. He didn't need to rub it in.

"Hornswoggle me?" she supplied, her voice bitter.

No reason to agree, so he changed topics. "I'm sorry about your mirror."

Katya shook her head. "It was the only way to sever the connection. Besides, I have others, but I may never want to use them again."

He tightened his grip on the hand he still held. "We learned a lot today. It was worth some inconvenience."

"Christ, Kon. I nearly added ten serpents to the ones already here. Except these were the original variety. They might have—"

"Hush. They're not here. Nor are they likely to be." He stood and drew his twin to her feet. "Time to leave. How are your hands."

"Better." She scooped up the piles of gems from her tears.

Good. He'd have been truly concerned about a dragon who left potential hoard material behind. Before they departed, he raised his mind voice to his bondmate.

"We need you back here now!"

His lesson from today was not for his twin to stop scrying, but to never attempt it again when her dragon wasn't present.

KATYA

Feeling like a failure, Katya trudged up a couple of flights of stairs after her brother's retreating form. The mix of gemstones clutched in her hands both soothed her and reminded her how closely they'd skirted disaster.

No wonder Y Ddraigh Goch had banished the serpents. They might have once been indistinguishable from dragons in form, but dragons were good and pure and principled. Judging from today's flight backward in time, sea-serpents had always been a devious bunch.

It was also clear the time they'd been caught bedeviling Y Ddraigh Goch's children was scarcely their first fall from grace, merely the first time they were apprehended.

Her dragon collided with her, clicking into place as if she'd never been gone. A few moments later, hissing filled her and fury shot from her mouth as fire mixed with ash.

"Did you know?" she asked her bondmate, not bothering

with telepathy since her magical reservoir was running on fumes.

"Know what?"

The dragon's question seemed overly cautious, particularly since she rarely answered a question with one of her own. Normally, if she wasn't going to answer, she said nothing.

"What did you think I was referring to?"

More smoke huffed through her mouth. *"I certainly had no way of knowing you were going to go mucking about in time travel. You had no business doing that without me."*

Katya stopped dead, planting her feet right outside the stone doors that marked the building entry point. Konstantin was a short distance ahead of her, but she'd catch up.

"You know damn good and well I wasn't time traveling."

"Amounts to the same thing. You ended up at least a millennium removed from now."

Katya gritted her teeth. "Did you know how corrupt the sea-serpents were? While we're at it, did you know their original magic was stronger than ours?"

The flood of smoke issuing from her jaws turned to fire. Great. Her bondmate was pissed, although probably not at her. She might have taken exception to the magical comparison, though.

"Many of us suspected they were immoral. We petitioned Y Ddraigh Goch to do something about them for a long time before he finally did."

"Even before the serpents tortured his children?"

"Pfft." More fire. *"Long before, but we were not of one mind.*

Some dragons took the other tack, that we could coexist with our serpent kinsmen. When Y Ddraigh Goch finally moved against them, he provoked serious discord."

"For what?"

"Some dragons believed were it not for the strike against his children, he'd never have done anything."

"So they viewed it as personal, not for the good of dragonkind?"

"Precisely."

Katya waited. The dragon hadn't responded to her second question, the one about whose magic was most potent. Nagging wouldn't move things along any faster. And it might mean her bondmate would end up not answering at all.

"I never believed their magic was stronger," the dragon said slowly. *"You were a fool. You ventured too near and waited too long. They wove their magic together and nearly bested you. Ten against one is poor odds."*

A wry grin wanted out. Convenient her bondmate didn't require explanations about what had happened. "Kon was there too," she said.

"Not from a position of strength, he wasn't. Whatever were the two of you thinking?"

Konstantin had stopped moving and stood a few meters ahead, but he wasn't looking her way. Was his dragon reading him the riot act as well?

"At least we learned a few things. And my scrying magic is still intact." She did her best to ignore defensiveness rolling through her and an irrational desire to chide her bondmate for leaving at an inopportune time.

No way either one of them could have guessed what would happen. Besides, casting blame was pointless. All it did was lead to anger.

"I'm not going anywhere until this is over," her dragon announced.

Katya shook her head unsure whether to be touched by her bondmate's love or annoyed the dragon didn't view her as capable of taking care of herself. She hurried to Konstantin.

"Did your bondmate have a few choice words?"

"You might say that." Her twin speared her with an exasperated look. "I wonder how many other tidbits we don't know about the serpents."

"Probably quite a few. Shall we see how everyone else is doing?"

"Everyone else as in our mates or the other shifters?"

Katya smiled. "Both." It alarmed her when Kon referred to Erin as his mate. And made her scared for him. If Erin ended up turning him down—and she might—it would crush him.

Katya had been surprised when Johan accepted the mate bond so readily.

She'd reminded him about the "no divorce" rule, but he'd been so sunk in lust at the time, he'd probably have signed a pact with the devil. Men were different creatures. Not that she didn't see herself as having a sexual nature, but things were different when you had a cock. Something that responded to almost every passing erotic event, no matter how trivial.

She didn't doubt Johan loved her, but men operated on a

fairly simplistic plane. Erin held secrets—and fears. Now that she was bonded with a dragon of her own, it was entirely possible the beast would fulfill all her emotional needs. Sex play with Konstantin would make her life complete, and she'd have no need to shackle herself to a mate.

"What are you thinking?"

Kon's question jerked her out of her musings; relief filled her he hadn't just helped himself to her thoughts. "Nothing much," she said brightly. Maybe her response was too cheerful, so she hurried to add, "I'm still recovering from back there." She looked over a shoulder at the door to the building they'd recently exited.

"I understand. My bondmate gave me grief over our scrying effort. He reminded me in no uncertain terms I wasn't blessed with that gift. But then, I reminded him if I hadn't been there, you'd have been unwittingly coopted into holding a gateway through time open. With disastrous results, I might add."

Breath whistled through Katya's gritted teeth. "I'll admit I wasn't very smart about things. When I first saw people around a fire, I assumed it was the first batch of humans—or close to the first batch—here on Earth. It wasn't until I moved nearer, I sensed dragon magic. Made no sense, though. We never sat around fires since we carry fire within us."

"The serpents used to produce fire as well," Kon reminded her. "No need for them to sit around one warming themselves."

She licked at dry lips. "I was putting it together when

that apelike fellow with all the black hair shifted. By then, it was too late. I was trapped."

Konstantin offered her a crooked smile. "You were quicker on the uptake than me. When he shifted, I assumed he was a dragon, and I was trying to see who since I know virtually all our kin."

"Thanks."

"For what?"

"I'm not feeling quite as incompetent," she replied. "Maybe we could not tell the others?"

"I was about to suggest the same thing," Konstantin murmured. "We will share what knowledge we gained but skip the part about our near miss with tragedy."

She gave him a quick hug. "You're the best."

"What are twins for?"

A cavalcade of all the tricks they'd played on each other marched through her mind.

"Those too." Kon grinned, and she blessed all her lucky stars he hadn't chosen an earlier moment to skim her thoughts. Mind-reading was one of his strengths. She needed to do better concealing her fears about Erin never becoming his mate.

"Are you planning to tell Johan?" he asked.

"No. Especially not him. He'd never let me out of his sight again."

Konstantin made a wry face. "The mate bond possessiveness. Tell me about it."

Before she could reply, his magic wrapped around her and whisked her to the familiar territory in front of their grotto. Various dinosaur grunts, stomps, and whistles blasted her as the ones that had been grazing near the lake headed their way.

A pterodactyl swooped close, shifting in midair and somersaulting to the ground in front of them. "We were about to hunt for you," Yle, the dinosaur's seer, announced almost before his beak had ceded to a mouth. Unlike most of his kind who had coal-black hair, his was silver. All of them had indigenous features with broad, flat foreheads, high cheekbones, and coppery skin. Silver eyes held a luminosity that was unsettling if you looked at them for too long.

His nostrils flared, and he bent closer to Katya. "You stink of scrying magic. What did you find?"

No reason to deny it, although she would have been content to let her twin take the lead and sketch out a few battle plans before they got around to what she'd been doing.

"You know how it is with these endeavors," she replied. "Nothing is ever certain."

Yle made circular motions with one hand, as in of course he knew and to get on with it.

Katya inhaled sharply. "It is possible serpents specifically targeted the *Darya*—"

"What's that?" Yle asked.

"The ship the new dragon shifters lived on. I saw serpents swimming around it before it was boarded by pirates."

"Fascinating. What else?" Yle nailed her with his disconcerting eyes.

"Apparently, the serpents escaped Y Ddraigh Goch's banishment a long time ago. Or a few of them did because we saw them in Germany around 1650 or so. Hard to tack down the time with much accuracy. I'm judging from the appearance of the buildings and carriages."

"We've already established they have a type of hive mind, which allows them to communicate over both time and distance," Konstantin spoke up.

"Makes sense the first group that escaped your god's imprisonment would have told the others how they managed it," Yle muttered.

"I still believe they staked out an acceptable existence for themselves somewhere," Konstantin said. "Something happened to their world, which is how they ended up here."

"Is there more?" Yle directed his words at her but halted shy of draping a truth spell over her.

"No." She stopped there. Yle looked oddly at her, almost as if he suspected she'd withheld something major, but he didn't press her further. He must have had a vision or two he'd chosen to keep to himself. It was true of all seers.

Around her, dinosaurs were shifting, probably to make it easier to communicate—and to save the magic they'd been husbanding while they ate and rested.

A shifter she recognized from their visit to the Fleisher group of borderworlds said, "You uncovered historical information, but nothing to help us right now." His black hair hung in many small braids in an approximation of a Celtic warrior pattern.

"Yes. That is true. I'm sorry. Revealing anything about either the past or the future has been difficult for me of late, so I keep my questions general. There was one vision, though, of the headlands above us that was confusing. No ice. No serpents. I couldn't tell if it was a scene from the past, validation the future will bode well for us, or something else, entirely."

"It's time for me to call everyone together," Konstantin said. "While they're gathering, Katya and I will make a quick trip to the surface to see if it's as infested with serpents as it was when we first returned here."

"One of us should accompany you," Yle announced. "Mixed magics work best if you're not as invisible as you hope to be."

Katya started to ask how he'd feel about riding on a dragon until she remembered he was bonded to a pterodactyl and flew as well as she did. In truth, he was probably more maneuverable since he had less bulk. He lacked fire, of course, but his beak was lined with serrated teeth.

"We'd appreciate your presence," Kon was saying.

She wondered if she should give Johan a heads up she was leaving, but she'd be back so soon, there was no reason to worry him unnecessarily. Besides, if she told him, he'd probably make a bid to come along, which would get Kon's dander up.

While Johan recognized Konstantin was in charge, it would take more than a few days as a dragon shifter for what that meant to sink in. Currently, Johan's understanding was more conceptual than rooted in practicalities. There'd been some gratuitous dick waving as he and Konstantin sparred over who actually made the decisions. She suspected there'd be more.

"Ready, Sister?" Kon was looking her way. From the

expression on his face, he seemed to be trying not to laugh. Maybe he'd caught her thoughts about dick waving, and they amused him.

She walked to his side with Yle keeping pace beside her. "We both are."

Her twin nodded. "My plan is to bring us out so we're hidden behind a large set of boulders lining the headlands. It's where I usually start from because I'm hidden from the ocean. Once we see how things are looking, we'll organize our next steps."

"How are you planning to communicate?" Yle asked.

"I'm not," Kon replied, "but that was a good question. If the ice is as pervasive as it was a couple of days ago, we'll take to the skies and do our damnedest to conceal ourselves behind wards. Serpents are quite sensitive to expended magic—if they're looking for it."

"Judging from what we saw on several of Fleisher's borderworlds, they're lazy," Yle said.

"Don't underestimate them," Katya spoke up. "I did on the third world, and the bastard nearly had me."

"Don't forget the dragons who ended up brood mares for the serpents' genetic experiments," Konstantin said.

"We missed that part"—Yle clamped his jaws in a tight line—"until you uncovered it."

Kon gathered magic. It eddied about them. "I will ferry all of us to the surface. It will be less noticeable than if each of us travels separately." He turned and locked gazes with the man sporting braids. "Summon everyone you can find. When we get back, we'll plan our first engagement and put it into action."

The man nodded acknowledgment. "I shall see everyone is here."

Katya had no doubt he'd do whatever was necessary. He had a no-nonsense way about him that inspired cooperation, and she assumed he was the dinosaurs' leader. The scent of her brother's magic thickened around her. Sunbaked clay and burning wood and aromatic herbs.

She wrapped wards about herself. No point in not being as ready as she could be. Just because they were emerging in a protected spot didn't mean a serpent sentry wouldn't notice a disturbance in the warp and weft of his—or her—magic. As she thought about it, she'd seen very few females.

What had happened to them? Were the inequities in their numbers creating problems?

The only familiar things once the spell settled were the boulders. A thick layer of ice covered the headlands. When she peeked over a hillock, the ocean was frozen as far out as she could see. Surely, humans had sounded a major alarm. This was summer in Antarctica, which mean dozens of cruise ships plied these waters daily. Were any of them stuck in ice, or had word gone out to warn ships not to come here at all?

Probably a little of both. Which meant the first batch of unlucky ships could be mired in ice. Kon tapped both her and Yle on the shoulder and pointed skyward. Shifting ate up a lot of magic. They probably should have shifted below and emerged as dragons—and a dinosaur.

Too late now. She hid behind warding as much as she could and spread her wings as soon as they'd support her weight. Kon's black dragon soared above her with the pterodactyl higher still. The dinosaur was large, but not bulky like dragons. Wings spread, he rode the air currents effortlessly.

Her bondmate wanted to bugle and paint the skies with fire. She muffled it amid a bevy of complaints that it was a sad day when dragons had to creep about like old women. Kon flew north. She followed, intuiting he wanted some sense of just how much of the ocean had frozen solid.

They flew toward the small stretch of open water humans had named the Drake Passage. She couldn't remember how it got its name, but it was known for rotten weather and rough crossings.

And shipwrecks. Those had come as a plus since most of her hoard had been gleaned courtesy of foundering ships.

So far, she hadn't seen even a single serpent, but she felt their foul magic. They had to be swimming beneath the ice. How the hell were they breathing? Last she checked, they had lungs just like she did. The pterodactyl flew in front of her and dipped his wings to one side, clearly wanting her to see something.

She glanced down.

The struggle she'd had with her dragon before paled in comparison to her beast's bid for freedom now. A ship was encased in ice. A good-sized one that could carry hundreds of humans. Helicopters hovered above it. One landed, took several passengers, and departed. As soon as it left, another took its place.

They were moving people off the stranded ship.

The humans were unaware of serpents closing on their stricken vessel. She felt their nasty emanations beneath the ice. Konstantin circled back to where she and Yle treaded air.

Kon had forbidden communication, but she didn't care. *"We have to do something."* She shielded her telepathy. Hopefully, the serpents were so intent on the feast they figured was theirs for the taking, they weren't paying attention to anything else. Surely, not something a couple hundred meters in the air.

"We could break up the ice," her twin agreed.

Yle flew in front of them and twisted midair so he faced them. *"No. Just because you can break up the ice with fire, is no reason you should. Humans do not need to know about us. It's bad enough a few of them may have guessed about the serpents at this point."*

"Meh. They've probably chalked them up to some iteration of the Loch Ness Monster," Kon mumbled, and then added. *"You're right. I've come to my senses. We'll only waste magic we can ill afford to lose."*

Katya battled anguish—and her dragon. *"We're warriors!"* her bondmate squealed into her mind. *"We oppose evil in all its forms. We do not walk away because it's inconvenient."*

"I have an idea," Kon said. *"Earth is fighting back. The ice is her doing. What if she could extend the freeze all the way to the ocean floor in this spot? It would keep serpents from reaching the ship. They'd have to turn around."*

"I like it," Yle replied. *"Can you reach the land?"*

"I don't know. So far, my attempts have not gone well, but I'm going to try again."

"Should we remain?" Katya asked.

"No. I'm retreating to the headland. No reason to be in the sky. You two should return beneath ground."

They covered the distance to where they'd emerged and shifted. Every serpent in the region was intent on the crippled ship. No one would notice their magic. She hoped.

Kon would be expending a lot of obvious power in his bid to reach the land. "Are you certain you don't wish at least one of us to remain?" she asked.

"Quite sure. It's bad enough my magic feels similar to those who are persecuting her. For there to be two of us might ensure failure."

Katya gave him a quick hug. "We're close if you need us."

Yle looked from one to the other of them, his silvery gaze serious. "Thank you for heeding my warning. My pterodactyl is much easier to manage than a dragon. He enjoys a good scrap, but he also recognizes losing causes."

Katya smothered grim laughter. "Dragons view themselves as invincible."

"So I'm coming to discover."

"Out of here, both of you." Kon sounded exasperated. "I'll return as soon as I can."

Katya gathered magic and set a course for her underground lair. At least her beast had retreated, but she still thought leaving was a mistake. A point she was making by sending fire, smoke, and ash splatting from Katya's mouth.

"I like your dragon," Yle said, "but she could accept sound advice more gracefully."

"Did you hear that?" Katya asked her bondmate. Instead of words, more fire spewed from her.

Katya brought them out in the midst of a large group that had formed near the shores of the lake. “If you believe dragons ever accept advice that runs counter to their wishes,” she told the dinosaur shifter, “then you know nothing about us. Nothing at all.”

ERIN

I hate to admit this, but I was relieved when Konstantin left the battle-training workspace. Not that he departed on his own. His twin, Katya, chivvied him out of here. She's a good woman, and she understands her brother. Probably better than I do.

It's not that I don't enjoy Kon's company. I do. But he reminds me of the old, crusty surgeons I trained under. He expects me to know everything—and be competent—right off the bat. I couldn't do it when I was wielding a scalpel. And I can't do it here, either.

Up until very recently, I'd relegated magic to the realm of the impossible. Children's fables, except my childhood was so far from idyllic no one ever read me a single fairytale. No wonder I never wasted energy believing in the impossible. I was too busy surviving. Things got a little better after I was six or seven and they dumped my poor excuse for a father in jail, but that's a tale for another time.

Or not.

It really isn't worth opening a door to examine the misery from my childhood. It won't change a thing. I got past it.

"Erin!" Johan yelled.

I ducked reflexively, and a ball of blue magic missed me by an angstrom. Several more were headed my way. I stepped out of the line of fire and shouted, "Can you shut that thing off for a moment?"

Whirring that had become part of the landscape quieted. I'd never known holographs made noise, but then I'd never come across one powered by magic, either.

"Are you all right?" Johan aimed a speculative glance at me out of his dark eyes.

"Yeah. I got caught up in thinking about stuff. I'm ready to try that last set of defensive moves again."

"Take a moment," he suggested. "Catch your breath." His English was excellent, but spoken with a strong Dutch accent. Up until I'd become a dragon shifter, English was my only language. Magic had corrected that little impediment.

Johan was a kind man, and his attentiveness to detail had served him well when he'd worked as a metallurgical engineer. He walked closer. "You can do this, Erin. I understand you did not grow up playing war games like little boys, but—"

"You have no idea how I grew up," I interrupted him. He was just being considerate, but something inside me splintered, jabbing me with sharp edges. Maybe because I'd been dangerously close to reliving my volatile childhood.

He held up a hand. "Sorry. I was trying to be supportive."

Remorse twisted my face into a scowl. "Yeah. Best thing for me is to get back to practicing. Whether I played 'war games' as a kid or not, killing wouldn't come naturally to me."

"No, I do not suppose it would." He took a deep breath and blew it out. "Whoever designed this workshop and the battle simulations was very skilled. The scenes are self-adjusting depending on your response to them. If something is too easy, it becomes harder."

"If it's so smart, why'd it chuck those last balls of juice my way?"

"Maybe it knew you had ceased to pay attention?" Johan shrugged. "We should switch to offensive maneuvers. My sense is that you already know how to defend yourself if attacked."

I grimaced. "Comes through loud and clear, eh?"

"Indeed. You can be as prickly as a hedgehog."

"Doctors, especially surgeons, don't especially prioritize social skills," I sputtered. Done waiting for Johan to reactivate the holograph, I borrowed a page from Star Trek and stomped closer to the far end of the room. "Alien battle, level two."

Johan snorted laughter.

"What's so blasted funny?"

"It responds to magic, not words. I discovered that by trial and error after Kon and Katya left."

"Where was I when you were doing that?"

"Staring after Konstantin."

Before I could protest I'd done no such thing, Johan

materialized next to me and raised a hand. Power flared from it.

From what I could tell, it was mostly fire with a jot of air mixed in. The whirring started up again, and I raised both hands and marshaled the power I'd discovered deep within me. My dragon was gone for the moment, but I was certain she'd return.

I parried a dart of white lightning, followed by a whole bunch of black ones. Soon the sum total of my attention was on figuring out where to send jets of power to stymie the holographic attack. At some point, I truly did move from defending myself to being a worthy adversary.

Sweat ran down my body, but magic sang sweet, kindling my nerves with the joy of destroying my enemy. I have no idea how much time passed, but I was breathing as hard as if I'd run a race.

Johan waved a hand and cut the flow of magic. "It is enough for today. We made progress."

I was still struggling to catch my breath, but I gasped out an agreement and sank into a crouch.

"You did well just now," Johan said. "What made the difference?"

It was a good question, and I thought about it. As usual, his observations were spot on. Something had finally clicked between me and my nascent magic and the holographic program.

I got my feet back under me and straightened. "It was rather like surgery when I'm in the zone. Everything is clicking, and I'm fully immersed in the moment. When that happens, there's no past and no future. Only now."

He smiled, and it lightened his austere features. "You sound like an advertisement for Zen mindfulness."

I grinned back because I couldn't help it. Something about Johan's moods were contagious. That was even true when he'd been lying in an ice cave with a broken femur joking with me.

"We'll never see that world again," I murmured. "The one where meditation ads are all over the web."

"You do not know that," he countered. "If we are successful, something will remain here on Earth."

"Yes, but we won't be part of it."

"Not in the way we once were," he agreed thoughtfully, "but you do not know how our futures will unfold."

I nudged him. "I have a pretty good idea about yours. You're mated to Katya, and you'll ride off into the sunset and live happily ever after. As dragons."

"And you shall be mated to Konstantin. Or will you?" He quirked one dark brow my way.

I did a quick spot check. My dragon wasn't back yet, so there was no one to spy on me and report back to Kon's beast. Breath whistled through my teeth. "I don't know. It's not that I don't love him, I do, but he has some arrogant aspects that set my teeth on edge. Like earlier today when he decided I was incompetent or incapable or something and simply stepped in front of me and fought for me."

Johan tilted his head to one side. "He is from an era when men protected women."

"Doesn't make it any easier to swallow—or accept."

"You stood up for yourself."

A rather rude snort blew past my lips. "And he moved six

inches away. It wasn't until Katya dragged him off to deal with some other task that he left. And he didn't want to go. I saw it on his face."

"What is the worst part of that for you?"

I regarded him through lids that sat at half-mast. "So now you're a psychiatrist rather than an engineer?"

He raised both hands until they faced palms outward. "The hedgehog returns, spines and all. I am trying to be your friend. As the only other human in this bunch, I understand more than you think."

Heat swooped from my chest to the top of my head. "Sorry. I can be a terrible bitch. Probably because of how I was raised, I've never let anyone get very close to me. If Kon had his way, he'd rule my life, and I value my freedom too much to let him do that."

"Katya and I have had several 'freedom' discussions. Turns out I was not as free as I presumed. Neither were you. This is not about independence, so what is it?"

Point to Johan.

Freedom was an amorphous concept, and a smokescreen. I nodded, feeling tired. "What if we end up hating each other? We're stuck. Forever. Doesn't that worry you about Katya?"

"Sometimes." The corners of his eyes pinched with concern. "I spent my life avoiding commitments. Oh, I had the best of excuses. One after another, but the upshot was I was still single and in my forties. And likely to remain so. I understood I would have to make some significant life alterations to accommodate a wife and children, and I was not ready. That was fine when I was twenty-five. Less fine ten years later, and edging into unacceptable when I passed forty, but I did not know what to do about it. Or I did, but I was not willing to make those changes."

"Sounds familiar," I ventured. "Not that I'm forty, but close enough."

"How did you square it with yourself?" Johan's dark gaze bored into me.

I shrugged. "I was busy. Doing critical work. Long hours on my feet. Even longer hours on call. A husband and children would never see me."

"Did it not occur to you to work less?"

"Sure, but I discarded it."

"Why?"

Here was the crux of the woman I'd become, and it hurt to admit it out loud. "I was afraid."

"Of?" he prodded, not willing to let me off the hook so easily.

"Lots of things. Making a mistake. Not being able to love someone enough. Being a terrible mother." I winced but forced a few more words past my unwilling lips. "Sparing you details, I had a perfectly wretched upbringing. Lots of foster homes and zero decent parental role models."

"I lack your excuses. I had wonderful parents and still doubted my ability to be a husband and father. Katya was worth laying my qualms aside." He dropped a hand onto my shoulder. "Nothing changes unless we do, Erin."

Boy, oh boy, was that ever true.

"Ready to look for everyone else?" I asked. Johan had given me a lot to think about, but I was done with introspection for the moment.

"I am. Shall we stop by the kitchen, first?"

"Sure." I visualized the great room one floor up, felt a rush of magic, and ended up there. Someone had tidied up the library, but not resurrected the illusory wall hiding it.

Was it a "fuck you" from Konstantin for the chaos I'd left, or was he simply being himself? Perhaps Katya had done the straightening. Regardless, I'd have to thank them for clearing up my mess.

Johan loped around me and was on his way up the stairs leading to the kitchen. He was as guilty as me for the disarray in the library, yet he apparently hadn't given it a second thought.

Because he's a man...

I chopped that line of thought off fast. I was prickly and quick to take offense. Even if Kon had cleared up the library, why couldn't I assume positive intent? What was wrong with me?

I didn't care much for the answer. When I played the injured party, it gave me a false moral high ground.

I could do better. And I promised myself I would. I'd said I was done with introspection, but I'd kept right on brooding. It truly was time to put a lid on things.

"Didn't find much," Johan was saying as I rounded a corner into the kitchen.

He'd laid out kelp and dried meat, and I realized I was famished. Somewhere around the second mouthful, my dragon slammed into me bugling, *"I'm back."*

"I noticed. Where were you?"

"My dragon has returned as well." Johan beamed, clearly delighted to be reunited with his beast.

"Did he say where they went?"

"I will tell you," my dragon said. *"You didn't give me a chance. We were in the dragons' world. Konstantin's dragon had something he wanted to accomplish."*

"It's all right," I said to Johan. "My beast just told me."

"Mine too," he said between bites.

I reached inward, happy to have my dragon nearby. She puffed steam through my mouth, so she was glad to be reunited too. *"You've been practicing fighting,"* she said, followed by, *"We must practice together."*

I pushed myself to move beyond how unnerving it was that she knew everything I'd done. Hell, she probably knew what had wandered through my mind too, which meant my discussion about Konstantin wouldn't pass unnoticed. Not much I could do about it.

"My beast thinks we should practice fighting in her form," I said, adding, "It's a good idea."

"Mine suggested the same thing," Johan said. "Do you want to go outside? Or back to the practice arena?"

"What do you think?" I asked my bondmate.

She preened, clearly appreciating I'd asked her opinion, but she'd had centuries in her dragon body and it still felt awkward to me. *"Outside. More space."*

Johan must have heard her too because he said, "You know we cannot go so far as the surface, but great untapped vistas extend beyond the first lake." He angled his head, clearly listening. "My dragon votes for outside as well."

We finished what was left on the table and trooped up the stairs. Being naked didn't bother me anymore, and it certainly made shifting more convenient. No clothes to remove and fold and remember where I'd left them. A few dinosaurs dotted the space between the house and the lake. I wasn't sure where the other types of shifters were. Kon had offered them rooms—or maybe assigned them—scattered throughout the dragons' former home.

Once more than fifty dragons had lived here, but now it was just Kon and Katya.

I held an image of my brilliant-red dragon in my mind and felt the now familiar stretching and tearing sensation. Thank god shifting had become doable. After my initial near-death experience, I'd been skittish as a colt about changing forms.

We stretched our newly formed wings and waited as fingers and toes ceded to talons. Next to me, Johan's green dragon took shape. He was gorgeous shades, with scales ranging from forest green to emerald. Soon we were both airborne. Flying as a dragon is such a treat, it's impossible to find words to describe how wonderful it is.

Our body is bulky and ungainly on land, but a thing of grace and beauty in the air. I still remember when I doubted we'd be able to fly. Brother, was I ever wrong. We winged our way past several lakes. Shifters clustered around the first three, but after that, we had the place to ourselves.

Remembering why we were here, I bugled and said, "Looks like a good place to practice. No one to hit below."

Fire blatted from my mouth, painting distant cliffs. I got the idea and flew at the cliffs from different angles, seeing if I could hit a defined area. Johan was doing the same thing about a quarter mile farther on.

"Build a ward," my dragon instructed.

I diverted magic and shaped a sloppy shroud around us. It took a few minutes before I had all of my dragon body covered. When I reached for power to blast the cliff again, there wasn't enough.

"There's a trick to this, eh?" I mumbled.

Dragon laughter trumpeted through our mouth. No wonder my bondmate had told me to ward our shared form. She must have known it required a balancing act.

Flying complicated things. It wasn't second nature, and splitting my attention three ways—remaining airborne, warding myself, and fighting—wasn't possible.

Not yet.

I landed, intent on mastering two out of three. Unlike Kon, my beast didn't intervene. She let me futz with various combinations of magic until I discovered one that allowed a passable ward with enough power left over to fight. Once I mastered it, we took to the air once more.

We didn't remain long, only until I convinced myself what I'd done would work. I'd blown through scads of magic experimenting. If we were called to fight right away, I'd be going into battle in a serious one down position.

"We're heading back," I bugled at Johan.

He was on the ground, a spot where I'd spent plenty of time as I worked through some of the finer points of titrating magic, so I'd have enough to stretch across simultaneous tasks.

"We shall leave soon as well," he told me.

I started to ask if I could help but remembered how put out I'd been by Kon's helicopter-parent routine. Johan was an adult. If he needed assistance, he'd ask for it without prodding from me.

We'd no sooner started back when telepathy reverberated through my mind. The practice session had been timely, indeed. We were being summoned to the lake near Kon and Katya's grotto.

A frisson rattled my scales. Part fear, part excitement, it filled me with anticipation. After all our talk about taking on the sea-serpents, we were about to engage them in our first major undertaking. Different from when Kon and I had lured two into their human forms and killed them, this would involve all of us and as many serpents as showed up.

"The basic principles are the same," my bondmate reminded me.

"Do you suppose they're still mortal as humans?" I had no idea what the fuck we'd do if they weren't. Not many options when you battled immortals, although the serpents had done a fine job of immobilizing dragons in ice on a borderworld.

"I do not know. We will fight what is in front of us. When we finish with one enemy, we shall move to the next. Until there are no more."

My dragon sounded supremely confident. I wondered if she harbored doubts, or if they weren't part of being a dragon. Regardless, I'd do well to copy her attitude. Focusing on the present had moved my brawling skills to a whole new level.

We cruised in and landed. Most of the shifters were human, so I reached for my other form despite grumbling from my bondmate. I scanned the assemblage and saw Katya but not Konstantin.

Where was he?

"He is our mate," my dragon said, sure of herself as always.

"What makes you think so?"

"I know these things, and I adore his dragon. I must approve your mating, and I heartily favor him."

I blinked back surprise. For a second, my beast had sounded like a besotted schoolgirl. I smothered a bevy of thoughts, most of them disagreeable. I'd be damned if I'd be railroaded into marrying anyone just because my permanent dragon bondmate liked his dragon.

Of all the reasons not to marry—or mate, or whatever their nomenclature was—my dragon liking his dragon was highly placed on the list. I'd tell Kon yes when I was good and ready and not a second sooner.

And I hoped to god I'd see my way clear to either a yes or a no soon. It wasn't fair to either of us to leave his offer hanging.

"Come close!" the dinosaur shifter with oodles of tiny braids covering his head invited. "We have a battle to plan."

The same sense of edgy anticipation I'd felt earlier rolled through me. If I'd still been human, I'd have happily sat out anything that smacked of war, but I'd made my choices.

I'd be the best goddamned dragon shifter I could. I'd make my beast proud of me. And Konstantin too, if he was in a generous mood. Blistering insight slapped me hard. One of my biggest reservations was no matter what I did, he picked it to shreds.

Maybe he was always critical—of everything and

everyone—but if he and I were to be a couple, he'd have to suspend that side of himself where I was concerned.

"Tell him," my beast piped up, proving she was always listening, and I'd never again have a private thought.

"Not right now," I said in as firm a tone as I could muster. *"And not until we get a break in the fighting. He is our commander. He has far more to concern him than me hashing out the fine points of our mating."*

Smoke and ash billowed from my mouth, and I added, *"You will not tell his dragon, either."*

I felt her unrest as she rolled within me, but she didn't reply. Probably for the best. Now wasn't a time to get into an argument. We had to be of one mind to get through the next few hours. I was sorry I'd squandered so much magic, yet it had been necessary.

Otherwise, I'd have been stuck either warding myself or fighting, but unable to do both at the same time.

KONSTANTIN

Konstantin had been crouched on the headlands between two boulders for a long time. His entreaties to the land weren't working, and his patience was growing thin. Normally, Antarctica's stark beauty was stimulating, with its tones of silver and gray and the restless Southern Ocean, but today he could have been anywhere. Because his magic was spread in a wide net, he felt the passengers' pervasive horror as the serpents broke through the ice and slithered up and over deck railings and onto their ship.

He'd never spent much time worrying about humans. How they felt. What they thought. None of it had ever mattered—until now. He'd watched human wars come and go, but those had been their own doing. This time, they were victims of magic that should never have been turned against them.

Magical creatures were governed by a covenant. Part of it

was to leave humans strictly alone. It was why Katya had been so angry with him for revealing himself to three Russian seamen. Of course, he'd killed two, but then he'd made damn good and sure the last one's crewmates saw him.

It had been foolish, but he didn't want the memory of dragons to die out. Whatever would replace them could never be as inspiring. He couldn't actually hear the people aboard the doomed ship screaming, but he didn't have to. Their emotions pounded through him until his dragon was so furious talons poked out as the beast tried to force a shift.

Fire shot from his mouth. "We must do something," his dragon shrieked, nearly deafening him as it commandeered his vocal chords.

"Quiet! We have no idea where all the serpents are."

"The hell we don't," the dragon sputtered. At least he was back to using mind speech. *"They're eating those poor, helpless people."*

Konstantin ground his teeth in frustration. It was precisely what was happening, but one dragon had no chance against an entire phalanx of serpents. He reached into the land beneath his haunches one more time and took off the gloves. Before, he'd tried for diplomacy, and it had gotten him nowhere.

"You are dying because you've given up. It doesn't have to be that way."

Nothing. Emptiness reverberated back at him as if he'd tossed his entreaty into a vacuum.

"Punish those who have misused you," he went on. "Take back the glory that is rightfully yours. It isn't too late. Unless you do nothing."

Maybe he was expecting too much too soon. He searched for a calm center and made a grab for it. Mu had taken months—perhaps annums—before she'd spoken with him. The problem was he didn't have that kind of time to spare. Mu had been an experiment, one he hadn't believed would pan out.

Earth could be a long-term project too, but not with the sea-serpents intent on overrunning it. He rebuked himself for not starting sooner. It wasn't as if he hadn't been here for a long time, but wooing the land and convincing her to trust him had never been a priority.

Until now.

"We have to do something," his beast insisted. *"Call the others. The serpents are out in plain view. We can immobilize some of them. Like we did with the renegade dragons on the ninth world."*

Konstantin wasn't at all certain their ninth-world strategy would work for a boat stranded in ice. Before, the dinosaurs had borrowed magic from a cooperative planet and buried three traitorous dragons in layers of dirt and ensorcellment.

Dinosaurs drew their power from the land. Whether their brand of magic would be as effective on the ocean was an unknown. Additionally, they'd lived on the Fleisher system of borderworlds forever. The land knew, and presumably trusted, them. Earth wasn't proving nearly as cooperative.

"Do something!" His bondmate was done waiting. And done with telepathy. Smoke and ash punctuated his words.

"Give it five more minutes, and then I shall summon the others."

Smoke, fire, and ash told him more clearly than words that his dragon disagreed. For every second they delayed, lives were lost.

Kon spread his hands across a boulder in front of him. "Last chance to help us." He sent his message as deep into the earth as he could. His threat had no teeth. Assuming the land was listening, she'd know full well that last chances came and went.

As he waited, he thought about Erin. He loved her, desired her, but didn't understand her. She'd made a decent point about never learning a new skill if he kept doing things for her, but she could have been nicer about it. He was almost certain she'd wanted him to leave, and it cleaved him to his soul.

They were almost mates. How could she not want him by her side? All of the time. Through good times and difficulties.

His nostrils flared in frustration. The almost mates part was a sticky wicket. Maybe the possessiveness beating a path through him would become more manageable once she was well and truly his. The overprotective instincts driving him to shield her were pushing her away. But how could he not hover? He loved her. Leaving her on her own ran counter to his better judgment in a serious way. Mates defended one another.

An idea formed. He hadn't given Erin any chance at all to go to bat for him because he always took the lead. If he sought her opinion, allowed her to follow her instincts—but made certain to be close enough to pick up the pieces—she might feel less put-upon.

"You do approve of my mating, do you not?" he asked his beast. He thought his bondmate liked Erin, but they'd never had an actual discussion about it. The dragon's blessing was a lynchpin, one he needed to make certain of.

Fire and ash turned to steam. *"Of course. Her dragon and I are in full agreement it is a beneficial mating. For us all."*

Relief streamed through him. If the dragons were on board, all would be well. They could sabotage matings. A corner of his mouth twisted downward. Three out of four pieces were in place. All Erin had to do was get over her ridiculous fear of commitment, and they'd be golden.

Mated just like Katya and Johan.

Why in the hell had it been so much easier for Johan? He'd dithered about a bit, but when the moment of truth came, he'd signed on the dotted line. Had Katya caught him in a moment of weakness? Say, for example, when they were in the throes of passion? He'd tried that method with Erin, but she'd mastered a veritable treasure trove of sex tricks that didn't include consummating the mating bond.

He sent one more entreaty deep into the land. With the same result.

Konstantin removed his palms from the boulder. He'd waited long enough. For the earth to respond and for Erin to embrace the inevitable. Not much he could do about the former. It was clear he wasn't going to establish a link with the land.

Not this land, and not today.

He raised his mind voice, intent on reaching Ylon, leader of the dinosaurs. *"Trouble up here. Have Katya fill you in. Meet me on the headland with a troop of shifters who are capable of flight."*

He didn't have to wait long before Ylon answered. *"Right away."*

"Finally," his bondmate muttered, still annoyed. Dragons didn't wait well. It surprised Kon he'd had the patience to woo Mu into acknowledging his presence. Maybe a similar strategy was needed with Erin too, except he wanted her with a singlemindedness that made putting their mating off painful.

Magic zinged through the air as shifters tumbled out all around him. He waited until the flood slowed. A quick glance showed around fifty shifters. All of the dragons except Erin and Johan. Fifteen dinosaurs, and the remainder a variety of birds.

Katya hustled to his side. "I told them about the ship. Are we going to free it? There's plenty of firepower here."

He scanned the crowd. Where were Johan and Erin? He bet they were probably together. Jealousy would have pricked deep, but Johan was Katya's mate. He and Erin were friends, though.

Another missing link. Humans valued friendship. There were many things he hadn't fully appreciated, but he'd prioritize a few of them. If he ever got clear of his duty to lead this shifter band against the serpents.

Johan and Erin were indeed together. They shimmered into being a few meters away. "Sorry we are late." Johan waved a hand. "Katya offered her assistance, but I insisted we could do this without her guidance."

"Turns out we could, but everything takes us longer,"

Erin said. "Apologies from me as well." Puffs of steam followed her words.

Answering steam billowed from his mouth. *"Stop that,"* he told his beast. Not a time to get mushy over the woman who neatly sidestepped his every move. Focusing on the assemblage, he said, "We will shift and fly to the stranded ship. Our job is to kill sea-serpents. Failing that, to immobilize them."

"More dinosaurs will be here soon," Ylon said. "We will build the same type of trap we constructed on the ninth world, but we must do it here. We cannot create such a thing in the sea."

Konstantin understood. "Assuming we cannot kill them, our task will be to chivvy the serpents here and drop them into your spell." He had no idea how they'd accomplish such a thing. The serpents would be intent on chowing through as many humans as they could. They'd never leave willingly, and flying with them for many kilometers held its own set of difficulties.

Ylon nodded tersely. "I cannot get the land to answer me. Perhaps you could encourage her to assist with our immobilization casting."

"She's not responding to me, either," Konstantin said.

"She will," Katya cut in. "She just needs more time. Remember on Mu—"

Kon chopped a hand downward. Fiery contrails shot from his fingertips. "We do not have any more time. We must work with what we have." He turned his attention back to Ylon. "Absent aid from Earth, do you still want us to bring the serpents to you?"

"If the land refuses to help us, our immobilization spell will be of limited use. We can snare them but not hold them without a continuous infusion of magic. How many serpents are we talking about?"

"A lot." Kon and Katya said in one breath.

"If we cannot dissuade the serpents with dragonfire," Konstantin said, "then we will direct heat to break a path through the ice and free the ship."

"What if there are not enough humans left to pilot it?" Johan asked.

"I have no idea. Shift. We leave as soon as everyone has wings."

His beast had been champing at the bit ever since it was clear Kon's attempts to communicate with the land were a waste of magic. When he opened the channel to his shift ability, the black dragon formed quickly.

Dragons and flying dinosaurs and birds took shape all around him. The dinosaurs and birds came in many variations. He was certain they all had species and genus names, but he wasn't familiar with them. Erin and Johan might be better versed than he was. Maybe later, he could ask them quietly so as not to offend the non-dragon shifters he knew painfully little about.

"Protect yourselves. Protect each other. Be creative. We must win this battle, or the serpents will never take us seriously."

He leapt skyward amid honks, squawks, bugles, fire, and smoke. Ash rained down from many dragon mouths. He switched to telepathy to make certain to reach everyone. If a serpent or two listened in, so be it.

"Your natural tendency will be to stick with your own kind. Shelve it. We are stronger deploying mixed magic. Form clusters that include dragons, dinosaurs, and birds. Fight from those groups."

He twisted midair to make certain everyone had heeded his instructions. For the most part they had, and new clusters were still forming. Good. He banked and flew as fast as he could straight for where they'd left the ship.

He smelled blood and entrails before the vessel came into sight. The boom of large bore rifles told him the humans weren't done fighting back. It also meant at least some of them remained. His group of shifters hadn't shown up too late despite his beast's gloom-and-doom predictions.

Fire shot from his mouth in a steady stream as soon as he was close enough to hit the thick tide of serpents covering every visible deck surface. Thank Y Ddraigh Goch there were no dragons. None visible, anyway. The reality of dragons joining with serpents smote him, made him ashamed for all dragonkind.

What had happened that they'd sunk so far?

He flew low enough to paint a ribbon of fire across three serpents. He was being foolish and overly sentimental about the dragon traitors. They didn't need compassion. They needed to die. Right along with the fucking serpents. Groups of shifters wheeled around him, each selecting and attacking a different portion of the beleaguered ship.

At first, bullets whizzed past them. But it didn't take the humans long to figure out that he and his shifters were on their side. Konstantin offered them points for being quick on the uptake.

Knowing death was stalking you had that effect. Serpent stench rose in a nauseating miasma from the ship. Rot and layers of decay from fresh to well-aged. If any serpents were left in the water, he couldn't pick them out. Decomposing brine mixed with decayed flesh coated his nostrils and tongue until he wished he could plunge into the sea to cleanse the taint.

The ice around the ship had broken up to some extent where the serpents punched through its surface. Intent on determining the extent of the icy barrier, he sent a thread of power streaking downward. Elation speared him. The ice was only about a meter thick. It didn't have the feel of serpent sorcery, so the land was making an attempt—albeit a feeble one—to protect herself.

Why had she been so loathe to acknowledge his presence. He could help. If the land would let him. Together, they'd be ever so much stronger.

His bondmate banked hard right, fire shooting from his jaws. Below them, a serpent bellowed as dragonfire scorched through its scales. The damage wasn't extensive, nor did it last long, but it gave him an idea.

The air was filled with ash and smoke and fiery contrails. Lacking fire, the birds and dinosaurs swooped through the ashy muck to peck with their sharp beaks. So far, the dragons had managed not to hit any of their allies. The dinosaurs were probably immune to dragonfire, but the birds wouldn't be.

Erin flew near, executed a midair flip, and splattered a destructive path along the upper deck. Serpents scrambled to get out of the way of her fire. "*None of them are dead yet. We need to do something different."* She tried for shielded mind speech. The result was garbled but understandable.

Konstantin bugled, hoping the others would understand without him using words. What he had in mind required split-second timing and stealth, so the serpents didn't sabotage it.

The dragons knew to come to him. Seeing them flying in a tight circle around him, the dinosaurs joined them. The birds came last. Several had singed feathers. Dragons' balls, but the damned serpents were a scourge.

"Open your magic to me," he commanded without offering a reason.

"What are you going to do?" Yle asked and snapped his pterodactyl jaws together.

"Best if you don't know."

Konstantin held his breath, or he would have if his beast weren't persisting in shooting fire at the serpents bellowing a challenge below. All about him, magic flashed and flared, some stronger than others, but all of it freely offered. He worked fast, weaving power into what he hoped would be unbreakable nets. Once he had three, he spoke words that should move the ship back in time. He aimed for a few days, but these castings were never precise. He could be off by as much as a month, which wouldn't be the end of the world.

It would mean, however, some of them would be forced to show up on the ship and warn whoever was captain what lay in their future. Not having lived through today's debacle, the humans would likely view them as deranged, but they had to try.

He was getting ahead of himself. Step one hadn't yet

been accomplished. If he couldn't nudge the ship into a time warp, his current strategy would be a bust.

The air smoked around him, developing a definite burned smell. Ozone wafted through the scorched parts with its sharply chemical overnotes. A whumping noise was followed by a maelstrom that formed out of the diverse magics he commanded. He tossed two of the nets over the boat and the whole mess into the swirling tumult of magic.

Another net sat in abeyance in case what he'd done wasn't enough.

Breath puffed past his jaws from the effort of commanding so much power. It had a mind of its own and nearly got away from his guidance multiple times.

The roaring intensified; everything around him turned black. He felt the pull of the vortex and fanned his wings hard to avoid being sucked into it. Lights blinked, looking for all the world like stars and galaxies. For long moments, he hung suspended in an airless void, much like the space between worlds when he was catapulting through it.

The vacuum gave him hope what he'd done was sufficient.

Alarm radiated through the bond he had with each shifter. He did his best to quell their panic. He understood completely. Their magic wasn't theirs to command, and, in the absence of air, they lacked the strength to reclaim it. Trust was a fragile commodity. They'd gifted him with theirs, and he would not let them down.

More time passed than he would have liked. Within, his beast was a steadying force. It knew what he'd attempted. Despite treading the edges of the impossible with his time warp spell, the dragon still cheered him on. His lungs were burning from lack of air, seizing every time he took a reflexive breath. Next to him, Erin's wingbeats were slowing. She wasn't as strong as him. He flew beneath the shimmery outline of her magic to offer a cushion. If they fell out of the sky, though, they might not hit the Southern Ocean.

He wasn't at all sure where they'd come out.

The maelstrom slowed. Unremitting black yielded to a silvery gray around him. He released everyone's magic, blinked to clear his vision, and forced himself to look down. Triumphant bugles shot from his throat. The ship was gone. His daring gambit had worked.

"Thank you for protecting us, but we are all right." Erin's red dragon spoke with dignity and flew off to one side.

"What did you do?" Johan's green dragon flew near. "Where is the ship?"

Kon forced his spinning eyes to slow enough for him to truly examine the water beneath him. Water, not ice. How far back in time had he taken them?

"You employed a time alteration casting," Yle cawed. "Nicely done, but we must locate the ship. Humans aboard will have no memory of a future that has not yet presented itself to them."

"If the ship is where it was a day or two ago, what happened to the serpents?" Erin asked in the dragons' tongue.

"None of us knows exactly where the ship is," Yle answered. "It might not be a day or two. It could be much more."

Konstantin's dragon was ecstatic, flying figure eights and

banking and swooping. He brought it to heel with difficulty. "I tried to capture as many serpents as possible in the time warp," he told everyone. "I sent them to a different spot than the ship. That part may or may not have worked. It's not a thing I've ever attempted before. Not that they cannot return, but at least they'll have to work to get back here."

He maneuvered his dragon to a position where he faced the others. "Thank you for trusting me. I couldn't tell you what I had planned. If the serpents had discovered my idea—"

"They'd have made certain it went to hell," Nikolai bugled. Leader of a flight they'd found stranded on the third world in the Fleisher borderworld system, he had copper-gold scales.

More delighted bugling and trumpeting and happy cawing and dinosaur cries drowned him out.

"Let's hunt for the ship," Erin said, sounding hopeful.

"Not that many spots it could be," Johan pointed out. His mastery of dragonspeak was better than Erin's.

"What do you mean?" Kon asked him.

"The ship was headed north through the Drake Passage on its way back to Argentina. It is a larger ship, so it would be limited in terms of where it could travel. My guess is it went to spots along the Palmer Peninsula or to the South Shetlands, and then turned and headed for home."

"What if we don't find it?" Erin asked.

"Then it will be in Ushuaia Harbor, not having yet left port," Johan replied.

"If we are more than a couple of weeks in the past," she countered, "it may not have reached Ushuaia yet."

"We fly south," Konstantin told the shifters to short-circuit the pointless logistics discussion unfolding between Johan and Erin. "Any of you who wish to return to my home may do so."

He set a course for the Antarctic landmass, keeping sharp eyes on the water. It didn't take long to run into ice floes that gave way to sheets of ice. So they weren't all that far in the past. If they had been, none of the ocean would have been frozen over.

All the shifters were strung out behind him. He was deeply pleased none of them had left. There'd been a few uncertain moments, but their faith in him and his leadership had paid off when his gambit worked. Nothing like success to breed confidence.

As he flew, he told Ylon what had happened, so the dinosaurs wouldn't be milling about expecting serpents who'd never arrive. At least, not today. When they'd exhausted the nearest portion of Antarctica's landmass, they split into groups to explore the islands that lay off the peninsula.

"Found it," blared through his mind after he'd nearly given up and chalked the ship off as having cloaking magic of its own.

Kon winged his way toward the voice, which turned out to belong to a raven. Noted for his keen distance eyesight, the bird had located the errant ship. Ice eddied about its prow, but it was doggedly chugging through it.

"I will do my best to talk them out of the folly of the Drake Passage," Johan said.

"Maybe I should come with you." Erin swooped close.

"Good idea," Johan said.

"We shall accompany them," Konstantin's beast instructed.

Kon overruled him. He had to show Erin he believed in her judgment. What better way than to not pull rank or make it appear he didn't trust her on her own.

"Katya will go along," Konstantin told them. "In case there's trouble, a seasoned magic wielder might come in handy."

His twin dipped a wing in acknowledgement and headed toward the distant ship with Erin and Johan flanking her.

If he hadn't already been in his dragon body, the beast would have given him a run for control. As it was, the dragon pitched and blew fire until the air around them heated to molten.

"We should be with them!" the dragon shrieked.

"Do you want her to be our mate or not?" Konstantin used his sternest tone. The one designed to bring errant dragons to heel.

"The two have nothing to do with each other."

"Ah, but I believe they do."

Bugling a summons, he led the flight of mixed shifters back toward the headlands where they'd begun. He'd have another go at opening a communication channel with the land. She must have witnessed what just happened. Perhaps his intervention would make a difference, and she'd be more open to joining forces.

If not, he'd have to proceed without her. It would be a blow, but he couldn't afford to squander any more time or magic on a losing cause.

JOHAN

As I flew toward the ship, the logistics of shifting seemed daunting. Humans milled about on deck, and I was certain a few of the ships' officers were peering through the many windows lining the bridge. It appeared to be on the uppermost deck, but most of these bloated cruise ships had at least one additional command center much lower in the vessel where personnel tracked a duplicate set of electronics.

Erin apparently shared my concerns about how we'd manage things because she asked, "How will we shift?"

Smoke trailed from my open jaws. Shifting was only one portion of the problem. Part two was we'd be naked. While I was almost used to not wearing clothing, the ship's crew would have a far harder time taking us seriously.

Katya circled around us, fanning her wings to hold her steady in the air. We were still far enough away, it was unlikely anyone would have spotted us. I rolled my mental eyes. The absence of gunfire was a sure giveaway. The moment someone noticed us in the skies, they'd haul out the automatic weapons.

Most of these ships plied polar waters seasonally. While they had no need for guns big enough to stop a polar bear in its tracks in the Antarctic, such firearms were a necessity in Arctic waters.

"We must think this through," Katya said in dragonspeak, keeping her words soft. "Neither of you are skilled enough yet to shift midair and land on that nice open deck toward the back of the ship."

"Even if we could, it is not a good idea. We will need clothes," I said.

Katya turned her spinning gaze on me. "Why?"

"We will be delivering a serious message," I replied.

"Indeed," Erin chimed in. "We'll be telling them they have to change course and maybe aim for Chile or Buenos Aires rather than the Drake Passage."

Katya's scales rattled as she shrugged her shoulders. "If they don't listen, it's not our fault. We will have tried."

"Yes, but if we don't present ourselves as professional and trustworthy from the gate, they'll never hear us out. We may as well not bother," Erin said.

"I agree with her." I blew a stream of smoky ash in front of me. What had I been thinking when I'd blithely said we had to warn the ship? Probably that I'd show up in my research duds from the *Darya*, be accepted as a scientific investigator, and say my piece. I hadn't gotten around to how I'd make it palatable for them.

Telling them we were dragon shifters was the wrong

approach. I may as well say we were faeries from the Scottish Highlands and dance a jig while I was at it. I narrowed my eyes. It seemed as if the ship had stopped moving. Closer inspection told me it was in the bay off King George Island.

"We might have gotten lucky," I said.

"Do you think they're stopping for the tourists to check out Arctowski Station?" Erin asked.

"No. The ship is too large, but they may be in trouble from all the ice. This is the only outpost in the region where they might secure assistance. Plus, Admiralty Bay is deep enough to accommodate even a ship of that size."

"Regardless," Katya cut in. "We can land, shift, and hunt for something to cover ourselves with. This is the Polish base, correct? The one you originally wished us to transport you to."

"Correct," I told her.

If it was either earlier or later in the year, we would have waited until it got dark, but what passed for darkness this far south wouldn't happen until toward the middle of the night. I wanted to be gone from here as soon as we'd discharged our duty and warned the ship what lay in wait for it.

I still wasn't certain quite which tack I'd take, but I knew many of the scientific staff at Arctowski. Because we were acquainted, perhaps it would lend me the credibility I needed to pull this off. Erin had been here, but she'd kept a much lower profile than me.

Konstantin had said something about trapping the sea-serpents in a time warp. If he'd been successful, maybe the ship might have safe passage, unless it became mired in ice once again.

Ice! That was the ticket. I'd tell them the ice was going to do nothing but get worse and they needed to avoid the Drake, a narrow strip of the Southern Ocean.

"We will do this." Katya's words broke into my train of thought. "Ward yourselves. The mountains a kilometer or so behind those buildings should be perfect to conceal us. We will land there. Surely, an installation such as this Polish base will have clothing lockers. I will conceal myself once I'm human and fetch garments for all of us."

"Be sure and dig down to the bottom of the pile," I told her. "Less chance of anyone recognizing we are wearing items stolen from their stores."

She shot me an annoyed look that seemed to ask how I'd put up with the suspicious fools humans were all those years. It hadn't been easy, but not for the reasons she thought.

I asked my beast for help warding his bulk. Soon, we settled smoothly on pockmarked ice fields at the base of a complicated series of cliffs. In the process, we startled a large group of fur seals. Determined to stand their ground, they barked up a storm and only moved a meter or two away. Snarling, they bared their teeth, reminding me they just looked fluffy and benign. Seals could be real bastards if you got on their wrong side.

The air glistened with expended magic as we traded our dragon bodies for our human ones. The seals yipped and scattered. Perhaps magic had accomplished what the dragons couldn't and scared the crap out of them.

"I will return as quickly as I can," Katya said and vanished before my eyes. If I blinked hard and looked from a different angle, I could see her loping toward the motley collection of brightly colored buildings that comprised Arctowski Station. Looking like railroad boxcars, the buildings were all prefabs that had been dropped here by cargo ships and assembled onsite.

Arctowski was comfortable, though. And they always had a pot of tea strong enough to chase the cobwebs away bubbling on the hob. The seals had gotten over their apprehension and waddled closer, curious as hell about us.

A large male barked.

Fire streamed from Erin's mouth, and he jumped back. She shook her head. "My dragon thought he got too close."

"They will not harm us unless they perceive us as a threat," I said. "Mostly, that one"—I pointed at the bull seal who was probably leader of this pod—"wants to make certain we aren't competition for food."

"So long as he's not seeing us as food, I'm good." Erin laughed. "What are we going to tell them after we go inside? Assuming any of the ship's personnel are there too."

"I have been thinking that through." It was cold, so I pulled warmth from the earth upward until it surrounded me. That done, I sank into a crouch.

"What did you come up with?" She hunkered next to me and wrapped her arms around her legs. "I figured we could tell them the *Darya* had been boarded and we escaped, but then they'll insist we remain here. At least until they can see us safely aboard a ship or a plane."

The same thought had occurred to me. "It is not a problem. Not really. We smile and make nice and once everyone goes to bed, we simply head back here, shift, and leave."

"They post twenty-four-hour sentries," Erin reminded me. "Just like on the *Darya*."

"It does not matter, Erin. It is unlikely we will ever be here again. We will ward ourselves until we are out of visual range."

She pinched her nose between her thumb and index finger. "Does that bother you?"

Her question was so open-ended, I had a hard time dissecting it. "Does what bother me?"

"That our time among our own kind is over?"

I patted her thigh. "They are no longer like us."

"No. I guess not, but part of me still sees myself as human. A big part. How could I not? It's the way I deciphered the world for almost forty years." Ash and smoke-tinged fire billowed from her mouth.

She spit out bits of black and said, "Sorry. This has nothing to do with how I feel about you."

I assumed she was talking with her dragon, trying to soften her statement about not having totally transitioned from human to magical being. Interestingly enough, my beast wasn't kicking up a fuss about anything. But then, him nearly getting both of us killed had shaved the crusty edges off his temper.

"Are you considering remaining here?" I asked her.

Her eyes widened. "Oh hell, no. Nothing has changed. The sea-serpent problem hasn't gone away. Besides, there'd be hell to pay if you vanished and I remained. Everyone would pester the crap out of me to see if I knew what happened to you. When that turned out to be a dry hole, they'd figure you fell into a crevasse, and they'd waste untold hours searching for you with the dogs."

She offered a crooked smile. "I can miss something without necessarily wanting to return to it."

I sensed Katya before I saw her. Dressed in black polar bibs and a red jacket, she looked jaunty and as if she'd been here forever. I hadn't quite figured out how to explain who she was. Maybe one of the researchers aboard the *Darya* who never left their workstations. We'd actually had a few like that.

"Do you want us to use your real name when we go back to the station?" I asked.

"Easier that way," she replied and dropped a bundle of clothing next to Erin and me. We dressed quickly. The boots she'd grabbed for me were painfully small, but I could manage for the short while it would take to deliver our message. Besides, they didn't allow boots inside the station. There was a mud room with cubbies for everyone's outdoor footwear. It cut down on the possibility of stray microbes that had been trapped in ice for millennia getting tracked inside.

"I like you better naked." Katya winked at me.

I walked to her and gave her a quick hug. "The feeling is mutual."

"Let's get this over with, then," she said. "We can leave the boots and apparel here before we depart. That way, someone is bound to stumble over them."

"Not a good idea." Erin glanced her way. "Someone will remember we were wearing these garments. They'll suspect foul play and turn the world upside down. It will be a tremendous waste of time and resources."

"Guess I'll have to live with my guilt." Katya grinned. "Dragons don't make a practice of stealing—unless it's gold and gems. Ready?"

"Yup." Erin started walking downhill toward the bright yellow-orange line of prefabs.

Katya caught up with her. I walked behind, wincing as my toes hit the front of my boots. Katya had the foresight to grab socks, so they cushioned things a little even though they made the boots even tighter.

"Are we visiting your flight?" my bondmate asked quietly.

"Not exactly. I am acquainted with many people who live here, but they are nothing like a dragon flight."

"How are they different?"

I struggled to find a short answer. Long ago, human groups had displayed the type of loyalty to one another common to dragon flights, but the advent of the electronic age had created a society of loners.

I knew it all too well because I was one. Or had been.

"We will speak of this at length later," I told my beast, touched by his interest in something definitely undragonlike. *"No smoke, fire, or ash,"* I added.

"Steam?"

"No. Nothing."

"It's a good reminder," Katya said, followed by, "Erin, make sure your bondmate doesn't get frisky."

"Already covered that ground." Erin turned a sunny smile Katya's way.

We were perhaps half a kilometer from the base when,

"*Hallo, Wer bist du*?" floated up the hill. The German carried a strong Eastern European accent.

"Johan Petris, Erin Ryan, and Katya Romanova," I called back. I'd had to make up a last name for Katya on the spur of the moment, and I hoped she approved of my choice.

Two figures took off toward us, running hard. Soon they were close enough for me to recognize Tomek and Kryzs, the *de facto* base managers. Both men were of medium height, but Tomek had Nordic coloring with wheat-colored hair and blue eyes. He was slightly built compared to Kryzs, who was put together like a tank. Black hair fell to Kryzs's shoulders, and his dark eyes were crinkled with pleasure at the corners.

"I am so glad to see you," he gasped in English, out of breath from his sprint uphill.

"Me as well," Tomek said. "We heard about the *Darya*. But we were told no one survived. Where have you been?"

"Officials from the Antarctic Treaty Organization are here," Kryzs said. "They will be most interested to hear the story from two survivors. Russia, of course, denies all knowledge."

"It was a Russian coup, was it not?" Tomek cut in.

"Yes. Russian. May we go inside?" Johan asked.

"Inside would be welcome," Erin spoke up.

"Da. Inside, please." Katya aped a Russian accent handily.

Kryzs clapped Johan across the back. "Of course. Where are my manners. You must be exhausted. Freezing. I fear summer has departed these latitudes, though I will be damned if I can figure out why."

"That ship is in serious trouble." Tomek pointed at the

cruise ship. "They are not equipped to deal with ice, and they limped in here. We are trying to talk them into waiting for a plane to ferry their passengers to Ushuaia."

"Why trying?" Erin said. "A plane is the only option that makes sense. We saw so much ice getting here. Places the ocean is frozen over and we walked on it."

"Excellent timing on several fronts," Kryzs said. "You can speak with the officials and the ship's captain. Hang on." He pulled a two-way radio from a vest pocket and fired off instructions in Polish.

Johan had no trouble following. He was telling whoever was talking with the captain that visitors with up-to-the-minute oceanic reports had arrived. The five of them walked slowly toward the research installation.

"Why has the captain or navigator not confirmed sea conditions via weather satellite?" Johan asked.

"That is a problem," Tomek said. "Satellite communications are down all through this region."

"But that happens frequently," Erin spoke up.

"Sure, but they always come back online. This time, it has been days," Kryzs told her.

I tripped because of my too-tight boots. Tomek made a clucking noise, having interpreted my stumble as the result of exhaustion. "We will get all of you nice, hot tea and fresh biscuits."

"Спасибо," Katya said.

I thought she was laying it on a bit thick with all the Russian. *"You know English,"* I reminded her.

She patted my hand. "Thank you."

We should all be on the same page with our story, so I

mumbled, "Tea will be so welcome. We have had Hell's own time. We were dumped at the chromium dig site and left for dead. After many tries, we climbed out of the mine and stole a Zodiac. That got us into the South Shetlands, but not easily. We encountered much ice; some we crossed on foot, dragging the raft."

"We lost it, one pontoon at a time," Erin helped me out. "Lucky for us, we made the far side of King George before the raft sank on us."

"You are lucky to be alive," Tomek said.

"We think so too." Erin nodded solemnly.

"You can fly out of here on one of the planes that comes for the cruise ship's passengers," Kryzs said.

"It is a better bet than a ship," Katya said. "I have never seen so much ice floating in the sea. Even in the winter months."

We had reached the main door. I ducked into the familiar mud room and sat to lever off my boots. Everyone else did the same. Parkas came off and were slipped over hooks. The station was always too warm, but it was welcome.

I made my way to a chair. Tomek brought steaming mugs of black, bitter tea and a plate of biscuits. I shut my eyes, doing my best to look too exhausted to be grilled by IAATO officials. I'd told Kryzs and Tomek what happened. They could pass it on.

If things went well, they'd convince whoever ran the ship to abandon it here and fly everyone home. Maybe I wouldn't have to do anything beyond what I'd already done.

"Humans are not forthcoming with one another." My dragon

sounded disappointed. *"You were not honest with those two nice men."*

"Do you want to end up on an airplane heading for Argentina?"

"We'd just teleport back here."

I selected another tactic. *"Are dragons always completely honest with one another?"*

Heat spread through my chest; I prepared to make a run for the outhouse if it got worse. *"No smoke. No fire."*

My beast grumbled within me, but the scorching sensation retreated. I noticed he ignored my last question. I waited, but he didn't ask any more of his own, either.

A tall, broad-shouldered man wearing a dark-blue ship's uniform over a starched white shirt walked toward us. He was bald and had a squared-off jaw covered with black stubble. His brown eyes looked tired. "Sorry for taking any of your time, mate," he began in a clipped British accent, "but I understand the sea ice is bad from all directions."

I opened my eyes. "Do not apologize. From what we saw, ice is a serious problem all around the Palmer Peninsula. I would not wish to risk hundreds of passengers in the Drake. It is a difficult stretch of water under the best of conditions."

He pulled a folding chair close and dropped into it. "Same conclusion I'm coming around to, old chap." He shook his head. "We seafaring types are superstitious as all get-out. You're the third person who has advised against traveling north. Three is a magic number. I will inform the captain, and we shall make alternative plans."

"Already in process." Tomek glided over from the next room, which was another boxcar attached to the one we sat in. He patted my shoulder. "You three will be on the first plane out of here. It should arrive in about two hours. No reason to make you wait while the ship empties 300 passengers."

"Very kind of you." Erin nodded her thanks.

"Indeed." Katya offered half a smile.

"You will get your wish," I told my dragon. *"We will be teleporting back here."*

"Better than sneaking off like a thief in the night," my beast retorted.

If I could, I'd have happily throttled him. Deep within me, dragon laughter warmed my heart.

KATYA

Katya was deeply pleased. Despite not having thought through how they'd leave Arctowski —without creating havoc—the problem had solved itself. And the serpents would never get their claws into the ship since it might well sit in Admiralty Bay until satellite communications came back up.

She had a feeling the outpouring of magic was responsible for the failure of satellite transmissions, but she didn't fully understand how the whole satellite thing worked. It would be a good question for her to ask Johan when they were well and truly alone.

Katya had never flown in an aircraft before. Why would she? She had wings of her own and the ability to travel to other worlds. Something this airplane could never manage. It was interesting, though, this metal tube that took to the skies with its noisy engines. Her dragon thought it was hilarious.

"I'm here if it crashes," she commented *sotto voce.*

"You'd better be here before," Katya shot right back. *"Less messy."*

The three of them were crammed into tiny chairs in the plane. A long, thin affair, it boasted twin seats on both sides of a narrow aisle. She and Johan sat on one side. Erin was directly across from her. A weary-looking man with short black hair and a red polar suit sat next to Erin. He'd closed his eyes as soon as he fell into his seat. He didn't appear at all well. His complexion held a pasty aspect, and dark circles carved beneath his eyes. Maybe he was just exhausted from his time aboard a struggling ship.

The plane had filled quickly, and they'd been airborne shortly thereafter. She supposed the pilot was in a hurry. He'd have to make at least three trips, perhaps four, to ferry all the ship's passengers and crew to Ushuaia. She'd asked how long the flight would be and been told two to two-and-a-half hours depending on wind conditions.

She assumed Ushuaia was a decent-sized city. She'd never been there, but losing themselves in an urban environment so they could quietly teleport back to Konstantin and the others shouldn't be all that hard. They obviously didn't have travel documents—passports—but both Johan and Erin had reassured a few folk back at Arctowski that they'd stop at their respective consulates as soon as they landed in Argentina. Katya just smiled and nodded. She had a paper with an official-looking stamp that should be enough to get her out of the airport.

In actuality, this whole playacting was ridiculous. She could cast an invisibility spell and spirit the three of them out of the airplane. It might leave a lot of jaws hanging open, but it wasn't as if anyone had the wherewithal to follow them.

Johan gripped her hand, pulling her wandering thoughts back to him. "For once, fortune smiled on us, eh?"

She nodded indulgently. "It would seem so, yes." She switched to mind speech. *"That officer from the ship did not give us any pushback at all."*

"Not only that..." Johan stopped and frowned. "No one to hear if I botch the, um, other type of talking, so I shall give it a whirl."

"May as well," she agreed, sticking with telepathy to encourage him.

"I was concerned I would have to fill out one of those interminable governmental reporting forms," he went on. *"That we all would."*

Katya winced.

"Was my telepathy attempt as bad as all that?" He drew his brows together into a thick, dark line.

"'Fraid so. If anyone else on this craft has any magic at all, they'll have heard you."

"What am I doing wrong?"

She thought about it. *"Try a lot less fire, more air, and a little water."*

"Too bad this is not a one-size-fits-all proposition. What works for you does not work the same way for me when I try to accomplish the same thing."

"That was better!" She jumped in with instant feedback—before he forgot precisely what he'd done.

He scrunched his eyes into slits as if he were

concentrating. *"It almost seems like we had it too easy at Arctowski. No grilling by an IAATO agent. The ship's officer barely asked us anything."*

"You don't trust the fortune you were crowing over?"

He shook his head. *"Not only that, I have begun to see magical boogie-men behind every bush."*

"If someone plans to sabotage this airplane, we will either switch to our dragon forms right away or skip that part and teleport back to Konstantin and the others as we are."

"Sounds simple enough," he ventured.

"Because it is simple. Talk to me about what makes this"—she patted an armrest—"not fall out of the sky." No longer needing telepathy, she let it go. Johan had done well. His private mind speech wasn't perfect, but at least it wouldn't broadcast to every magic-wielder within a half-kilometer radius.

"Not so different from dragon wings." He stuck with telepathy. *"All wings are airfoils, which means air flows faster over the lower edge than the upper one. It is how anything with wings remains airborne. Obviously, this craft uses engines to provide propulsion. Dragons use magic and muscles."*

Katya chuckled. *"Magic and muscles. My dragon liked that. A lot."*

"Actually, mine did too."

The man sitting next to Erin groaned. Erin had been slumped against the window shade, but her eyes snapped open.

"Oh-oh," Johan mumbled.

"What?" Katya cast a thread of seeking magic toward

Erin's seatmate. He writhed in his seat, and a fine sheen of perspiration formed on his brow.

"I recognize the expression on Erin's face. It's the same way she looked at me right before she told me she was going to fix my broken leg. Kind of an 'I won't take no for an answer' attitude."

Erin was indeed poking and prodding. The man didn't react to her touch. "Crap on a cracker," she muttered and basically crawled over him and loped toward the front of the plane.

"Do you know what she's doing?" Katya asked Johan.

He shrugged. "If I had to guess, she is trolling for medical gear."

Katya continued to probe with magic. She hadn't forgotten Erin was a doctor, but magic was so much better at healing everything, she discounted whatever Erin might or might not have in the way of skills. It had been her, Katya, who'd fixed Johan's broken leg. In minutes, not months.

As she dug deeper examining Erin's seatmate, what she found wasn't promising. An illness, not unlike the Black Death, was ripping through the man's organs. Blood was everywhere, not nicely encased in vessels where it should be. Sure enough, it started leaking out of his mouth and eyes and ears. Purplish blotches were forming on his face from blood pooling beneath his skin.

Erin raced back, a box with a red cross painted on it clutched in one hand.

"Do you know what is wrong with him?" Johan asked.

"Of course, without lab tests, it's difficult to know for certain—" she began.

"Never mind," Johan broke in. "What do you think it is?"

Erin glanced at the people seated closest. About that time, a dark-haired woman dressed in a black uniform skirt and jacket joined her. A name tag identified her as Lupe Morales. "What can I do to help, Doctor?"

Before she had a chance to answer, the man started gagging. Erin twisted his head forward about the time bloody bile spewed from his mouth. "Move the two rows around him to another location," she told the cabin attendant.

"But we have no other seats," Lupe protested. "It isn't safe for them to—"

Erin leaned close to the uniformed woman. Katya had no difficulty hearing her whisper, "I believe this man has a type of viral hemorrhagic fever. If I'm correct, it's very contagious."

The woman's dark eyes widened, but she didn't hesitate before she clapped her hands smartly and started herding people as far from the sick man as she could move them "We will remain where we are," Katya told Lupe.

"But the doctor said—"

"I am a doctor too." Katya sharpened her tone. "Dr. Ryan will have a difficult time managing this patient on her own."

"As you will." Lupe's tone clearly intimated it was Katya's funeral. Johan's too.

Katya switched back to telepathy, this time directed at Erin. *"This sickness, is it like the Black Death?"*

"Only insofar as it has a high mortality rate," Erin replied in kind. *"The plague was caused by a bacterium. This disease is*

caused by a virus. It's actually far more contagious than the plague ever dreamed of being."

Johan must have been listening, at least to Erin, because he asked, *"Will everyone aboard die?"*

Erin looked up from where she'd been catching more bloody vomit in a plastic bag. "Um, it's likely, yes."

Something crackled annoyingly loudly before an accented male voice filled the cabin. "This is your captain speaking. We have illness aboard. Everyone will don masks handed out by the cabin crew. We will land in Ushuaia in approximately forty-five minutes. The plane will be quarantined until medical personnel can clear each of you. Do not worry. All your needs will be attended to."

Katya craned her neck around and saw Lupe and two other women dressed just like her passing out paper masks. Many of the passengers were agitated. A few were crying. A man jumped from his seat and shook a fist at Lupe. "I will leave this aircraft. Do you understand me?"

"Yes, sir. Certainly, sir." Apparently well trained in dealing with abrasive passengers, Lupe tried to press a mask into his fisted hand.

"I'll make all of you sorry as hell if you try to hold me." His face was splotched an angry red.

Katya had had enough of his attitude. A judicious shot of magic sent him sprawling back into his seat. His mouth opened and closed as he gasped like a landed fish. Too bad. He was lucky she hadn't killed him and been done with it. Although if Erin was right, the disease mowing through the man half a meter away would make short work of the others too.

The cabin filled with a foul odor as the man's bowels turned to a watery mix of blood and shit that sluiced across the seat covering and onto the floor. Erin straightened, muttering, "This man needs to be in a hospital. I have nothing to give him."

Something about her words struck a chord in Katya. She got to her feet and stood next to Erin. *"We should leave while we can,"* she suggested, seeding her words with the tiniest bit of compulsion.

"But he's sick," Erin protested. *"If I go, he'll have no one."*

Katya nodded, fully understanding why her twin had fallen in love with Erin. She had a compassionate side that shone through, and a selfless nature that was almost antithetical to being a dragon.

"Is there anything you can do with magic?" Erin turned to her, entreaty in her blue eyes with their thick golden rims. Katya had no idea why no one had noticed how otherworldly their eyes were, but no one had said a word.

Katya considered it. She didn't want to lie to Erin. As she thought through what she'd have to do to pull this man's life out of the unfortunate place it hovered circling a cosmic sewer, she checked other passengers who huddled nearby.

No one had said much of anything, but it was as if they already knew they were goners.

Katya hooked a hand beneath Erin's forearm. *"Yes, I could probably reverse the illness. In him. But every single person I checked has the same thing. We do not have time to cure everyone. Never mind all the questions we'd end up having to answer. Medical miracles. Phenomenal cures. We'd be stuck in Ushuaia—or worse, Buenos Aires—for weeks."*

"It would knock a big hole in our original plan to slip in and out unnoticed," Erin muttered.

Katya had already suggested they leave. Right now. Before the stupid plane landed and officials quarantined it. Erin was a doctor. Katya had lied about being one. She had no doubt both of them would be pressed into service. No one would split hairs verifying her credentials.

Unfortunately, there wasn't an unobtrusive way to teleport out of the plane. Their presence would be sorely missed. No reason to waste extra magic on wards to hide them before they vanished.

Before she could generate more arguments in favor of leaving, Erin went on, *"It feels wrong to desert these people. They're sick. I took an oath to help the sick as best I'm able..."*

"Even if you know they're all as good as dead?" Katya pressed.

Johan materialized by her side. "This discussion looks serious," he said in a low voice.

"You have no idea," Katya mumbled.

"Katya thinks we should teleport out of here now," Erin said.

"I happen to agree with her," Johan replied.

Katya's eyes widened. Apparently, engineers weren't suckers for lost causes like doctors were.

"We do not want to get in the middle of being quarantined," Johan continued. *"I have been there. It was not pleasant. Especially for us since we will not sicken. Some do-gooder researcher will decide we are immune, and they will turn us into pin cushions taking blood to attempt to fashion a vaccine."*

Erin turned curious eyes his way, not bothering with telepathy. "What and when?"

"Yellow fever. The Belgian Congo ten years ago. I had a natural immunity since I had never been vaccinated."

Katya tightened her hold on Erin's forearm. Below them, the man moaned piteously and vomited more blood. His face had turned into a mass of blood-filled pustules. Even from where she stood, Katya could feel heat pouring off him as his fever spiked.

"I can end his suffering," she told Erin, *"but then, so could you. Simply reach inward and stop his heart."*

Erin jerked her arm out of Katya's grasp and whirled to face her, features contorted in fury. Katya met her gaze calmly. The human world was changing. Soon, not much recognizable would remain. Erin needed to grow a tougher skin.

"Tell her how fortunate she is to be a dragon," Katya's beast urged.

"Not the time. She has some decisions to make," Katya replied.

Johan had moved to Erin's other side and placed his mouth right next to her ear. "We must go," he urged.

"But I can't," she protested. "Don't you see?"

"Of course, I do." His voice was rough. "We have a far more pressing obligation than this plane." He switched back to telepathy. *"Erin. Even if you had a full-blown trauma center, what would you do for these people?"*

"Treat their symptoms and hope they make it," she admitted, looking as if she wanted to kill Johan for making her face facts.

The man's body started to shake as he seized. Katya closed on him, intent on ending his travail. "My patient,"

Erin snarled and placed a hand on his head and another on a shoulder. A clean white slice of magic cleaved right to his heart. It shuddered, and then stopped beating.

Katya was inside Erin's mind and heard her silent entreaty. *May God forgive me.*

She wanted to tell Erin that the only god who mattered a whit was Y Ddraigh Goch—and that he could give a fuck less about humans—but wisely remained silent. Instead, she harnessed magic as unobtrusively as possible. Most of the other passengers were off in their own private worlds, no doubt wondering if they'd be next to start puking blood.

She wove her teleport spell around Johan and Erin as surely as she'd once woven various colors of wool into patterns on her loom. When she was certain everything was in place, she kindled her casting. Brilliant light blazed around them to the accompaniment of screams and pounding feet as Lupe and her fellow cabin attendants ran toward them.

Katya poured more magic into the mix. The cabin slipped away along with hands making a grab for her. Good. She didn't want to have to kill anyone. If the sickness that had afflicted the man was as virulent as she suspected, they'd all succumb before long.

She inserted a course alteration and brought them out on a deserted spit of land toward the southern end of the Beagle Channel. They'd talk through this before returning to Kon and the others.

"Where are we?" Johan scanned a small group of falling-down buildings with corrugated roofs as her magic cleared.

"An abandoned whaling station."

Erin planted herself in front of Katya and crossed her arms under her breasts. "We could have saved those people. All of them. Using magic."

Katya stood taller, grateful she'd had the foresight not to drag this quarrel into the midst of the other shifters, who were probably deep into crafting battle plans. "Yes," she agreed, keeping her tone mild, "we could have."

Erin shook her head until blonde hair danced around her shoulders. "Look. I get the part about the serpents being a danger to all life on Earth, but we played god up there." She jerked her chin upward.

"How so?" Katya asked, genuinely curious and wanting to understand Erin's reasoning.

"We—rather, you—made a field decision and jettisoned the men and women on that plane. That man had Ebola. Or maybe Marburg. Those diseases have something like a 95 percent mortality rate."

"How long an incubation period?" Johan spoke up.

"Two to twenty-one days," Erin replied dully. "Researchers are of two minds about this, but I believe people can be contagious the whole time."

He nodded. "What, exactly, does that tell you?"

Erin's eyes widened. "Oh my fucking God. The entire ship is infected."

"And everyone at Arctowski," Johan pointed out.

"So we made the right choice," Katya said, and then could have kicked herself.

"Your interpretation, not mine," Erin spat out through gritted teeth. "We could have leveraged magic and cured all those people. The plane wasn't going anywhere. Certainly not back to Arctowski to pick up another batch of passengers."

"Not that particular plane," Johan agreed in a decidedly neutral tone, "but what about the next aircraft? If they even send another one, which is far from certain. Had we remained, the local infectious disease control team would have ascertained the three of us were not ill from an examination of lab tests."

He stopped there, letting his words sink in. Katya offered him credit for being a better diplomat than she was.

"How much magic would it burn through to cure several hundred people?" Erin asked.

"A lot," Katya said. "And time too. We would have gone through several cycles where we would have had to rest and replenish our ability." She narrowed her eyes to slits. "This is assuming we could fling power about. Such is not allowed. Humans must not know about us, or about the existence of magic."

"So it's fine to kill someone with magic, but not acceptable to cure them with it?" Erin's tone held a glacial edge.

"What you did was hidden within the man's body," Katya pointed out. "For us to have had a fighting chance to help any of the rest of those people would have required visible displays of power." She blew out a breath. "I'm sorry I was so obvious about the way we left the airplane, but I didn't have much of a choice. If I'd fashioned warding first, we'd have vanished from sight. It would have created as much of a stir as the flash of brilliance that presaged our departure. And wasted magic. For nothing."

Katya ground her teeth, annoyed at having been backed into an impossible corner. No choice would have netted her the anonymity she wished for. "Most of those people will die," she muttered, "but not before they tell a whole lot of somebodies what they saw."

Erin's harsh expression crumpled; her eyes sheened with tears. "This is difficult."

"It is," Johan agreed. "Nothing is the same."

"My instincts haven't changed," Erin murmured. "Healing is my life. Or it was." Steam puffed from her mouth. Solace from her bondmate.

Her mouth twisted downward. "My dragon knows."

"Knows what?" Katya asked.

"Everything." Erin's nostrils flared. "In this particular instance, she knows this is far from the first patient I've edged across the veil when there was no hope of recovery and they were suffering."

"Is that a common practice?" Johan angled a dark brow upward.

Erin nodded. "We all do it from time to time. It's a kindness when no hope remains." She stood straight. "I'm ready to join the others."

"They're not far," Katya said. She wanted to hug Erin but sensed the other woman was holding onto her dignity by a thread. Sometimes composure was more important than solace. Besides, Konstantin would sense her distress and console her.

"I can take us back," Johan offered. "I need practice."

"You both do," Katya said. "Before we leave, there are a couple of things I want to say. Things for you to think about.

I have no idea what will be left of this world, mostly because I don't have a way of judging how much damage the serpents will do.

"Regardless, Earth will be changed from the world you knew. Changed so greatly as to be virtually unrecognizable. You will be called upon to make decisions—difficult ones such as Erin faced today. You cannot base those choices on who you used to be."

Erin nodded, looking sad. "My dragon said exactly the same thing. She would have spirited us out of the airplane the moment the man started looking bad, long before I determined he had a terminal illness. Once I understood he was a dead man walking, my bondmate became almost uncontrollable. She was screaming at me so loud, it was hard to think."

"She would," Katya said. "Her job is to ensure your safety."

"But the man didn't pose a threat to me," Erin pointed out.

"No, but your place is in the magical world, not the human one."

"I have our spell ready to roll," Johan said.

When Katya glanced his way, power shimmered around him. Damn, he was beautiful, as if he'd been born to wield the magic jumping to his call. Perhaps he was. She remembered a wise dragon shaman—the one who'd nurtured her seer magic—saying there were no coincidences.

She'd noticed Johan—and Erin—and been drawn to them in ways she didn't understand. She hadn't questioned her intuition, though. Nor had she fought her twin very hard when he'd floated the idea of drawing the two humans into their realm. Maybe somewhere an old dragon matchmaker was rubbing her hands together, having finally come up with bait that jolted Katya off her perpetually single pedestal.

Muffling a smile, she slipped in next to Johan and motioned Erin to his other side. Once they were in place, she said, "You said you wanted to control this casting. Take us home."

KONSTANTIN

A Short While Earlier

Konstantin retreated to a distant corner of the headlands, determined to make one more bid to encourage Earth to communicate with him. If he could get the land on board, it would make such a difference. He'd left Ylon and Nikolai in charge of crafting a roadmap for their first actual skirmish. He wasn't certain just how much of a jump backward in time his little sleight-of-hand maneuver had bought them.

Probably not much, given the location of the ship and the large chunks of brash ice floating in the ocean. He hoped he'd been successful trapping a fair number of serpents in the time warp. It would remove them as threats for a few days. Maybe.

He crouched on a spot of open ground between two large rocks and splayed his hands on the dirt in front of him. It was fortunate he had something to occupy himself, otherwise he'd be mired in worry about Erin.

He never should have let her go off by herself.

Konstantin slapped one hand against the ground and told himself to stop it. He'd had good and sufficient reasons not to order his not-quite-yet mate to stick by his side like glue. If he did too much of that, she never would be his. Katya was with her, and she'd let him know if anything went wrong.

It wasn't quite as effective as being there, but almost. He could teleport to damn near anywhere on Earth in a heartbeat. As settled as he was likely to get, he made an effort to clear everything but the living, breathing land from his mind.

"I know you're there," he told Earth. "We could help one another."

He pushed a gentle flow of magic through his fingertips and deep into the rich, loamy ground.

And waited.

Time dribbled past just like with his other attempts to coax the land to recognize him. He chided himself for all the wasted years when he hadn't bothered. If he'd begun this process when he first selected Earth, the land might have been far more trusting.

The longer he thought about it, the more certain he was that he'd stumbled onto something critical. The past hundred annums had been very hard on this world. Damage from mankind had snowballed, become irreversible. The incursion of sea-serpents had probably been a death knell. The land was fighting back, but it seemed the heart had gone out of its efforts.

Given the similarities in their roots, sea-serpents probably felt a whole lot like dragons to the land. She might be laboring under the illusion his flight of dragons were simply precursors to the serpents.

An idea formed. Earth had an extensive subterranean network of channels. In addition to the underground lakes, mountain ranges soared, far higher than anything on the world's surface.

"I'm not leaving." He kept his voice soothing, reassuring. "I'm moving closer to the heart of you, so we can talk more easily."

Konstantin stood and walked quickly to the thick knot of shifters with Ylon and Nikolai in the middle. His bondmate was still kicking up a fuss about Erin. The dragon thought they should go after her first. Once their almost-mate was back by their side, Kon could do whatever he wanted.

"She'll return once she's done," he told his beast, and then added, "Katya is with her. If you're worried, check in with Katya's dragon."

Smoke and ash rained from his mouth, evidence the dragon didn't agree with his assessment. Erin was theirs. She needed them by her side.

The circle parted to let him through. He scented the air, intent on checking for sea-serpents and not finding any. "Whatever you're about," he said, "keep it going. I'm not having any luck up here, so I'm going to travel closer to the heart of this world. If I guessed right, she will have a much harder time ignoring me."

"And if you guessed wrong?" Ylon angled a pointed glance his way.

Konstantin snorted. "Then I'll be back damned fast."

"Have you heard from Katya?" Nikolai asked.

"No. I just suggested that my beast get a full report from hers, though."

"Good." Yle scrunched his forehead into thoughtful lines. "I can't put my finger on it, but I had a bad feeling about that research base."

Heat built in Kon's chest. He opened his mouth to let fire escape. Once it cleared, he said, "I'm sure everything is fine." He wished Yle had kept his doubts to himself, but that cat was out of the bag. All it had done was get his beast even more ramped up than he already was.

"Probably is," Nikolai chimed in. In his human form, rust-colored hair fell in tangles to the middle of his back. He was tall, but not quite as gaunt as he'd been when Konstantin ran across him on a borderworld. "After what happened on the third world," Nikolai continued, "where I almost lost six of my flight to dark sorcery, it's hard not to worry."

Konstantin clapped him across the back. "Like I said, I'm certain all is well. Katya would raise me with telepathy if it weren't."

"Once you're mated," Yle spoke up, "you'll sense what's afoot through the mating bond."

More fire, smoke, and ash rolled from his mouth.

"We should have bedded her before we let her leave," his dragon ranted, clearly incensed.

"We did not let her leave," Konstantin corrected his beast.

"She is an independent person. I have no jurisdiction over her decisions."

"She owes allegiance to you," the dragon blustered.

"Allegiance is one thing, mating quite another," he informed his bondmate.

"Regardless of what happens below ground, I shall return before one turn of the glass," Konstantin told everyone. Visualizing a spot not far from his lair, he teleported to it.

And then, he addressed his bondmate. "Erin was human until a very short time ago. You cannot expect her to eschew every single value she's ever held dear overnight."

He stopped to take a breath, but his beast wasn't talking over him. He took it as a promising sign. "We have to meet her at least halfway," he went on. "If I start ordering her about, it will be a death knell. She will never be ours."

"What if you're wrong?"

"Then I'm wrong," he retorted. "Clopping her over the side of the head and raping her isn't going to endear me to her. It may force a mating bond, but she'd be miserable. And make our life hell."

"She'd get over it." The dragon sounded certain.

"No. She wouldn't. Besides, she has to want me for me, not because I forced her to do something she was deeply ambivalent about."

Konstantin waited, but the dragon didn't say anything further. "Can we move on?" he asked his bondmate.

Sulky ash spewed from him, but at least it wasn't tinged with fire.

Walking quickly, he covered the distance to the third lake

from the one nearest his lair. A shaft off to one side led deep into the Earth. He'd been down there once. Narrow and steep, it was adorned with rich veins of ore that appealed to his dragon's soul.

He stemmed his body into the nearly vertical shaft, leaning his back against one side and his knees against the other as he slithered downward. A mage light glittered into being below him to light the way. It reflected off crystals embedded in the walls, creating a multihued display that flickered and sparkled.

Soon, he reached the bottom, and he took a moment to revel in the beauty of a cavern banded with silver, gold, copper, and chromium. Chunks of minerals littered the floor. It took willpower not to snap them up and teleport them straight to his hoard.

He followed a path he'd discovered a long while back. It ran out of the cavern and along a curved tunnel with a gently downward cant. One side of the passage dropped away. He brightened his light, and it reflected off jagged mountains. A long row of them rose from unseen depths and towered far above his head. Rather like a world within a world, the rocky crags beckoned to him, but they weren't why he was here.

Konstantin walked until he located a flat ledge. Perching on it, he said, "I have come a long way to meet you where you live. I can travel lower still. It would be new territory for me, but if I hunt for a route, I'm certain I can locate a path to the bottom of this trough."

He dropped his barriers, made himself as accessible as he could. Nothing happened.

"Try my form," his beast suggested.

It was a decent idea, but first Konstantin said, “Other worlds have trusted me. Mu warned me when her destruction was imminent. In return, dragons eased her way through her ending. The Fleisher group of borderworlds put their faith in me.”

He blew out a fire-tinged breath before going on. “In the dim reaches of the past, the sea-serpents were cousin to dragons. No more. Our god, Y Ddraigh Goch, severed that tie and penalized the serpents by removing their wings—and their fire. They can no longer fly. Dragons and serpents might have the same feel to you, but we are nothing alike. Serpents are our enemies as well. It is why I am here as a supplicant. Working together, we can rid Earth of the serpents.”

“Dragons are as faithless as sea-serpents.”

The words reverberated off the walls and created a circular repetitive echo. Konstantin was ecstatic. The land had broken her silence.

“It is partially true,” he replied. “Some dragons have become corrupt. Our god is doing his best to destroy them.”

Moments dripped by. A lot of them before the rich, low voice said, “Why should I believe you? Men lie.”

“I am not a man, but a dragon shifter.” Before the land replied, he opened a path to his beast. The dragon formed quickly and spread his wings. The ledge that had accommodated him before was suddenly much too small. A few flaps and they were dipping and climbing in and around the craggy mountains. They were lovely and isolated. He might be the only one who’d ever laid eyes on them.

Spying a particularly rich vein of gold, he flew toward it,

wanting a closer view. He extended a taloned foreleg to break off a quartz crystal studded with gold that was sticking out but changed his mind.

Stealing from the land was the wrong approach. He located a broader area a few meters lower and landed on it, waiting to see what would happen next.

Maybe nothing, but he'd gotten so much farther today than with his other attempts, he felt encouraged.

"You want something. What is it?" The voice was back. No longer rich and honeyed, it sounded suspicious and tired.

He folded his wings and directed his whirling gaze toward where the voice had come from. "I want us to be allies." He used the dragons' tongue, but the land was old. She should understand.

"Allies presumes we do things for one another." The weary aspect edged up a few notches. "What, precisely, are you expecting me to do for you? Before you answer," the land went on, "know that I am dying. Mankind has stripped me of every conceivable commodity to make themselves wealthy. They have been neither kind nor careful."

"I am sorry."

"Pffft. Pretty words. How sorry are you? You and your kinsmen have been here for a long time. You arrived when I was still robust, yet you did nothing to aid me as I weakened. Surely, you recognized I was in danger."

If he'd been human, he would have winced. How to explain the complex covenant that governed those like him without sounding petty. As if upholding the precept that dragons did not reveal themselves to humans was more important than a dying world.

Besides, he'd been quick enough to break that rule when he decided humans should never forget magic was real.

"What happened, Dragon? Did you run out of pretty words?"

His beast wanted to bugle and shoot fire. Konstantin kept their mouth firmly shut while he summoned shift magic. This transformation was neither quick nor simple because his beast fought him every step of the way.

Finally, he stood in his human body, feeling like a two-faced bastard. He spread his hands in front of him. "What can I do except apologize? Yes, we understood men with their digging and drilling and industry were damaging you. Shy of leveraging magic and killing bunches of them, I'm not certain what we could have done."

"Talk with them? Men love to talk."

"When money is concerned," he pointed out, "they become conveniently deaf." He pushed his shoulders straighter amid cracking vertebrae. "I assumed this world would warm and oceans would rise. Once that happened, many men would die off. Fewer humans would have meant less impact on your resources."

"You were planning on leaving long before any of those things occurred."

His eyes widened. Only one way the land could have known that. "You've listened to Katya and me."

"Perhaps a time or two. Not much else to occupy myself with. If you're expecting an apology—"

"I'm not. You have a right to know everything that occurs on your world," he hastened to reassure her.

"Thank you for that. I am old. And weak. If I were honest —which I frequently am not—I don't believe I could be much help with your serpent problem."

"It's yours too," he told the land. "If they win, the wickedness that's plagued you will seem like nothing compared with the ruin they'll create."

"You said you aided Mu at the end…"

Konstantin understood the rest of her unstated request.

"We would help you as well. Set a truth spell to test my words." He bowed his head and waited. The jab of unfamiliar magic augured into him from all sides.

After a lengthy pause, the land murmured, "I must think on what you've said." Unlike before, her voice was faint, distant.

"Please, don't go yet." But when he reached out with a thread of seeking magic, the land was gone.

"What do you think?" he asked his beast.

"She spoke with us. It's a beginning." Steam puffed past his jaws.

Konstantin reversed his steps, climbing toward the ledge where he'd begun. From there, he'd walk to the steep shaft before teleporting. He could have traveled from where he stood, but he needed time to think.

It had damn near killed him—and broken his heart—to hasten Mu's destruction. A promise was a promise, though, and he'd offered it freely. Mu had warned him to vacate her world in plenty of time to accomplish the task. It was only when dragonkind were almost gone that she'd begged for assistance.

She'd said much the same thing Earth had. That she was weary to her core and had lost the will to go on. If he'd refused her, his lack of generosity would have haunted him for the rest of his days.

A long time, given his immortality.

He'd had no idea how hard it would be. Mu's tortured screams as her core blew apart had pierced his soul. He was the only one who'd heard her because he was the one with the link to the land. The other dragons he'd rounded up to help him were spared the sound of her agony as magma blew outward. Coaxed by dragon magic, the process had happened fast.

He'd always wondered if it would have hurt less if they'd used a different incantation. Mu had asked for a quick and merciful end, though.

Her demise had been quick but far from merciful.

He'd reached the bottom of the nearly vertical shaft. His mage light had shaded to gray, mirroring his bleak thoughts.

He'd have to talk with Earth, let her know dragon aid came with consequences.

"Mu's end was...difficult," his beast said, sounding sad. Not a typical emotion for a dragon.

Konstantin held off summoning a teleport spell. His bondmate rarely admitted to any feelings beyond anger and entitlement.

"Mu was much like our world," the dragon went on.

Interest kindled. For all his years bonded to a dragon, he knew less than nothing about the dragons' world.

"So it was like destroying the mother land where dragons were born."

"Did the other dragons who helped feel the same?"

Ash rained from his mouth in a wordless affirmation.

"But we were the only ones who heard Mu's screams."

"Sometimes one does not have to hear to feel reflected agony," his bondmate said.

Konstantin dug deeper. "You're telling me this because you believe we'll have a difficult time persuading other dragons to help Earth find a way out of her misery."

Fire and smoke joined the flood of ash. *"None of the dragons who took part in Mu's end would willingly do that again."*

"Would you?" Konstantin waited. Without his bondmate, his promise to ease this land beyond her suffering hadn't been much more than the pretty words she'd accused him of.

"I am your dragon. We shall do what is necessary."

It wasn't exactly an answer, but it was as good as he was going to get. He'd lived with his bondmate long enough to recognize probing for more would be fruitless.

He set a teleport spell in motion, aiming for his grotto. He wasn't totally settled on what would come next, and commanders who went into battle without a clear plan were at a disadvantage. The breadth and depth of the sea-serpents' strategies were disturbing.

They'd clearly been planning a coup for many months, perhaps years. Hence the breeding farms on nearby borderworlds. Had Earth always been their target? The more he thought about it, the surer he was he was right. Centrally located, Earth provided a convenient jumping off place for other spots. It was large enough and diverse enough to provide a defensible home for his erstwhile kinsmen.

The breeding farms he'd destroyed on the ninth world in the Fleisher system had been arranged in pods, suggesting possible intent to move the operation at some point in time.

His beast had been quiet after stating the obvious, that he was a dragon, and dragons didn't back away from distasteful tasks. Kon walked through a gateway and stood gazing at the still surface of the lake nearest his lair. He and Katya had remained here far longer than was prudent. Hidden away from other dragons and all other worlds, they'd missed early signs that might have alerted them to the serpents' plans.

"Can't go back," he muttered as his thoughts turned to Erin. Were she and Katya and Johan back yet? If so, had they convinced the ship to either alter its route—or abandon it altogether?

"We have visitors." Nikolai's mind voice held an unreadable note.

"Who?" Kon shot back.

"Come and see for yourself."

Annoyed at being interrupted before he had a firm plan —and backups—well in hand, he reopened the gateway he'd just stepped through and rode it upward. Visitors presumed someone with magic—besides dragons—knew where to find them.

If Nikolai had said "a visitor," rather than "visitors," he'd have assumed Y Ddraigh Goch had paid them a call. Konstantin nodded to himself. That had to be it. Last time he'd seen the dragon god, he'd had minions with him.

Excellent. They could use aid, and assistance from Y Ddraigh Goch was as valuable as help got. Who'd traveled with the god? Would it be the same red and blue dragons he'd met on the seventh world in the Fleisher system?

He blew out a tense breath but then reminded himself he had good news. Earth had deigned to talk with him. Not the most auspicious of starts, but at least it was an improvement over her continued silence.

ERIN

I admit I was pretty spun out about the fellow with hemorrhagic fever. In the first place, where the hell had he come down with it? Judging from his garb, he was part of the ship's crew. Maybe he was new and had replaced someone else? I wasn't sure how many days the ship had been at sea, but probably not long enough to wait out the far end of the incubation period.

During his time aboard, he might have infected everyone he came into contact with. Others too since the virus can live for hours on hard surfaces. I did my damnedest to clear my mind, but all I could think about were those poor people. There are far easier ways to die than leaking blood out of every vessel and orifice.

What surprised me most, though, was what happened after I staked my claim to an undeserved moral high ground about essentially murdering the sick man. Somehow my bondmate knew I'd euthanized patients before. Not just a couple, either. Probably more like two dozen over the years I'd practiced medicine.

She was quick as lightning to remind me of that niggling fact.

Among other things, it meant she not only read my current thoughts, but had access to my memories as well. I sure as fuck wasn't thinking about those other men and women I'd eased out of this life, but the dragon knew, anyway.

Katya must have blown a few minds when she spirited us out of that plane with a blast of magic bright enough to wake the dead. Where would the passengers pigeonhole what they'd seen? They'd have to put it somewhere, and none of them had a mental locker labeled "Supernatural Phenomena."

It was wise of Katya to let us hash our crap out privately, well away from the other shifters. It didn't take long before I came to my senses. Whether we'd teleported out of the plane while it was still in the air or done the same thing to escape an interminable quarantine period after we'd landed didn't matter. The end result would have been the same.

Humans would have been exposed to magic.

I understood it was forbidden, and it didn't take too much of an imagination to figure out why. Men were real dicks about mobilizing to obliterate what they didn't understand. Since it wasn't a war they could possibly win, all it would yield was a string of human casualties.

Dragons and others with magic would feel bad, but not for long. In their minds, they'd have done what was necessary. No more and no less. The unvarnished truth was I had no idea how the phalanx of infectious disease specialists, who would have converged on the quarantined plane, would have felt about us tossing sparkling streamers about.

They'd probably have pitched a fit, stuffed us into hazmat suits, and carted us off to the local looney bin as soon as everyone else was dead.

"We'd have left long before then," my bondmate observed.

"Yes, we would have," I replied. It made our abrupt exit from the plane somewhat more palatable.

Leave now... Leave later...

Katya's spell spat us out a few yards away from the other shifters, who'd packed up into a snug circle with Ylon and Nikolai toward the center. Katya kept a ward around us while she splashed magic about, testing the headlands for intruders.

"Whew! No serpents nearby," she muttered and barked a few words in Gaelic. Her spell dispersed. Actually, both of them did. Teleport and warding.

The others noticed us immediately. I'm certain they felt the bite of Katya's magic. Welcoming calls warmed me. I'd always avoided human entanglements, which translated into no real friends who weren't professional colleagues. We'd gone out for the occasional dinner, but more often we saw one another at medical conventions where we'd smile, wave, and retreat to our own bubbles.

I scanned the group for Konstantin, but he wasn't among them.

Where was he?

"Is he all right?" I asked my dragon. Surely, if anyone

would know, she would. She already considered him—and his dragon—our mates.

"Yes."

I waited for her to add details, but she didn't say anything more. We reached the others and were ushered through them to where Ylon and Nikolai stood. I'd already begun coaxing warmth upward. The dragon shifters' method of warming ourselves was becoming second nature.

I hoped all the other bits and pieces would fall into line soon. I wasn't particularly proud of my performance on the airplane. I'd been an angstrom away from telling Katya and Johan to leave. That I'd figure things out as I went, but I'd been assessing the problem through my human filters.

The ones where doctors dropped everything when faced with medical crises.

"Report." Ylon snapped off the word.

I opened my mouth but shut it fast. I'd defer to Katya, wait and see which parts she highlighted and what she left out.

"We were successful diverting the ship," Johan said.

Him grabbing the point surprised me. I'd assumed Katya—the one who'd been magical millennia longer than us—would be our group voice.

"Excellent!" Nikolai actually smiled. In the short time I'd known him, this was perhaps only the second smile I'd witnessed. The other had been when five of his ensorcelled dragons were rescued from their icy crypts. Unkempt, rust-colored hair hung around his shoulders, and his golden eyes with their deep green centers glowed with delight. A robe fashioned from tawny-striped animal skins hung from his shoulders. The cloak was more decorative than anything, and he'd been wearing it since the first time I laid eyes on him.

"Did you run into any serpents?" Ylon narrowed his silver eyes.

Katya shook her head. "I sensed they'd passed quite near the research base but hadn't actually set foot on that particular patch of ground."

"What about the ship?" Ylon pressed.

"We did not go aboard," Johan explained.

"We were in close proximity to about a hundred passengers and crew, though," Katya said. "None of them felt contaminated by sea-serpent spoor."

I waited, but she didn't elucidate that the people aboard that ship had been plenty contaminated—by something else. Probably, in the grand scheme of the magical world, human viruses didn't warrant so much as a nod.

"We reached them in time, then." Ylon sounded relieved.

I couldn't in good conscience let him believe all was as sanguine as he believed. "Um, not exactly," I said.

His unsettling gaze poked right through me. "What does that mean?"

"They were infected with a serious human disease, one that kills 95 percent of whomever contracts it."

Ylon turned to his seer. "Have you any idea what this means?"

I knew he'd asked Yle, but I felt compelled to add, "It might not mean a thing. Diseases have run rampant through human populations since we crawled out of the primordial slime."

He ignored me, didn't even twitch an eyelash in my direction. It annoyed me, but I bit my tongue. All around me, shifters were nodding to one another with knowing looks stamped on their faces. No one asked a thing about the fate of the infected humans. Clearly, that aspect was deemed of scant import.

Johan leaned across me and nudged Katya. "What do we not know?"

She held up a hand and tilted her chin at Yle, the dinosaurs' seer. Silver hair fell past shoulder level. A gunmetal shade, it was lighter than his eyes. All the dinosaurs looked like indigenous tribesmen from South America with high cheekbones, broad, flat noses, and well-formed foreheads. Or they would have looked like Native people if the natives had been seven feet tall with heavily muscled shoulders, arms, and legs.

They were naked just like the dragon shifters.

"It might be a sign this world's latter days are closing fast," Yle said. "Or, as Erin mentioned, it could mean nothing at all."

I'd been keeping my eyes open for Konstantin. While I sensed traces of him, he'd clearly left a while ago. No one appeared worried, but I wanted to know where he was.

Steam puffed through my mouth. Obviously, my beast approved of me being concerned about his whereabouts.

Nikolai clapped his hands to direct attention back to himself and Ylon. "We have finessed two victories. We cancelled the damage the serpents were in the midst of dishing out to that ship. And we made certain the ship will not put itself back in harm's way."

"Three if you count the serpents lost in Konstantin's time warp," Ylon tossed out.

Cheers rang. A few shifters danced a jig in place. Obviously, no one was concerned about the viral hemorrhagic fever. Human deaths were collateral damage—unless said humans provided fodder for serpents. In that case, we'd intervene. My inner dialogue was tinged with bitterness, but I had no reason for such a sour mood.

None at all.

Everything was relative. Shifters viewed humans in much the same way I'd once viewed insects or rodents. Some were loveable. Many were even somewhat necessary, but they weren't worth much in the way of time or energy.

"How are your battle plans coming?" Katya asked. "And where is my twin?"

"Kon is still working on establishing contact with the land," Yle replied.

"We have a couple of fledgling strategies hashed out," Nikolai said. "Pending Kon's approval, of course."

"If he secured Earth as an ally, it will help a lot," Boris, a dark-haired dragon shifter, said.

Relief surged from my toes to the top of my head. I'd been far more worried than I'd acknowledged about where Konstantin was. For all I knew, he'd run off on his own to battle Surek, the serpents' leader. It was very like something he'd do. So far, he'd been patient with me, but I'd have to give him a firm answer soon.

Yea or nay.

It wasn't that I hadn't fallen in love with him. I had. The mating decision was just so bloody permanent. Dragons didn't get do overs. Whoever they mated was who they sat out eternity with. My gut twisted uncomfortably, and for once it wasn't my beast wreaking havoc. I'd never been willing to keep seeing any man who started making "let's live together" noises. Nope. At the first sign of anything that smacked of commitment, I ran like hell.

Technology made it simple. All I needed to do was block a few things, and I could pretend I'd never met Mr. X. Or Dr. X. I rolled my mental eyes. Doctors were the absolute worst. They made the assumption you were lucky they'd blessed you with their time, attention, and interest.

Cringing, I had a moment of insight where I recognized I'd done much the same. Play by my rules, or I'm out of here.

Anyway. Kon was no doctor. And I was confused as fuck about what I might or might not be these days. Clearly, the person I used to be had limited utility in my current situation. That had been amply proven on the airplane.

Johan bent close and put his mouth next to my ear. "Are you okay?"

I shrugged. "More or less. You?"

"It is different for me. Had I been trained as a doctor, leaving a hundred sick people would have been far more difficult."

"I didn't just leave them," I hissed back. "I left them to die."

"Yes, but what could you have done?"

His stark question brought me zinging back to reality. "Nothing," I said dully. "Nothing at all."

"Can you let it go?"

I could have hugged him. Would have if Katya might not

have misinterpreted my motives. Dragons were possessive as hell. I'd barely scratched the surface of that, and I already understood it took very little to set them off. I'd been surprised when Konstantin had patted my shoulder and sent me off to Arctowski. It must have cost him, which told me how desperately he wanted me to say yes and become his mate.

A very old phrase from the hippie era blazed through my brain. "If you love someone, set them free." It was true in an oddball way, the metamessage being you couldn't force anyone to love you. They either did, or they didn't.

"Can you?" Johan asked again.

It took me a moment to resurrect our earlier conversation about the doomed passengers. "Yes," I said, and meant it. "In fact, I already have."

Just like that, my edgy unrest from earlier dropped away. The mind was incredibly powerful—if you didn't waste it wallowing in "might-have-beens."

"Good." Johan patted my arm. "This is difficult. You and I, we have a foot in two very different worlds—"

"What was that?" Ylon growled. Miniature bolts of golden lightning arced between his raised hands.

The shifters fanned into a single, long row. The air thickened until the earthbound scents of shifter magic, with a strong ozone undernote, sucked every bit of moisture out of my nose and mouth.

Katya stepped in front of Johan and me. I felt the weave of her warding surround us. "Stop that!" Johan struggled to remove the gold-and-silver netting from around his shoulders.

"But we don't know what's out there." Katya flicked her protective shroud back into place.

Johan's nostrils flared. "I do. This smells the same as that cave in Scotland."

Katya's nostrils quivered as she tested his theory. "I'll be damned. You're right. The bloody faeries tracked us down. I assumed it was just idle talk. They never leave the British Isles."

An intriguing flood of emotion marched across Johan's austere features. I picked out satisfaction, anger, and curiosity before he smoothed his face into its usual, bland expression. One that could mean anything.

"You might have been a tad bit more diplomatic," he told his mate.

Katya drew her brows together. "About what?"

"Not acting so shocked I figured something out on my own. We men are a tough bunch, but we do have our pride."

She rolled her eyes. "Sorry, sweetie. I'll try harder not to wound your sensitive ego."

"Please." The corners of his mouth twitched with his usual dry humor. He extended a hand, and she laced her fingers with his.

"Compared with Kon, you're easy. That one holds grudges. For years." Katya tugged on their joined hands. "The Sidhes' portal is forming. Shall we see who decided we were worth a visit?"

I wanted to ask what she meant about Konstantin. Holding onto resentments, letting them smolder into even bigger aggravations, could be a worse problem than his overprotectiveness. Mostly because I sometimes did the same thing. Thirty-five years had passed, and I still hadn't forgiven my father for being a prime bastard.

More than my worries about the man who wanted to marry me, though, I longed to see the faeries. Wonder filled me such creatures were more than the stuff of myth and legend.

Now that I knew it was there, even I could feel oddball magic—quite different from shifter emanations—filling the headland. I sniffed, picking out goldenseal, rosemary, cloves, and perhaps allspice. The scents were piquant and didn't carry the soothing quality I was used to from shifter magic.

"Get back here!" Ylon ordered Katya and Johan.

She turned to face the line of grim-faced shifters with power glistening around them. "It's the Sidhe. Johan and I ran into them. Possibly by accident. Or not. Given they're here, I vote for the 'or not' option."

"We didn't hear that tale," Nikolai said.

"I'm sure Kon didn't think it worth the telling," Katya retorted. "Neither of us believed they'd actually show up."

"Why not?" Yle frowned. "Doesn't cost much magic to teleport anywhere on the same world."

Katya cast a sideways glance at a spot magic brightened the marine air. It didn't look anything like a gateway to me yet, but I trusted her assessment.

"Because," she replied, "neither Kon nor I have ever known the Daoine Sidhe to leave the UK. Something about the *Dreaming* feeds their power. I don't believe they can travel too far from it, or they will fade."

"Pffft. You picked that up from one of your lore books," Ylon said.

Katya nodded affably. "Indeed I did, but I've never seen one beyond the British Isles. Have you?"

"No, but we shall find out soon enough," Yle said and ran lightly toward the shiny place that was growing outward.

I positioned myself next to Johan and Katya. What would the faery folk look like? Would they be tiny? Decked out in precious jewels? Did they have wings?

"Right on one, wrong on one, and the third can go either way," my bondmate piped up.

"You've seen them?"

"Of course. They're arrogant as hell, not prone to hiding themselves away."

They sounded exactly like dragons, but I held that thought to myself and buried it deep.

The glistening place morphed from sparkles to a gateway in seconds. Four men and one woman marched through. I realized my mouth was hanging open and shut it fast, hopefully before anyone noticed I was gawking like an idiot.

Dripping with gold, silver, and gemstones, the faeries were so beautiful it was a chore to look at them. More than the eye could take in, actually. Masses of golden hair shot with silver and bronze fluffed around them. The woman's fell nearly to her feet. Fawn-colored robes sashed in a rainbow of colors covered their tall, regal figures. They were barefoot, but the icy earth didn't appear to bother them.

Katya bowed low. A split second later, so did Johan. I figured I should too, since I was standing next to them.

When Katya straightened, she offered a warm smile. "Keir and Gavin. I didn't expect to see you again so soon."

"Of course, ye did," a dark-eyed faery told her.

"If you say so." Katya kept her voice agreeable and even-toned. I remembered her theorizing with Kon that her side trip to the Scottish Highlands had been far more than happenstance.

The dark-eyed man inclined his head. "I am Keir. This is Gavin"—he tapped a man with sky-blue eyes standing next to him."

The female stepped in front of the rest of them. "Goddess's tits. I shall punish you for your lack of manners, but later. I am Titania. Oberon would be here, but he is...indisposed."

I leaned closer. Indisposed was right up my alley. I almost opened my mouth to stupidly offer doctoring services when I remembered myself. I tried to wrench my gaze away from the faery queen and had a hell of a hard time. It was as if once I looked at her, I was lost.

A subtle jolt of magic did the trick, courtesy of my beast. *"You must be careful,"* she murmured. *"Their power is ancient—and quite cunning."*

Ylon made his way to the Sidhe and nodded pleasantly. "What is Oberon's ailment, and how can we assist?"

Titania craned her neck, scanning the assembled shifters. "Where is the dragon shifter who speaks with the land? I do not sense his presence."

"Right here." Konstantin's deep voice boomed from farther inland. He loped into view.

Happiness seared me. What manner of magic was in play? Had Konstantin bewitched me to be so delighted by his simple presence?

"No magic at all," my bondmate said. *"I have told you. He is ours."*

"Come to me." Titania's clear, ringing voice could have lured sailors with the same efficiency the Sirens had possessed.

Konstantin stopped dead behind the line of shifters. "No one orders me about. You stand on my territory, Faery Queen, and you would do well to remember that."

"As ye will." Titania glided toward where Kon stood.

I didn't trust her, not for a minute. He was mine. I shook my head to clear it. Where the hell had that come from? Or had my possessive nature finally risen to the fore? Regardless, I hustled around the far edge of the row of shifters, reaching Konstantin a second or two after Titania. My dragon wanted to coat her in ashes, but I held it back.

Konstantin didn't take his eyes off Titania, and I didn't blame him. "Why are you here?" he asked.

I gave him credit for not getting sidetracked about whether the Sidhe had waylaid Katya and Johan on purpose.

"Are ye the dragon prince who speaks to the land?" she answered his question with one of her own.

"I am. What is it to you?"

I felt power, a warm, seductive heat, slither from her and wrap itself around Konstantin. Fire shot from his mouth. He averted his head at the last moment, and the flames piled into a large rock cairn.

"Sheathe your magic," he growled. "Tell me why you're here. You have until I count to ten. If you haven't managed a credible reply, I shall leverage magic of my own and—"

"Enough," she shouted in Gaelic. "No one speaks thus to me."

"Fine. Both of us are laboring under god-complexes." Kon skewered her with his spinning gaze. The dragon was very near the surface and not about to take any crap. From anyone.

Titania spread her hands in front of her. She had long, tapering fingers and skin the shade of warm cream. Rings adorned all but her thumbs. "Oberon is a land-linked liege. The land is...beleaguered. So careworn, she has all but given up."

"You were hoping I'd establish a link to the land and tell her to shape up?" Konstantin furled his tawny brows.

"Something like that." Titania looked away. Rosy spots dotted both cheeks. Anger. Or shame. I couldn't tell which.

"I am not insensitive to your problem," Konstantin said, "but my gift doesn't work that way. The land does not answer to me. Or to you, apparently."

"Apologies for bothering you." Titania spoke stiffly. "We shall be on our way."

"Hold up." Kon's voice cracked like an old-fashioned lash. "You are free to go, but before you leave you should know that sea-serpents are intent on taking this world for their own. If that happens, and Oberon is still land-linked, he will sink into evil."

Something—the faery queen's glamour?—splintered to shards; Titania looked ancient and terrifying. Nothing soft was left of her ageless face. Fury poured from her. "Do ye think me daft? Of course, I know such to be true. 'Tis why I am here, groveling at the feet of a magical inferior."

I assumed Konstantin would react with fire and anger. Instead, he softened his voice. "I'm sure this isn't easy for you. We could work together, your people and mine. It might ensure the serpents never gain the upper hand."

Keir, Gavin, and the other two men materialized around their queen. "What do ye wish of us," Keir asked Titania.

"Aye, we anticipated their refusal and left our portal open," Gavin added.

"Shut it! Before all manner of darkness realizes it's there and grabs a free ride. We must remain, at least for now." Titania's voice was lined with bitterness and resignation. "What choice do we have?"

KONSTANTIN

"You have infinite choices." Konstantin kept his voice smooth, soothing, more to mask his anger than to calm the high-handed bitch who ruled Faery with an iron fist. Stories of Titania never painted her in anything but manipulative colors. "You could sever Oberon's link to the land and start anew on a different world."

"Never. Our roots are here," one of the other Sidhe said.

"So? Put down roots elsewhere," Kon countered. "It's better than being lost to sorcery."

He was careful to shutter his thoughts. The last thing he wanted Titania to know was that he'd spoken with Earth, and that the land was considering going out in a blaze of glory. Just like Mu had done. He'd have to bear in mind that Earth was cagey. Akin to many ancient, magical creatures, she kept her own interests front and center.

Surely, she knew Oberon's fortunes were tied to hers. Did

she also understand she'd obliterate the Sidhe if she chose Mu's way out of a distasteful situation?

Mu had no choice. Earth did—for a while, anyway. Dying was a relative term. This world was changing quickly, but becoming less able to support the millions of lives sucking the marrow from her bones might be her salvation.

Titania pushed her shoulders back. Her glamor had broken when she'd become too angry to funnel magic into it. Still magnificent, her beauty held an otherworldly aspect. No one would ever accuse this version of the faery queen of being a mortal.

A swooshing sound told him someone had sealed the gateway.

"You're in time to join our strategy session," he told Titania. "Any chance of securing a few more Sidhe warriors? Your fighting ability is legendary."

"Perhaps."

Konstantin wanted to drop his hands onto her shoulders and shake the crap out of her, but he didn't need an internecine war. They had enough problems. Everybody had their own agenda. His was to annihilate the sea-serpents. Earth's was to find a way out of her loneliness and pain. From her point of view, humans had abandoned her, so she saw no reason to stick around for them. Titania wanted to save her husband—and all of Faery.

Even if they managed to drive the serpents out, the other two issues would remain. Many worlds had chosen oblivion. Was it simply that they'd lived too long? Rather like dragon shifters who wearied of immortality and either gave up the link to their bondmates or signed on to work for Y Ddraigh Goch?

Everyone was looking at him. He clapped his hands together and said, "Ylon and Nikolai, outline what you came up with during my absence."

The ragged line of shifters formed a half circle so everyone faced him. He'd been delighted when Erin had approached about the same time Titania planted herself in front of him. He motioned to his almost-mate to stand next to him, but she shook her head and strode to where Katya and Johan were.

Ylon and Nikolai flanked him, facing the assemblage of magic wielders. "Before I begin," Ylon said in his deep, rumbly voice, "were you successful contacting the land?"

"You were gone longer than your estimate," Nikolai cut in, "so we assumed things went better than they have before."

Konstantin debated whether to simply lie and have done with things, but it went against the grain. He was the *de facto* commander of this group. Eventually, they'd discover he hadn't been truthful, and it would drive a serious wedge between him and the others, and erode his position.

If the Sidhe weren't here, he wouldn't have had any problem at all sharing precisely what had occurred, along with his concerns Earth was playing him to gain her own ends. She was the one who'd brought up Mu's fiery demise —and reminded him of his part in it.

He inhaled deeply, blew out the breath, and did it once again as options blazed through his head. He'd invited the Sidhe to fight with them. He could just as easily uninvite their participation. They could run back to their hidey hole in the UK and live with the outcome of a war that played out half a world away.

"Konstantin?" Nikolai's voice held a worried undernote.

"Yes. I was considering how to spin things, and then I got over it. We are either allies"—he narrowed his eyes and scraped them across everyone's face—"or we are not. Allies means there are no secrets since we fight a common enemy."

He squared his shoulders and kept rolling. "The way I see things, our primary problem is the serpents. If they gain a toehold, we will be battling their evil forever to the exclusion of all else. Until we give up and leave Earth to them."

"Why are you so certain they'd win?" Boris called from a spot toward the center of the throng.

"I'm not," Kon replied. "But it is a possibility we cannot discount." He held up a hand and counted off on his fingers. "One. We have no idea how many serpents there are. Two. We have no idea if there are more breeding farms for atrocities on distant worlds. Three. There's the niggling problem of renegade dragons who've signed on to fight with the serpents. Four. I assume comingled magic flows two ways, which would mean serpents can reclaim their lost dragon essence and become stronger than we are."

"But Y Ddraigh Goch is hunting them down," Nikolai said.

"He is, indeed." Kon nodded. "It's a process that could well take many annums. The logistics of searching every borderworld will tax even him."

"Apparently, there is much we do not know," Titania

spoke up. "Ye dinna answer your underling about whether or not ye talked with this world."

"No, I did not," he agreed. "But I will get around to that. Your turn," he told Ylon. "The current topic is serpents and battle plans."

"We came up with two," Ylon answered. "Most of us were in agreement we should go on the offensive. Find them where they've concealed themselves and figure out if they're still mortal in human form."

"What if they are not?" Konstantin pressed.

"That was where cooperation from the land came into play," Ylon said. "We could do something similar to our method on the ninth world where we bound them with dinosaur enchantment and the land secured them. Forever."

Konstantin kept his gaze firmly on Titania when he said, "The land did talk with me. Reluctantly. She is not certain what she wishes to do, or if she will assist our cause. She sees herself as weak, tired, but she did not say no outright. She is thinking about my proposal."

He stopped there. He wasn't about to go into what he'd promised, nor that he'd given his word with incomplete information to hand.

"Pffft!" Titania spat on the ground. "All of us are ancient, weary to our bones. It doesn't excuse us from doing the right thing."

"But what if that 'right thing' is in the eye of the beholder?" Konstantin challenged her. Before she could dress him down for impertinence, he went on, "For the shifters gathered here, the right thing is doing everything in our power to deal with the sea-serpent threat. For you, it's ensuring your mate's survival, so the Sidhe will not fade. For Earth, it might be that no one has cared about her for so long, she's sick of being taken for granted. For her, closing up shop may feel like the proper path."

"But we pay homage to her," Gavin protested.

Konstantin eyed him and shrugged. "While I'm certain that's true, a handful of Sidhe don't balance well against a hundred million humans all out for their own ends."

Wind whistled up out of nowhere. It held a warning note. Konstantin sent seeking magic auguring outward. The sound of ice floes cracking against one another echoed in his ears, and he reeled in his casting. While they'd been occupied in philosophical chatter, the serpents had crept close. They'd obviously warded themselves. If they hadn't, he'd have smelled their foul essence long since.

"If you got as far as developing battalions, now would be a good time to form them." Konstantin raised his voice, amplifying it with magic.

"We did." Nikolai sprinted forward, motioning the shifters into groups of ten or so.

Kon noted the mix of shifter magics with approval. Power shimmered around the five Sidhe. When it cleared, their robes had been traded for form fitting hunting leathers. Golden bows hung from their shoulders, along with quivers full of black-tipped arrows.

"Join with one of our groups or form your own," he told Titania. No time to check how the Sidhes' brand of power would mesh with theirs. The arrows looked lethal. He hoped they were magical enough to deal death blows to those who were immortal. If that was true, they also posed some level of risk to him and his shifters, but he didn't believe the Sidhe would be so stupid as to sabotage their only chance of wresting Oberon away from danger. If Earth should fall to dark sorcery, they were all in this together. Surely, Titania recognized that.

"Erin!"

She ran lightly to him and said, "I'll be with Katya and Johan. You've got plenty to do. If I'm nearby, you'll worry too much about me."

"I'll worry about you no matter where you are."

"Order her back to the grotto." His dragon puffed steam until it shrouded them from view.

"I heard that." Erin smiled ruefully. "My dragon respectfully declines. So do I. What kind of mate would I be for you or any man if I hid myself away at the first sign of trouble?"

He wanted to ask if her statement meant she'd come to a decision about him, but there wasn't time for that conversation. Instead, he dragged her close, arm around her shoulders, and kissed her once. Quick. Hard. Desperate. He did his best to infuse all his longing and love into that kiss. Her tongue tangled with his before he let her go.

"No heroics." He tipped her chin up with an index finger.

"You should talk. See you on the other side." She trotted to where Katya, Johan, and several other shifters had formed a group. Nikolai was part of it. Good. He was as solid as dragon shifters came.

All around him, shifter magic glistened as his army found their animal forms. His dragon pressed for its freedom, demanding ascendency. Kon kicked his magic wide open, glorying in the miracle of scales and talons. No matter how long he'd lived, how many tens of thousands of times he'd shifted, he'd never lost his sense of wonder at the transformation.

He spread his wings and let the wind carry him skyward. He'd oversee all the groups, adding his magic where it was needed most. Surely, by now, the sea-serpents knew about the wholesale destruction of their plans—and their kinsmen—across several borderworlds in the Fleisher system.

Before, their skirmishes with the sea-serpents had been small, inconsequential. He'd viewed the serpents as more of a minor inconvenience than anything. But that was before they'd kidnapped half a dozen dragons and turned them into broodmares, tapping their essence to nurture evil.

Tarnishing dragon purity had made the fight personal. On both sides. Konstantin didn't doubt for a moment that the dead serpents they'd left on the ninth world had riled Surek and his companions to a fever pitch.

He scanned the ice-crusted sea. Sure enough, it teemed with serpents. Gray. Black. Dull red. Green. Blue. Dragon colors, but lacking their luminosity. No time like the present to find out if their human forms were still vulnerable. He focused drawing magic on a horny-headed gray just hauling his bulk onto the beach.

Before his incantation even got rolling, one of the Sidhe danced close, arrow at the ready. When the beast opened its mouth to snarl a challenge, revealing rows of double teeth, the Sidhe loosed his arrow. Almost too fast for Kon to follow it, the shiny black shaft dove into the serpent's open mouth.

And vanished.

The serpent clawed at his throat with both forelegs. It rolled onto its back, bellowing in what sounded like agony. Other serpents flowed around it, giving it a wide berth, almost as if the havoc the arrow had created might be catching. Kon considered blasting the wallowing serpent with fire, but he wanted to see if the Sidhe arrow would take care of the beast on its own.

Ice cracked in long fissures. Groups of shifters converged on serpents as they crawled out of the sea. They were smart enough to wait until the serpents had put a few meters of shore between themselves and the water. It allowed the shifters to form a line behind the wyrms and cut off their exit.

Serpents were their strongest—and most maneuverable—in water. Once they retreated to their native element, pursuing them would become nearly impossible.

Bugles, bellows, caws, howls, grunts, and screams battered his ears.

"Look to the fallen," Titania's unmistakable voice blasted through his mind.

"What am I supposed to see?" He didn't have the time or inclination to play guessing games, but he assumed she meant the serpent that was still writhing and roaring.

"His scales are splitting. Your task is to seed the gash with fire."

Fire spewed from his mouth, painting a vertical line down the serpent's belly. Kon's dragon was far more accommodating than he would have been. He resented the hell out of the Queen of Faery ordering him about.

His whirling gaze spun faster as the gouge in the serpent turned into a burning crater. Where his fire connected with what he presumed was Sidhe magic, sparks flew. With zero warning, the serpent imploded in a booming blast.

"Neat trick," he told Titania.

"Our people have fought together before. Apparently, you were not yet born."

He ignored the dig. *"Do you have enough arrows to dispatch all the serpents?"*

"Yes, but insufficient magic. They must work together."

"Do what you can," he told her and flew toward a group that looked to be in deep trouble.

"They might have told us about their arrows," his beast groused. *"I, too, was unaware of them, and I have lived at least as long as Titania."*

"Doesn't matter," Konstnatin replied. *"What we need to know is how much magic it takes to ignite an arrow. And if the Sidhe can replenish themselves as we do."*

"No. They must return to the Dreaming."

Kon considered asking how his bondmate knew that, but it didn't matter, either. He flew lower, aiming a flood of flames at two serpents who chivvied a wolf between them. Yle flew low, directing his pointed pterodactyl beak at the serpents' eyes, but they anticipated him, swinging their heads out of harm's way whenever he got close.

Two more wolves growled, hackles raised. One leapt onto a serpent's back. Its claws slipped on the slimy scales, but it recovered. No matter how the wolf closed its powerful jaws, it couldn't break through the serpent's tough scales. Before it could try another angle, the serpent bucked it off. The wolf rolled to its feet, barking its fury, and gathered its powerful hind legs for another leap.

The air grew dense with smoke, fire, and the stench of various magics. Konstantin had never figured out why the rancid reek of dark magic trumped the clean smell of his own. He bugled. Fire streamed from his jaws, but he had to be careful not to hit the trapped wolf.

The serpents were playing with him, getting high on his panic and pain and impotent fury. The wolf jumped and spun, trying to leap sideways out of the serpents' trap. They brayed laughter and tightened the magical web they'd built between them.

Kon's dragon was incensed, but its fury matched his mood. Killing cleanly was one thing, or trying to, but playing with your victims was unconscionable. Below him, the wolf's eyes widened until white showed all the way around. It was only a matter of time before one of the serpents caught him in their jaws and crushed something.

The wolf wouldn't die. But he could suffer forever, and he knew it. Kon bugled at Melara, a dragon in the group below. She bolted skyward, silvery scales reflecting every shade of the rainbow.

"Keep them busy," he told her not bothering with shielded telepathy. The serpents shared enough dragon magic, they'd hear whatever he said.

Melara understood him well enough. She hated the sea-serpents even more than the rest of them since she'd been one of the dragons trapped as a breeding ground for their hybrid horror show. Another dragon, this one red, joined her. Together, they initiated strafing runs, mixing up their angle of attack until the serpents' attention had to be divided between their shifter captive and protecting their flanks from fire.

Kon waited. Timing was everything. He added more fire to a blast burning a hole through one of the serpents' backs. When the soft tissue beneath its scales caught fire emitting a noxious stench—roadkill that had spontaneously combusted—he swooped low, carved through the serpents' spell, and snatched the wolf with his taloned forelegs.

Long before the wolf was done thanking him, he dropped the shifter well behind the battle lines and returned to see if he could finish off the serpents. Or at least the one that was on fire.

Skidding to a halt a meter away, he chanted furiously, intent on drawing the serpent's human form forward. He repeated what he'd done when he and Erin had come across shifters many days ago, except this time the bastard just leered at him through whirling dragon's eyes.

Fuck!

They had no right to look anything like him. It was an affront to all that was good. To the purity of his magic.

Konstantin upped the ante on his spell, borrowing shamelessly from the shifters ranged around him. He was puffing fire, ash, and smoke like an old-fashioned locomotive before the serpent's gray scales took on a hollow aspect. A different strain of power threaded with his just before Yle landed on his shoulder.

The mix of dinosaur earthbound magic with his own forced the serpent's human form into ascendency. A tall, rawboned man with long, greasy gray hair stumbled upright, shaking a fist at Konstantin. "You will never win this war, Dragon."

His scales clattered as he shrugged. "I seem to be holding my own, *Serpent*." He did his damnedest to make the word sound like the curse it was. Konstantin changed up his incantation to what he hoped to hell would kill the fucker sneering at him.

The other serpent who'd taunted the wolf had begun slithering backward. "Do not let him leave," Kon shouted in between the stanzas of his casting.

A chorus of, "We won'ts," and "We've got this," allowed him to focus everything he had on the serpent in front of him.

"Your breeding farms are gone," he said. So long as he had this serpent as a captive audience, he may as well troll for information.

"What makes you think you found all of them?" the serpent jeered.

"Third world. Seventh world. Ninth world." Kon dusted his forelegs together. "Clean sweep." He watched the serpent carefully but didn't glean any clues. "I could be persuaded to spare you. In exchange for information."

The man skinned his lips back, baring yellowed teeth. "Nice try. Go ahead and finish me off. Betrayal isn't on today's menu."

"Others weren't so quick to toss their lives onto the trash heap." Konstantin beat back elation. The serpents were still mortal as human. Or else the serpent wouldn't have invited Kon to finish him off. Had their magic become so perverted it had turned into a permanent flaw?

Getting ahead of things here. I'm probably wrong about that.

"Who?" the serpent growled. "I would have names of the traitors."

"What makes you think I know any of your names?" Konstantin folded his forelegs across his scaled chest.

"Descriptions, then."

Konstantin seeded compulsion into his next words. "Appears I have something you want, and you have something to trade for it. How badly do you want those descriptions?"

"You first." The serpent tossed his head.

"Ha! You must think me stupid. You first, or we have no deal." Konstantin relied on bluster since he knew full well he had zero information about serpent traitors.

The battle raged around him. Shifters who'd been part of this standoff had moved to other nearby skirmishes, adding their magic where it was needed. He'd been doing spot checks on Erin. She was more than holding her own, and he was proud of her.

"What do you want to know," the serpent gritted out.

"How many dragons are part of your ranks? What incentive convinced them to join you?"

"Not today, Dragon. Not tomorrow, either." Harsh laughter blatted from the serpent. He was still howling, doubled over laughing, when Konstantin tired of the game he'd set in motion. A judicious blast of dragonfire turned the serpent's laughs to screeches of agony, but soon even they fell silent.

He scanned the headlands. He'd figured by now they'd

be well on their way to a full-scale rout with serpents teleporting away as fast as they could pull power.

No matter how much he wished it to be true, he was wrong. From the looks of things, they'd be damned lucky if today ended up a draw.

They couldn't lose. The initial battle was always a bellwether. They'd just have to try harder. Where the fuck were the goddess-be-damned faeries? He didn't give a crap if they burned every Sidhe's power down to dregs. They were going to get all the mileage they could out of those magic-imbued arrows.

JOHAN

Not that this will come as a surprise to anyone who's actually fought in a war, but reading about battles is nothing like slugging it out in the mud. Or in this instance, ice. I don't know what I thought would happen, but I had faith in magic. I figured we'd hit the serpents hard and heavy and be done with them in an hour or so. Perhaps less.

I seem to have miscalculated. Badly.

My dragon has been amazing. He clearly knows a whole lot more than me, so I've just turned him loose. He loves tossing fire about. I suspect he'd love it a whole lot more if the serpents died, but we're working on that aspect. The Sidhe arrows seem to do the trick when mixed with dragonfire. Only problem is the faeries ran out of magic—or something—a while back. And vanished.

"They went back to the Dreaming," my bondmate told me.

"Why? It is a long way."

"You're thinking with your human brain. Do you recall how fast your magic recovered in the Highlands?"

"Of course." There'd been a mild euphoria that had come along with our time in the Sidhes' cavern. Perhaps it had been a by-product of tapping power from the *Dreaming*.

All the while we were talking, my bondmate was dipping and weaving and coating every serpent in sight with fire and ash. Not that it even slowed them down, but at least it felt like we were making a good faith effort.

The harsh astringent stink of the serpents' poison occasionally snuck through, but it hadn't incapacitated any of us. Not yet.

The wolf Kon rescued had joined my troop or brigade or whatever we were calling our various contingents. He seemed none the worse for wear, but I suspect he was embarrassed for causing so much furor. We surged forward as a group intent on attacking three serpents, who hissed at us. And then we withdrew and did it again.

"Why are they not employing the aerial poison they used when you were by yourself?" I asked Katya. *"I smell it, but it hasn't knocked any of us out of the sky."* When I'd found her that time, she'd been in bad shape with a black, suppurating hole in her side the size of my fist.

"It didn't force me to land that day, either. I've warded everyone in our group. Once burned, twice shy, and all that."

She sounded happy. Just like my bondmate. I wasn't miserable or anything, but we weren't making any headway. Not much, anyway. My tactician's brain was in full rebellion, shrieking we needed a different strategy, or we'd be here forever.

I'd been hopeful once I discovered the Sidhe arrows were lethal, but they hadn't killed more than a handful of serpents before the faeries slipped away.

Konstantin stood perhaps a meter in front of a serpent who'd shifted to his human form. I suspected Kon had forced the shift. What I didn't understand was why he hadn't killed the serpent yet. The bastard was laughing his ugly head off.

"Duck!" Katya screeched.

My bondmate didn't require encouragement. He'd feinted down and to the left before Katya shouted a warning. We came out of a dive face to face with a jagged slice someone had ripped in the ether.

A gateway to somewhere.

Low-key buzzing grew louder and louder until my bondmate closed off a membrane that protects our ears. The slice ripped open a few more meters, and a gaggle of giant bees with bird wings shot through. Their stingers were at least half a meter long, and I could smell the poison from where I hung suspended in the air.

Different from the serpents' toxin, but I bet it was just as lethal.

Fire roared out of me. Three of the bee things plunged to the ground as their wings burned to cinders, followed by the rest of them. My dragon capered about, picking the hybrid horrors off as soon as they became visible. He was beyond thrilled at something that died so obligingly.

"I want in on the fun." Erin flew next to me and killed the next four bees.

"This doesn't require two of you." Katya said.

Something about her tone, even in the dragons' raucous tongue, alerted me she was worried. I left Erin to it and flew next to Katya. "What?" I still didn't trust my non-mastery of private mind speech.

"Too easy. It's a diversion. The problem is, I don't yet know for what. It's also a message we didn't locate all the hybrid breeding farms."

I was annoyed with myself. I should have made that connection immediately, except I hadn't. "Did the Sidhe really go back to the UK?" I asked.

She nodded amid plumes of smoky ash. "They burned through their magic shockingly fast with those arrows. I expected they'd last through at least a dozen, perhaps as many as fifteen serpents, but they were done after five."

"Did they used to be stronger?"

"Much."

"Will they return?" I asked. It was Kon's job to deploy our resources, but I was still running my own mini war in my head, complete with a mock-up of pseudo computer-generated probabilities courtesy of my gaming days.

She turned her spinning gaze my way. "I have no idea."

Which meant we needed a master game plan that didn't include them. If they returned, great. If not, we had to come up with another way to force the serpents to retreat. They were still emerging from the ocean. It was a lot less frozen than it had been. Not so much slabs of ice anymore as chunks.

The serpent who'd been channeling Comedy Central had turned into a flaming pyre. But one less serpent was starting to feel like one less ant on the occasions my kitchen had been overrun with them. Maybe not quite that bad. But almost.

A quick count yielded fifty serpents, give or take a few.

The bee things had slowed down. What was left of their charred bodies littered the ground. The slash in the air was pulsing, moving in and out as if it were breathing. The analogy creeped me out. I imagined a dark puppet-master lurking on the far side of the hole clapping glove-clad hands and saying. "Hurry now. You're up next."

Kon was flying toward us. He cast a disgusted look at the portal, and a ribbon of blue-white magic streamed from his upraised talons. The gateway shuddered and folded in on itself.

"Why'd you close it?" Katya demanded. "They'll just open another one."

I wanted to ask who "they" were, but I was pretty sure she had no idea.

Her twin didn't answer. A peremptory bugle summoned us all to a spot well removed from the crowd of sea-serpents. "This isn't working," he said.

Something that had been tightly wound within me relaxed. Not that we were safe or home free or anything like that, but at least our commanding officer viewed the world through my set of filters.

The next obvious question was what would work better.

I gave myself a harsh mental slap. Good thing I'd never been conscripted. The first time I piped up with ideas that contradicted authority, I'd have been court-martialed.

"Where are the Sidhe?" Kon asked, having obviously noticed their absence.

"We suspect they retreated to the *Dreaming*," Nikolai replied.

"How many serpents did it take to drain their magic?"

I furled one scaled brow, impressed. Konstantin was on top of a whole lot of things with a knowledge base I'd gladly have killed for.

"Five," Nikolai said. "No. Six."

Smoke poured from Kon's slack jaws. "Damn. Did they say if they would be returning?"

All around me, heads shook back and forth.

"At least we know what we have to work with," Konstantin continued. "By the time we get back to the shoreline, we can count on at least ten more serpents having showed up. We need to track down where they're coming from."

"What about the gateway?" Katya asked. "The one you just shut."

"It's a diversion, nothing more. A ruse to drain our power on inconsequentials. And to make certain we know we didn't kill off all the hybrids. Don't waste magic on whatever emerges from them, just close off the portals."

"Who is behind them?" I asked, unable to keep my mouth shut.

"A very sound question." Kon switched to telepathy. *"They are working with someone who is very strong magically. I believe it's how they convinced dragons to join their side."*

"Yes, but who?" Erin asked.

"I have a feeling we're going to find out, but probably not today," Kon replied. He shook his head until his scales clattered. *"The serpents seem lethargic to me, not fighting back*

as staunchly as I've seen them do before. It was difficult to force one into his human body, though. Much harder than I expected."

"Maybe it was easier to change things up at that end than to make them fully immortal again," I suggested.

"I thought the same," Konstantin said. His ready acceptance of my assessment warmed me. Good thing because his next words poked a hole in my happy bubble. *"No more telepathy for you until you have a better handle on limiting its spread."*

"Got it," I mumbled in dragonspeak.

"You're doing really well," my beast spoke up.

"Thank you, but I need practice. A lot of it."

Katya hovered protectively next to me. From time to time, I felt her make adjustments in the warding she had draped around me, Erin, and herself. It was chauvinistic and stupid, but I vowed there would come a day when I took care of her, not the other way round.

Brilliant light forced my third eyelid shut, and I instinctively bent my head against the glare. Not good if it was another of those blasted portals. The magic had a different feel, though. One I recognized.

Sidhe, but a whole lot more of them than before.

Sure enough, a gateway blasted into being. No wasted time with shimmers or a slow burn. One minute it wasn't there, the next it was complete with utilitarian silver edges and a veritable army of Sidhe pouring through. Every single one had a bow and a quiver of arrows. I recognized Titania, but this time a man stood by her side. Black hair streaked with silver and beaded with gems that made my dragon drool fell to his waist. A golden circlet sat atop his brow, and his robes glittered as if crafted of pure gold.

I understood without being introduced, this had to be Oberon, King of Faery. His classically handsome face was set in resolute lines. Nothing soft about him. Titania had said he was ill, but he seemed to have thrown off whatever was ailing him.

"Pair up, two Sidhe to one dragon," he shouted at the faery horde before turning to Konstantin. "We must work quickly while our magic is at its zenith. My warriors will open the way with arrows, but your dragons must seed the gap with dragonfire as soon as it is exposed. Once that is done, move to the next serpent."

"We shall fight alongside you as well," Ylon said. "Dinosaur power is just as deadly, but we leverage earth rather than fire."

I expected at least a small amount of pushback from Konstantin. Instead, he inclined his head. "Thank you for your aid, Oberon. Once this battle is concluded, we shall sit and talk."

The king focused multihued eyes on Konstantin. "Agreed."

Erin nudged me. *"Wonder what was wrong with him?"*

"Probably nothing Western medicine could have solved."

Eager to offer the dragon shifter part of things, I half ran and half flew to the group of Sidhe still pouring through the gateway. Joining up with the next two faeries to emerge, I headed for the shoreline half a kilometer distant. Clumsy on the ground, I flew above them. My companions were both male, and both fair. Dressed in soft beige hunting leathers and calf-high lace-up boots, they reminded me of the elf in Lord of the Rings, minus the pointy ears. It took me a moment to resurrect his name. Legolas.

The Sidhe had an elegance and grace to them at odds with the vicious cast to their eyes.

Kon's prediction about the serpents seemed accurate. There were more of them, and they'd packed up in groups of three and four. Some Sidhe had already reached them. The serpents roared a challenge, open jaws displaying double rows of teeth. The similarity to dragons was unnerving, but I didn't let myself dwell on it.

The sour astringent reek of their poison thickened the air. I hoped the faeries knew to ward themselves. I didn't want to risk irritating them by stating the obvious. My companions had nocked arrows and ran toward a cluster of serpents. Two grays and a red.

I wasn't certain just how this would work. Could the arrows penetrate the serpents' scaled hides? Or did they have to wait for a perfect shot right into the creatures' mouths? I hovered, keeping up a steady stream of ash and smoke. Maybe it irritated the serpents, made it tougher for them to breathe. I hoped so. My beast was conserving fire until we needed it. I felt heat building within us as my bondmate made good and sure our contribution would be hot enough.

A faery jumped sideways and loosed an arrow into one of the gray serpents' eyes in a single, fluid motion. The shaft didn't remain with its feathered end sticking out like a normal arrow. Almost as soon as it connected with the serpent, it continued to sink until nothing visible was left.

The creature bellowed and roared as the scaly skin around its eye socket pulled back. The eyeball bubbled and liquified, running down the bastard's snout.

"What are ye waiting for?" the Sidhe screeched at me.

I didn't bother to answer. My jaws were open, and my beast poured a stream of flame into the ruined eye socket. I'd been expecting a long gash to open somewhere in the serpent. Good thing everyone else had this nailed down better than me.

The second of our three serpents was on his way out too. This time, I'd saturated a festering hole in his side with fire. It took the fuckers a while to burn even after my bondmate doused them with flames. I was starting to figure out that every serpent was different, and I couldn't take anything for granted.

The air was dense with the stench of burning meat, and smoke was so thick it was tough to breathe. My Sidhe partners danced around the third serpent, but it must have been taking smarter pills because magic blasted outward from it, dark jagged shards that chopped through the faeries' leather garments. When the grayish cloud of darts and poison cleared, the serpent was gone.

I landed, intent on checking on the Sidhe. One didn't look good to me. Face contorted in pain, he clutched a long slit in his side where the leather had split. When he brought his fingers away, they dripped blood.

I scanned the shoreline. Not many serpents remained. Not alive, anyway. My guess was the word had gone out from Serpent Central to retreat.

"Are you all right?" I asked the Sidhe.

"Do I look all right?" His words held a breathy quality, and blood bubbled from his mouth. Crap. Even I knew he had a punctured lung. What I didn't know was if he had enough magic to fix it.

"Katya!" I bugled.

Her golden-scaled form materialized fast, and she landed next to me. The other Sidhe had his arm around the injured one, and the two of them had begun walking slowly up the headland.

"Wait," Katya bugled. "We can fly you."

The faeries turned, and the one with blood staining his leathers gasped out, "Thank you, but ye canna fly us to the *Dreaming*."

Oberon shimmered out of nothing. He was just there. Placing his hands on the wounded man's shoulders, he hummed a few notes and followed them with Gaelic so old, it even took my bondmate a moment to understand his meaning.

Oberon was sending his warrior to the faery equivalent of Valhalla. Guilt arrowed into me. This was my fault, somehow. I hadn't been quick enough to corral the serpent and his sorcerous magic. Or to anticipate what he was about. Worse, I hadn't told the Sidhe to ward themselves. My silence had cost a life.

"Can we not save him?" I asked.

Oberon kept on chanting. I was afraid I was trampling on something sacred, so I shut up. Katya dropped a foreleg on my shoulder, and I bowed my head. A golden glow started at ground level and gradually grew, surrounding the man. The strained expression left his face and he shook off the other faery who'd been holding him upright.

The glistening shroud pulsed with hope. I may have misinterpreted, but it promised the Sidhe he would resurrect himself and live again after he'd healed in the *Dreaming.*

When the shiny veil cleared, the man was gone. Oberon's shoulders sagged, and his hands fell to his sides. His face had lost most of its color. I could only guess what the outpouring of magic had cost him.

Konstantin's bugle was followed by instructions to teleport to their lair.

"I assume ye know where that is." Oberon's voice was raspy.

"We will take you there," Katya said.

I turned in a full circle, surveying the shore. Smoke from numerous pyres stained the sky. We hadn't killed all of them, so the others must have left in much the same way our target had. I wondered if there'd been more casualties.

I'd always found the Southern Ocean awe-inspiring, but as I gazed at the gray water and gray sky and chunks of ice bobbing on the waves, protectiveness surged. Hot, vicious, lethal. Evil would not gain the upper hand here. Earth would not turn into a breeding ground for hybrids like the third and ninth worlds in the Fleisher system. Or into a command post for serpents to finetune their plans to chivvy everything good and decent out of the universe.

Outraged bugles rang from me. A challenge to anyone who might be listening. I might be young. I might be untried, but goddammit I would not stand by and allow wickedness to win.

A very old truism from Edmund Burke ran through my mind. "All that is necessary for the triumph of evil is that good men do nothing." Surely, it applied to good dragons as well as good men.

"Johan?" Katya prodded me.

"Sorry. I am ready to—"

Above me, a green wing poked through the thick gunmetal cloud cover. My beast wrenched control and spread his wings, intent on taking flight and challenging the intruder—who could only be another dragon—to aerial combat.

"No!" Katya screeched.

When I twisted my head to look at her, I saw Oberon swaying on his feet. The other Sidhe attempted to support his liege, but Oberon shook him off.

"Get control of your bondmate," she yelled.

"Leave," I told her. "I'll be right behind you."

"I'll hold you to it." Magic built around her. She lumbered next to the two Sidhe and snapped them into her spell.

My beast was still trying to move us into the air. The green wing had expanded to include a neck and another wing. This had to be one of the dragon traitors. I recalled all too well what had happened on the ninth world. I'd nearly died. It was all the incentive I needed.

"We are following Katya," I told my beast, leaving spaces between each word. "Our mate. I made her a promise."

"But I know him. He doesn't deserve to live." Fire shot from my beast but fell short of the bastard in the sky by a kilometer.

I tried to open a teleport channel, but my bondmate blocked me. He was still intent on destruction. "We are alone here," I told him. "Alone."

"So? We don't need anyone else." A mighty surge nearly upset the death grip I had on our wings.

I reached deep. Dug for what power I could command. "We. Are. Leaving." I have no idea what I did differently—or maybe my beast gave up—but the shoreline turned dark, replaced by the lake near Konstantin and Katya's grotto.

So long as I had the upper hand, and a very pissed off bondmate, I followed the teleport spell with shift magic. I was afraid the dragon would make it hard, but I fairly catapulted out of his form and into my familiar human one.

When the magical dust cleared and I reached within, intent on making peace, he was gone. Crap! He said he knew the green dragon. I should've gotten his name. I did my best to seal up my passageway so the dragon traitor couldn't follow.

Probably should have done that first, but this magic crap is still new to me. Hoping my sloppiness wouldn't create problems, I hustled toward the house.

KATYA

Katya had read about the Daoine Sidhes' renewal casting, but she'd never seen it done before. The spell held a poignant beauty that made her long for Scotland's lochs and Highlands. The reason the faeries were immortal was because of Oberon's link to the land.

He'd managed to marshal and hold the magic for his spell, but it had cost him a shocking amount. When had the Sidhe grown so weak? It wasn't exactly a question she could ask, but she bet it had something to do with the sulky, recalcitrant land. She hadn't gotten the full story from her twin, but reading between the lines of what he had said, she guessed this world was tired, feeling disenfranchised and just didn't care anymore—about the impact of her actions on anyone.

Her probable reasoning was easy enough to understand. No one gave a fuck about her, so why should she put herself out for anyone.

Mu had gone down fighting. That world hadn't given up until there truly was no hope. Its core temperature had reached a point where destruction was imminent. Earth had centuries of life left but felt terminally sorry for herself. Katya understood the downsides of immortality as well an anyone. How the prospect of endless days drained you, sucked the joy out of everything.

She brought Oberon and the other Sidhe down gently very near her front doors and shifted. "You are welcome to bide within, Oberon, Faery King, and you as well," she told his companion.

She was worried about Johan, but controlling his bondmate was the first and most critical lesson when it came to being a dragon shifter. She'd wanted to stick close until his dragon retreated, but Oberon was fading. If he sank too far, she had no idea what would happen. Could another Daoine Sidhe cast magic and send him back to the *Dreaming*. Perhaps Titania could manage it, but Katya wasn't certain.

Oberon cast his multicolored eyes—gold, silver, and violet—about. "What is this place?"

She held up a hand with talons changing into fingers to let him know she'd answer him in a moment. Once her shift was mostly complete, she said, "A world within a world. A string of lakes extends for many kilometers, and there are terrain features that mirror this world's surface, including high mountains."

"Aye, but how did ye find it?"

She was getting used to his odd eyes. They were more green now, but a moment ago, they'd been pale lavender.

"Konstantin located it. When we first came to this world, there were many more of us."

"What happened to your kin?" the other Sidhe asked.

"They grew dissatisfied with living underground. Our crops failed, and we had no easy way to replenish them."

"They left?" Oberon raised a dark brow. She nodded, and he went on, "Have you heard aught from any of them?"

"No. Nothing. Both Kon and I thought it odd."

Johan's distinctive energy bloomed not far away. She blew out a relieved breath. Good. He'd won the struggle with his bondmate.

Titania strode close and aimed her words at Oberon. "I felt your spell."

"No choice. He was dying. I had to send him back."

"But the cost—"

"I am recovering," he cut her off.

The harsh cast to her face softened, and she tucked a hand beneath his arm. "Come. Walk with me. Everyone is gathered next to a lake. The waters hold renewal."

Katya watched while the three Sidhe walked away, and then made her way to Johan's side. "Was your beast upset?" she asked.

"Very. In fact, he is missing. He said he knew the other dragon, and—"

Anger ran hot, courtesy of her beast, who was outraged. "Who is he?"

"That is just it. I did not get a chance to ask before he went off in a snit."

"He'll return." Katya wrapped an arm around Johan's back. His skin, silk stretched taut over muscle, felt tantalizing beneath her fingertips. “I’m glad you’re all right. I felt torn up there on the shoreline, but Oberon needed to leave more than you needed me to stay.”

“I understand, and I appreciate your vote of confidence more than I can say.”

“I’m sure your bondmate does too, or he will once he gets over himself.” Katya smiled.

Johan hesitated. “Do you suppose dragons were behind today’s attack?”

She nodded slowly and made a face. “It pains me to admit it, but yeah. Kon said the serpents seemed lethargic. It might have been because they were caught up in a spell.”

“But why would we not have sensed dragon magic if it was in play?”

“One of the things I love about you is all your questions. They mean you’re always pondering.”

Johan angled an indulgent look her way and threaded an arm around her shoulders. “That would be me. The Thinker. You did not answer my last query, though.”

“With all the dragon magic floating about, do you think we would’ve noticed a wee bit extra?”

“Probably not. I am just beginning to recognize the differences in magic among the various shifter types.” He cast a questioning look at the double stone doors leading inside and dropped a hand to cup her ass.

“Uh-uh. I’d like nothing more than to vanish inside with you, but we need to join the others. Sooner rather than later too.”

“You have the finest ass, woman.” He squeezed it again and nuzzled her neck. “I love you, darling.”

"I love you right back." She spared a glance at his thickening cock. "You have a whole lot of prime real estate too, but it might be a long time before we get even five minutes to ourselves." Wriggling out of his grip, she set a quick pace for the lake.

Most of the shifters seemed to already be there, and she hoped to hell Konstantin wasn't waiting on her and Johan. The Sidhe sat on the ground, except for Oberon and Titania. They swam in the lake. Oberon's color had returned, and she risked a subtle scan with magic to test her assumption about him being better.

Surprisingly, his power had rebounded from when he stood on the shores of the Southern Ocean. Of course, it had nowhere to go except up, but something about either this location or the lake were helping.

Titania had said the waters held "renewal." Katya hadn't paid much attention to her at the time, but maybe she hadn't fully appreciated the lake's potential. Or perhaps it was synergistic with the faeries' brand of magic. She and Johan went to stand with the other dragon shifters. Katya did a quick nose count to ascertain if they'd lost anyone beyond the one faery.

One raven shifter appeared to be missing.

Konstantin strode to a small knoll. "We fought well, but we must do better. Losses are unacceptable, and today we lost a bird shifter and a Sidhe."

Gustaf, a thick-bodied bird shifter with flyaway brown hair and green eyes took a step forward. "He is not lost. He's been captured. We must do everything we can to get him back."

"Can you still sense him?" Konstantin asked.

"No," Gustaf admitted. He looked as if he wanted to say more. If Katya read his expression right, it cost him to be part of this conclave when what he wanted to be doing was helping his companion.

"If we can rescue him, we shall," Kon promised and turned his attention to the Sidhe. "How is your magic holding up?"

"Better down here," Titania said.

"Aye, we are closer to the core of this world." Oberon climbed out of the lake and shrugged into his golden robes. Titania remained in the water.

"A dragon showed up just as we were leaving," Katya said. She aimed for a neutral tone, one where she simply imparted information.

Every set of eyes skewered her along with many variations of, "Do you know who it was?"

Katya glanced at Johan, who nodded. "Bennet. The name of his human side is Bennet. My beast just told me."

Katya had known his bondmate would return, but not quite so soon. She understood she was focused on that to avoid what felt like an inescapable conclusion. She'd ignored Loran and his brothers—traitors one and all—because only one of them had been part of their flight. But Bennet had been another.

Had all of the forty-seven dragons who'd settled beneath the Antarctic ice sheet with her and Kon turned their backs on honor? On what it meant to be dragon shifters?

Wordlessly, she looked at Konstantin. The same agony

chopping a trail through her was reflected on his face. "It can't be all of them," she blurted.

"It's probably not." Her twin's expression had clouded over with ire—and disappointment.

"You're talking in riddles," Ylon sputtered.

"Indeed. Tell us what you think you know," Gustaf said.

Kon's shoulders slumped. Katya's heart ached for him. From the looks of things, what he was about to admit would be a serious splotch on dragon shifters from now until the end of all worlds.

"When Mu was dying"—he spread his hands in front of him, showing half-formed talons, which meant his dragon was very near the surface—"some dragons refused to believe she was doomed. It was mostly the very old ones, the ones who had called Mu home for thousands of years. Y Ddraigh Goch came to me and asked if I would create a flight of my own to ensure every dragon left Mu. I asked him how he thought I could accomplish such a thing, and he assured me he would help."

Kon flexed his fingers—that had mostly turned into talons—and kept talking. "I still do not know exactly what our god tried to accomplish, but a handful of the dragons were angry. They blamed me—and Y Ddraigh Goch—for their plight and swore retribution. To my face."

He narrowed his eyes as if he were dredging up a memory, and murmured, "They said to me, we live long, our kind. Never turn your back too far, Konstantin. A day of reckoning will find you, no matter how vigilant you are."

A sharp hiss ran through the dragon shifters. Erin and Johan would have no way of knowing, but for a dragon to lift its claws against another dragon was cause for banishment. It was almost the worst thing you could do to a dragon. Y Ddraigh Goch would be better served to kill a beast outright than to ban them from the dragons' world.

"I did my best to smooth the waters." Smoke puffed from Konstantin's mouth. "Told them they did not have to accompany me, but they'd obviously talked among themselves. The only response they gave me was 'We live long…'"

"You did not know," Johan said right next to Katya's ear.

He hadn't asked a question, which spared her responding. Good thing since she didn't trust herself to talk. Angry at Y Ddraigh Goch for placing her twin in such an untenable position, she was amazed the dragons who'd come to Earth with them had stuck it out as long as they had.

Her bondmate must have known about the other dragons' deep discontent. And said nothing, keeping Kon's troubles private. Of course, Katya had her own set of problems with her dragon leaving for such a long time, but she'd have walked through burning coals if it would have helped her twin.

Konstantin was talking again. "We waited until the last possible moment to leave Mu. Y Ddraigh Goch did a fair job splitting the recalcitrant dragons among the flights that fled Mu's destruction. Twelve ended up with me."

Only twelve. Not every dragon in their flight.

Katya couldn't keep her mouth shut. "Did everyone but me know?"

"No, Sister. Part of our god's requirement was silence. It

was wise of him. Had he openly identified the rebels, the rest of dragonkind would have turned their backs on them. It would only have made the problem worse.

"I gathered the twelve dragons together. We met in secret after we escaped Mu. I told them they were free to leave Earth, that I wouldn't hold them against their will—or report their egress to Y Ddraigh Goch. They mourned the loss of their home, and I hoped the presence of other familiar dragons would soothe them.

"At first, I thought they were settling in, but what they were really doing was sowing the seeds of discontent. Dragons are quick to anger, but it takes us time to figure out how we can get back at whoever wronged us. They worked one angle after the next until they'd convinced all the dragons in the flight to leave."

"And then they ran straight to the serpents and joined up with them." Nikolai sounded bitter.

A snarl emerged from Konstantin. "We do not know that. I refuse to believe every dragon who left went immediately to the dark side. So far, we've identified four traitors. Five if you count the one Johan and Katya saw today."

Titania had left the lake and was back in her formfitting hunting leathers. Long golden hair dripped where it hung about her shoulders and down her back. Katya had been so focused on Konstantin, she'd missed the faery queen's transition.

Oberon stood next to his queen. "Before ye say aught else"—his clear, ringing voice commanded attention—"we shall depart. Our presence offered an edge in today's battle, but shifter wars are not our wars."

"How can you say that?" Katya blurted. "Everything is connected."

"Not to our way of thinking." Titania tossed her shoulders back and stood tall.

Konstantin caught Katya's eye and shook his head. He bowed toward the faeries. "We are most humbly grateful for your assistance. As Titania noted, our magics were designed to work together to dispatch immortal creatures. I will do everything in my power to convince the land to find it within herself to continue."

"It is appreciated," Oberon said. "Ye can leave Earth. We cannot. Our power is keyed to the harmonics of this world. My magic is part of the warp and weft of Earth's loom. I never expected our reign here to last forever, but neither am I ready for it to end quite yet."

He blew out a weary breath. "Long ago, Bran and Gwydion advised me to place the *Dreaming* elsewhere, on another world, but it would have required a continuous infusion of magic to maintain. Far more than keeping it here, and so I declined their counsel. Bran is the Celts' seer. I should have listened to him."

"Splitting the source of your power would have given you alternatives," Kon murmured.

"Precisely." Oberon sounded tired. "But it is far too late to extricate the *Dreaming* from Earth's grip. We, Titania and I, shall go to the Celtic gods' council chambers in the ruins of Inverlochy Castle and request an audience."

"I hope they look favorably on whatever requests you put before them," Konstantin said. "If you change your minds about fighting alongside us, we would welcome you back."

Katya gripped Johan's hand far too tightly. She had to be hurting him, but he didn't complain. Her twin couldn't just let the Sidhe leave. They needed them. Absent their intervention, they wouldn't have killed a single serpent today.

"I cannot hold them against their will," Kon's voice whispered deep in her mind. He must have read the outrage and despair on her face. Or else her beast had talked with his.

Clouds of the earth-tinged power she associated with the Sidhe rose around them. When it cleared, the faeries were gone. The low hum of worried-sounding side conversations eddied around her. Konstantin bugled to quiet everyone.

"This is only your battle if you wish it to be. I said much the same when we stood on the sixth world. Those who wish to remain and fight with us are more than welcome, but I respect your decision if you choose to leave."

Katya glanced about, tightlipped. She half expected a mass exodus, but no one stirred.

"We managed to immobilize dragons on the ninth world," Konstantin reminded everyone. "There we combined shifter magics and the power inherent in the land. Earth has not yet answered me, which makes me hopeful she will assist us. If she were going to say no, she'd have already done so."

"Maybe she was waiting to see the outcome of today's battle," Katya's beast muttered.

"Does anyone have any idea how fond she is of Oberon?" a red-haired wolf shifter with hazel eyes asked. When Katya looked closer, it was the same female who'd tried to move in on Johan before they'd formalized their mating bond.

"Not really. Why?" Kon asked.

"Well, I might be reading this wrong, but the Sidhe—or Oberon, anyway—seem intent on seeing if there's a way to correct concentrating their magic here on Earth. I was just wondering how the land would respond if the faeries pull gobs of magic out of her."

"Not well, but we can't afford to worry about something we have no control over that hasn't happened yet." He scanned the assembled shifters. "Thank you for choosing to remain. It may not feel like it, but we won a definitive victory today. We killed enough serpents to buy ourselves some time. They are still vulnerable as mortals. It's one more way to deal with them.

"For now, I'm going to take another crack at convincing Earth to aid us. Once she makes a commitment, she will follow through. I'm certain of it. The rest of you are free to do as you wish for the next day or so."

"We will attempt to aid our lost kinsman," Gustaf said.

"I will return to the surface," Katya spoke up. "I want Bennet to face me and explain the allure of serpents and dark magic."

"Be careful," her twin said. "He's not the same as when he lived with us."

"Neither is he all that different," she shot back. "Unlike Loran's youngest brother, Bennet had a mate, hatchlings. What happened to them?"

"May I go with her?" Johan asked.

Kon nodded. "I appreciate you asking and not just assuming. Keep her safe."

"Not the easiest task," Johan mumbled.

"Is that any way to talk about your mate?" Katya elbowed him. Together they walked back toward the doors leading into the house.

"What? You have a problem with the truth?" He cast a sideways glance at her.

"Of course not." She exhaled thoughtfully. "At least we know a little bit more about what happened to the dragons who used to live here. I was relieved it was only a few. When Kon started talking, I feared the entire flight was corrupt."

"And you were the only one in the dark?"

Katya nodded. "Kon could have confided in me."

"Why do you suppose he did not?"

They'd reached the entrance. Katya stopped. "My brother doesn't like to fail. I assumed he was upset because the flight left, but it ran deeper than that. He did his best to soothe the dragons who'd threatened him. It must have taken enormous willpower not to turn them in to Y Ddraigh Goch for treason. Our god would have killed them, and it would have been the end of things."

Johan held up a hand, palm outward. "Not the way I read the trail of events at all. Granted, I am new at this, but dragons strike me as reliant on a social structure. Surely the twelve dragons had friends among the others. If Konstantin had turned into a self-fashioned judge and jury—and dragons died because of his negative assessment of them—what do you suppose would have happened?"

"Other dragons would have resented him." Katya cringed

as a fuller interpretation of her twin's impossible situation sank in. "I'm beginning to understand why he kept the dilemma to himself."

Johan cast a longing gaze at the double stone doors. "I would love nothing better than to steal some time for ourselves, but we must return to the shore."

"I was considering if we should ask some other shifters to accompany us," she said.

"No. They are as close as telepathy, and two can be more circumspect than a crowd."

She could see arguments for both sides. Curious, she asked, "Where did you learn about strategy?"

He furled his dark brows. "Video games."

"What are those?"

"Simulations on a screen where the enemy you vanquish pops up again and again, forcing you to come up with new and more creative ways to kill them." He placed a hand on her shoulder and squeezed lightly. "The sooner we leave..."

Katya dipped into her magic. It was still perilously low from earlier but had begun to recover. When she had juice enough to teleport, she loosed her spell. "I'll ward us," she said.

"I will take care of that part. Be sure and jump in if my effort is lacking."

"I don't know about jumping in, but I'll tell you how to correct it."

"Even better. It is the only way I will learn."

JOHAN

I battled to force my mixture of fire and air into submission fast. The trip to the surface would be over in seconds, and I had to be ready. In case something lurked on the headlands just waiting for one of us to make an appearance. So far, the serpents hadn't made much of an effort to locate our lair, but it was only a matter of time before that changed.

I could see their problem. Their serpent bodies were awkward and ungainly on land, and their human forms were vulnerable. They'd need strong magic to penetrate the wards around the underground grotto, which argued for their serpent forms, but it would be difficult for them to mount a realistic offense.

What had happened to Surek? Was he still behind the scenes directing the action? Or had he ceded that task to a group of dragons? We'd done well with the ship—or we would have absent the Marburg/Ebola epidemic.

How important was it to seek out and destroy whatever hybrid breeding enclaves remained? Would they wither without magic to fuel them? As usual, I had a whole lot of questions and very few answers. The headland took form around us. It was darker than when we'd been here earlier, so I guessed it must be nighttime. It never truly got dark this time of year at the extreme end of the southern hemisphere.

I wrapped the netting of my ward more tightly around Katya and me. It was visible to my psychic vision, but not to my earth eyes. I couldn't yet multitask with magic, so I was relieved when I felt Katya sprinkle seeking power in a wide arc. The smoke from earlier hadn't totally cleared despite a brisk breeze. We'd dispatched a lot of serpents. I hadn't counted, but I bet the number hovered north of forty.

I was surprised by how justified I felt about those killings. I'd clearly thrown off the veneer of twenty-first century civility in favor of a far-more-primitive mentality. Early man had killed without a second thought back when it was a matter of survival.

No one worried about mastodon rights when the fucker was bearing down on you because you'd wedged a spear in its side.

Katya gripped my arm. I wanted to ask what she sensed, but I was stuck. Normal, out-loud talking would carry a long way—even if I whispered. Telepathy would be worse, at least the way I did it. I may have improved, but I had a long way to go before my mind speech was truly private.

She crept farther from the ocean and then broke into a run toward a line of rocky crags perhaps a quarter kilometer distant. I followed her, doing my damnedest to keep us both warded. It was amazing how much harder it was to hold magic where I wanted it while my body was in motion.

Ja. I needed a whole lot of practice. Opportunities weren't exactly popping out all over. I ducked into the same slit in the rocks where Katya had vanished. I would have bet money she'd been here before. A rounded affair came into view, courtesy of the blue-white mage light bobbing next to Katya's shoulder. I hadn't been cold—drawing heat upward from the Earth's core was one magic I'd mastered—but it was a relief to be out of the incessant gusts of unsettled weather.

I was about to ask as innocuous a question as I could, but my darling mate anticipated me. *"We wait. No talk. No questions."*

Mmph. That pretty much cut the wind out from under my sails. I glanced around and summoned a light of my own to see better. Sure enough, petroglyphs lined the walls of this grotto. If human histories were to be believed, prehistoric man had never been to this pole, but the cave drawings proved those accounts wrong.

The paint was faded, but I made out something that looked like a wooly mammoth. A whale was in another panel. And a rather ungainly craft that might have been a cross between a birchbark canoe and a rowboat. At least it explained how the artists had gotten here. I moved deeper into the cave and found exactly what I expected: piles of bones. Some were probably humanoid.

Archaeology had always been a sideline interest of mine. I'd run into plenty of sites not unlike this one in my metallurgical engineering career. Minerals and bones had one thing in common. Both were frequently found in the same spots, sunk into the earth.

I'd let my warding disperse once we entered the cavern. Katya hadn't rebuked me. I made my way back to where she crouched. She'd been drawing runes in the dirt floor with a sharp bit of rock.

I knelt next to her and examined them, sensing she'd told me a story. It was smart of her to use runes. Much like Asian characters, a single rune took the place of many words. These looked Norse in origin, and my beast happily took over.

Surprise lined his words. *"She grew up with Bennet. He courted her. She refused his troth, but they remained friends."*

"Why sound taken aback? You must have known." I figured it was permissible to talk with my beast since the chatter was internal.

"I did, but the courting element was so long ago, I'd forgotten about it."

I figured out the next part easily enough and took the rock from her to write, *"Is Bennet coming?"*

She nodded and mouthed, "Very soon."

I scribed, *"Why?"* into the dirt. She shrugged.

We'd find out soon enough. I rocked back on my heels, waiting. This felt a lot like when Erin and I had been trapped in a cave that turned out to be a gateway to Konstantin and Katya's lair. Several lifetimes had passed since then. At least, it felt that way. In reality, probably not more than a month had elapsed.

If that.

My mind was busy. Who had located whom? Had Katya

asked this Bennet fellow to come to us? Or had he thrown down a gauntlet? Should we be concerned about an attack? Would he come alone? Or with other dragon traitors.

Katya patted my thigh and murmured, "He will not hurt us."

"How can you know that?" I scrapped writing in the dirt for whispering.

She placed a finger over her lips. Frustration soured my nerves. How the fuck were we going to talk with this Bennet fellow? Or would all the conversation be in mind speech? Leaving me out of the loop.

I didn't care for that alternative at all, particularly given the other dragon shifter had been interested enough in Katya to want to marry her. *Mate with her*, I corrected myself.

Well, she was already mated. To me. My beast's possessiveness roared to the forefront, obliterating everything else. Yes, those twenty-first-century customs were gone for good. I was ready to challenge Bennet to a fight to the death—never mind, dragons were immortal—and I'd never even met him.

Magic blasted through the rear wall, and the other dragon shifter was just there. No transition while he materialized. He'd come in his human form. Russet hair was braided away from his face and hung down his back in several plaits. He had a high forehead, sharp hawk's nose, and a squared-off chin. Naturally, his eyes were golden with deep green centers. Like us, he was naked.

I would have liked it better if he was short and squat and ugly, but he had the same type of build as Konstantin. Broad shoulders and acres of muscles.

Katya shot to her feet. So did I, and I made a point to stand shoulder to shoulder with her. For a ridiculously long time, the three of us stared at one another.

"What are you doing?" Katya asked in a low, strained voice.

"There is much you do not know," he replied. "Wait." He raised a hand and turned in a full circle as small white darts flew around us. Once he'd closed the circle, the projectiles grew together and formed something like a translucent tent surrounding us.

"It will not last long," Bennet warned, "but it will allow us to talk without being overheard for a short time."

"How could you have anything to do with serpents?" Katya glared at him.

"Power is a strong motivator, Kat."

"Strong enough to leave your principles at the door?" I sneered.

He rounded on me. "I will allow criticism from her. I've known her my entire life. We were young together. You will hold your opinions. I have no idea who you are, and no wish to alter that status."

Fire poured from me. My dragon was incensed.

He angled a pointed look my way. "Precisely what I mean. You've yet to learn how to control your beast."

"Leave him alone," Katya snarled. "This isn't about him. You always were good at diverting attention away from what you didn't want others to look too closely at. Third time, Bennet. How could you?"

He shrugged. "Some offers are too good to refuse."

"What could they possibly have put on the block that

was so attractive you'd walk away from everything good and decent? I can't believe your dragon didn't at least try to talk you out of this."

A corner of Bennet's handsome mouth twisted downward. "Oh, he did, so I found a better beast. One of the original versions of us. Before that piker who passes as a god exiled the serpents."

He ran his gaze over Katya, taking her in inch by inch in a way I didn't like at all. "I came because I had to see you once again."

"What happened to Mina? And your children?" Katya crossed her arms beneath her breasts.

"She felt much the same way you seem to."

Sadness flickered across Katya's face. "I feel sorry for you. You cast aside everything that was important in your life. Your mate. Your children. Your bondmate. You broke rules at the heart of what it means to be a dragon shifter. And what did you gain?"

"We live a long time, Kat. Nothing is permanent. You should know that by now. Come away with me. I can offer you—"

"Over my dead body." I stepped in front of her. "She is mine. You lost whatever chance you may have had when she refused you eons ago."

"Is that so? Shall we let the lady speak for herself?"

Heat built in my belly and chest. Smoke, ash, and fire sprayed outward, but Bennet batted them away.

Katya moved from behind me and wrapped an arm around my shoulders. "I never wanted you, Bennet. Never. You were always too arrogant for your own good."

"You're making a mistake. You will lose this world. You'll cede it to us after you get tired of losing."

"We did not exactly lose today," I growled.

"Eh. First skirmish is just a warmup. Besides, those faery bastards appear to have left. I can't scent their reek anymore.

"Last chance." He leered at Katya.

I doubled up a fist and punched him square in his sanctimonious face. I heard the *thwack* as his nose broke. I waited for blood to sheet down his face. Instead, his nose bounced back to where it had been before I hit him. The whole thing reminded me of a cartoon sequence with Wile E. Coyote and the Roadrunner.

"Take your last chances and go fuck yourself," Katya barked in a harsh tone like nothing I'd ever heard from her.

He shrugged, a motion that made muscles ripple across his chest and down his arms. "I fought against this too. You'll see the light. And when you do, I'll be there. I've always wanted you, and I'm finally powerful enough to take everything that's due me."

My beast wanted out in no uncertain terms. Katya was ours. OURS. He bugled, challenging Bennet's dragon to aerial combat. While I was struggling to hold onto my human body, Bennet vanished in a cloud of smoke and magic, laughing his head off.

A crazed edge to his laughter set my teeth on edge. "There is something wrong with him," I muttered. At least my beast was becoming more manageable now that his adversary had left.

"There always was," Kat murmured. "I'm sorry. When I sensed his presence not far from us, I invited him to meet. I was hoping for information. I had no idea he was so far gone, or that he was still carrying a torch for me."

"He certainly healed fast."

She nodded. "His magic is strong. More robust than dragon shifter magic has any right to be. After you hit him, I was afraid he'd strike back. I don't understand why he didn't."

"I do." I'd received that message loud and clear. "He was letting me know he is a bigger man than me."

She rolled her eyes. "I never did do well interpreting all that dick wagging. He did say something I want to follow up on, though."

"The part about breaking his bond with his original beast?" At her nod, I went on. "That was the beginning of my dragon demanding ascendency. He was outraged. I guess Bennet's dragon was a friend, but I'm not sure. My bondmate is still too angry to talk with me."

"Mine isn't saying much, either. She's rampaging about, screeching. The dragons all know one another, but I had no idea any dragons from our original creation remained." Ash and smoke blew past her lips. "I saw a group I thought were early sea-serpents in a vision, but it occurred thousands of years in the past—at least, that was my interpretation."

"Serpents from before our deity exiled them? What happened?" I'd heard bits and pieces of the story, but never the whole thing.

"Y Ddraigh Goch banished the serpents and took their wings after they tortured his children. He made a few changes to the dragons' configuration at the same time, probably to ensure we would have different habitats than the serpents. It's why water isn't exactly a natural element for us any longer."

I shook my head. "I was asking about your vision."

"Oh." She closed her teeth over her lower lip. "I was with Konstantin. That image was the last of a series we viewed that day. At first, I thought the bunch sitting around a fire were cave men. Then I thought they were dragons. Finally, after it was too late to extricate myself easily, I understood they were serpents, but before Y Ddraigh Goch had taken their wings."

"What did they want?"

"To use my magic to forge a path through time. Kon broke my mirror and ended my scrying spell."

I put two and two together. "You could not close off your casting in any other way?"

"No. I tried."

Protectiveness flooded me, but the incident had already happened. Even if I'd been there, I'd have had no idea how to intervene. I wrenched my attention back to the other dragon shifter.

"Could Bennet have been lying about breaking the bond and crafting a new one?" It seemed logical to me. Men who had no honor frequently played fast and loose with the truth.

"Yeah, he could have. It's likely, now you mention it. We lack the magic to break things off with our beasts. Only our god has that power."

"Do you sense any other dragons or serpents on the headlands?"

"When I checked after we first got here," she answered,

"the only one I found was Bennet. Doesn't mean much, though. They could have been warded much like us."

I tried for subtle and sent a thread of seeking magic outward. I asked my beast to help interpret the results. "I believe we are alone," I said once I'd searched. The dragon didn't contradict me, but he was still spun out about Bennet's beast.

"My take too. Shall we go back? I need to tell Kon and the others about this. And we need Y Ddraigh Goch. He will know if any of the original dragons remain."

"If what Bennet said is true," I spoke slowly, "it means the dragon god no longer has control over the dragons' original configuration."

"Which is why Bennet was probably lying." Katya's tone was brisk, and she set a teleport spell in motion.

I was all for leaving. The cave stank of Bennet. Unlike other dragon shifters, he smelled like the serpents with a cloyingly rotten undernote that grew worse the longer I breathed it.

"There is nothing left of the dragon I knew inside Bennet." My beast finally recovered his voice.

"But is it the same dragon?"

"Yes and no. He is changed, and not for the better. His capacity for independent thought has fled. It is as if he's been ensorcelled." More fire shot from my mouth. *"It's an outrage. No one tampers with dragonkind."*

"Katya?"

"Yes, I heard. Even though your beast is correct about it being disgraceful, still I am relieved we aren't dealing with a resurrection of whatever we were before the serpents' exile."

"Did your bondmate weigh in, yet?"

She shook her head. "Long ago, she urged me to accept Bennet's offer of mating, but that was when she was pushing me toward any male who showed an interest in us. She's probably feeling guilty."

The clean feel of her power surrounded me. The cavern gave way to the verge around the lake. It had emptied of shifters except the odd dinosaur grazing on marsh grass. Three were in the lake, splashing about.

"Where's Konstantin?" Katya called.

Something that looked a lot like a Spinosaurus called back, "He left to talk with the land."

"How long ago?"

The dinosaur shrugged, shaking water in a wide circle. "A while."

"Thank you."

"Do you want to hunt for him?" I asked.

"No. Let's go inside for a bit. I'd like to consult the lore books. And see if I can't set the wheels in motion to raise Y Ddraigh Goch."

I threaded my fingers with hers. Together we walked inside and down one flight to the level with the sleeping pallets. Both of us stopped, and she wrapped her arms around me.

I drank her in, still not quite believing she was mine. "You are so lovely," I murmured and brushed my thumb across her cheek. My bondmate took up his chant about the mating flight where we would shift and make love in the air. I felt for his plight, but the odds of us taking the time to travel to the surface to mate were nonexistent.

Lost in passion, we would be exposed to whoever lurked there.

Her nipples pebbled where they pressed against my chest. Despite being mates, we'd only made love once. My cock rose in a column and pressed against her soft belly. Her eyes glowed with love and tenderness.

"We shouldn't," she said, "but what harm can five minutes to ourselves do?"

I wanted a whole lot more than five minutes. The only other time we'd gotten together hadn't lasted much longer than that, but beggars couldn't be choosers. She snuck a hand between our bodies and curled her fingers around my shaft. Not that I'd been undecided before, but her touch clinched it.

Still clinging to each other, we sidestepped into the nearest room. The door slammed shut behind us, and we half fell onto a pad pushed into one corner. Katya was on top of me, straddling my legs. She rose far enough to seat my cock at her entrance, and then she sank onto me. The heat of her surrounding me was enticing, irresistible.

Reaching up, I filled my hands with her breasts, rubbing the erect nipples between my thumb and forefinger. She moaned and pressed herself deeper into my touch. Her muscles clenched around me, and she rotated her hips from side to side. The musk of our combined arousal stoked the heat racing through me.

She dropped her hands onto my shoulders and steadied herself as she danced up and down the length of my shaft. Her mouth crashed against mine, and I wrapped one arm around her back and grabbed a hip with the other hand.

Between the two, I moved us faster and faster. My heart thudded against my chest wall, and my breath turned to ragged pants.

Within her, my cock was as achingly hard as it ever got. I willed her release. Fucked her harder. Faster. I wanted the sensation spilling through me to last forever, but these were stolen moments. Time we should have been researching Bennet's claims and begging the dragon god for his time and assistance.

She'd been biting my lower lip when she dragged her mouth from mine long enough to say. "We chose this. Dragons are jealous. Think only of me."

"How could I not?" I somehow managed to get the words out. "You are everything I have ever dreamed of in a woman."

She crinkled her nose at me. "Brash. Outspoken. Headstrong."

"Gorgeous. Smart. Insightful. Compassionate."

Her hair streamed down around us. She captured my mouth with hers again, and I took firm hold of the amazing rounded globes of her ass. Upping the tempo, I walked a fine edge, holding on until her soft moans and the rhythmic contractions around my cock told me she was cresting. No reason to hold off any longer.

I let go of everything and lost myself in the woman I loved.

Panting and laughing, we hung on for dear life until our passion ebbed enough for us to untangle our limbs. "Not much more than five minutes." She grinned at me.

"Worth every second." I grinned back. "Not having

clothing to get in and out of has advantages." I rolled to a kneeling position and held out both hands. "Shall we?"

"We shall. I believe we were on our way to the library?"

"We were, indeed. Might we detour through the kitchen?"

She snorted. "We could, but there might not be anything left."

I scrambled to my feet and lifted Katya to hers. "If not, we shall remedy it later."

Her expression sobered. "I have a feeling hunting on the run will be our new normal. At least until we either dispatch the serpents or give up and leave."

"Never. Earth is worth saving."

"Let's hope she feels the same way. If not, there won't be a whole lot we can do to convince her to hold on."

A thought occurred to me. "Much as I view this as an absolute last-ditch scenario, if the land is hellbent on destroying herself, perhaps we can arrange things so she takes the bloody bastard serpents with her."

"I like the way you think. In fact, there's not much about you I don't like."

Her words pleased me as I trailed down the stairs after her. My stomach rumbled, and I hoped to hell there was at least a pan of dried kelp left to munch on. "What is your first priority in the library?" I asked.

"Dragon shifter history," she replied. "I want to make certain what I believe is what actually happened and not a watered-down version we were fed as youngsters because it was more palatable."

“I am glad humans are not the only ones who rewrite history to whitewash atrocities.”

“No one has a corner on that market.” She whooped. “We’re in luck. No one found the rest of the seal meat.” Scooping booty into a cloth square, she ran for the library with me right behind her.

I swear, that woman has the finest ass. I could watch its curves forever and never tire of the view. A shot of magic from Katya eradicated the illusion that kept the library hidden from casual view. She plopped the cloth sack on the desk and headed for a particularly dusty shelf. I grabbed a bit of dried seal and settled in with a stack of scrolls Erin had collected that mostly had to do with how dragon shifter magic worked.

We’d figure this out. We had to. Rather than dwell on Bennet’s magic and why it was so potent, I chalked him up as a nut case and began to read.

KONSTANTIN

Konstantin was partway down the steep shaft when the earth rumbled menacingly around him. Rocks cascaded downward, bouncing off the walls. "Stop that!" He infused command into his words. Earth was turning into a fickle bitch, but he'd be damned if he'd let her bury him under tons of rock. He could dig his way out with magic, but it would take time he didn't have right now.

A terrified shriek cut into his soul. Erin. What was she doing anywhere near him? Had she decided to tag along quietly? The cry had come from above. He dug his feet and knees into the soft dirt to stop his downward trajectory. A blast of magic propelled him upward.

But he didn't get very far. The upper end of the shaft had filled in with soft crumbly dirt and rocks. "Erin!" he yelled and followed it with a thread of seeking magic. Sure enough, she was between him and the ledge that led to the shaft, presumably mired in dirt and boulders that had fallen into the chute.

A whimper reached him, followed by garbled telepathy. *"I'm sorry. I'll get myself out of this. Last thing I want is to add to your problems."*

He rebuked himself for being overprotective. For not teaching her to teleport properly. Her dragon could step in, but would she? Intent on freeing Erin, he levered himself upward, clawing dirt out of the way as he went. He mixed in streams of magic to make things go faster.

"I'm out," reached him.

"Stay there." He snapped off the words, sounding far more pissed off than he actually was, but she'd have no way of knowing that. He quit digging his way upward, trading manual labor for magic as he teleported to the ledge system a few meters from the head of the shaft.

Erin stood, hands on her hips. "Look," she sputtered. "I told you I was sorry. I am. I was curious about this Earth person, or spirit, or whatever the land is. I didn't think it would hurt anything if I followed you." She flapped her hands his way. "Go on. I can find my own way back."

"This isn't about you finding your way back to the surface," he said, not wanting her to leave. "I didn't mean to sound so abrupt, but when you screamed—"

"I was surprised." She spoke over him. "I've climbed. A lot. I tested the shaft. Last thing I expected was for the fucking thing to collapse around my head. At first, I couldn't breathe, but that was only because I forgot I have magic these days."

She turned her back on him and began walking away.

"Erin. Stop. You're touchy as an unseasonable winter."

She stopped but didn't turn around. "Maybe it's because I feel like an idiot." She did turn then. "I do best when I believe I'm contributing something of value. I, um, thought that maybe if I could hear whatever the land had to say to you, I might pick up something beneath her words. Then this would be a project we could work on together. You and I. Not always me tagging along like a puppy who knows nothing."

"What aren't you saying?"

She closed her teeth over her lower lip. "How did you know I'd left something out?"

He walked to her until they were nearly touching. "I love you, Erin. I want you for my mate. Because I care, because you're important to me, I pay attention to...everything. You haven't complained before about feeling useless, so something moved you in that direction. What was it?"

She shook her head and looked away.

"You can tell me anything. I won't judge you."

Her blue eyes with their thick golden rims did meet his gaze then. "You'll think I have no faith in you, and that's not it at all. But I'm worried. Without the Sidhe..."

He nodded solemnly. "I wish they would have remained as well. And they may yet return. I have no idea what counsel their gods will offer. It is never just one thing that wins a war, though, but a coordinated approach. The serpents have at least one fatal flaw, which is their loss of immortality in their human form. It's almost as if someone punished them, and they can't find a fix for it."

"So if we find out more about their recent history?"

He nodded. "I was hoping the land would ally with us, but she created that mini cave-in on purpose. I thought she was doing it to annoy me, but now I believe she targeted you. Not so much to aggravate me as to warn me off."

He dropped his hands on her shoulders and lifted his head. "Hear me plainly. This is my woman. Mine. If harm befalls her at your hands, I and my dragons and all the other shifters will leave you to your fate. I understand you don't care anymore, but that is because you haven't had to suffer pure evil raping you at every turn.

"Men are a bunch of rowdy, unprincipled jerks, but most carry at least a flicker of decency. Once they're all dead—and they will be—the only thing left will be serpents. And dragons who've joined the dark side. You think your existence is difficult now. Let me tell you, you have no fucking idea how bad things can get."

He blew out an exasperated breath. "You think about that. If you change your mind, or have an epiphany about who your allies really are, you know where to find me. But do not tarry. I'm not overly fond of waging wars that benefit the ungrateful."

"That was harsh," Erin muttered.

"Yeah, well, kindness didn't get through. Or compassion." He shook his head. "I feel sorry for Oberon. I hope the Celts can free him from the magic shackling him to this world."

"That could possibly help us. If the faeries aren't constantly having to run back to the *Dreaming* to replenish their magic, we might be able to kill off all the serpents and be done with it."

He tipped her chin up with his index finger. "You're beautiful when you're in a bloodthirsty mood, my dear."

Erin snorted and tossed her head. "I'm beautiful all the time. I'm also not ready to walk away from Earth. This has been my home. Granted I had no idea about all the shit playing out behind the scenes, but it's the only place I know."

"I will try my hardest to preserve it for you." He moved his hands back to her shoulders. "Will you accept my troth?" Steam puffed from his mouth as his dragon added a plea of its own. His bondmate had been incredibly patient, but Konstantin understood he'd long since given up ever having a dragon to fly and mate with.

"Yes. I will be your wife. Or your mate." Erin tilted her chin at a defiant angle. "On one condition."

He would have whooped, except it wasn't dignified. "Anything, darling."

"You might wait to hear what it is."

He nodded, the totality of his attention focused on her.

"We will be equals in all things. When you allowed me to accompany Katya and Johan to Arctowski, I knew it was a concession. You were doing your level best not to make me feel like you had a leash around my neck."

He winced. She'd nailed precisely how he'd felt, and his bondmate had been livid because he hadn't insisted she remain by his side. Telling her she didn't understand dragons wouldn't endear him to her.

She was one.

Nor would he blurt a bunch of excuses to make himself look better.

"I can't promise I will never do anything to anger you," he said, "but I will treat you with the respect you deserve. You haven't been a dragon shifter long, but surely you've come up against your beast's possessive streak. It is very close to the foundation of what it means to be a dragon. We love fiercely, and when we stake a claim to something, it is ours."

Before Erin could say anything, he hurried on. "But that cuts both ways. You will want me with the same singlemindedness I long for you."

Her expression softened. "I already do. Resisting your mating bid has cost me, and not just because my dragon labeled me a coward."

He moved to her side and tucked a hand beneath her elbow. "We must return to the others, but the gods won't fault us if we stop at my hoard. I would have you pick something special. A symbol of our troth."

Steam billowed from her. Erin's dragon clearly loved the idea. It was rare for dragons to bring anyone—even mates-to-be—to their hoards.

A soft smile curved her lips. "My beast is all over that one."

"And you?"

"I'd love you just as much if you weren't offering gold or gems."

Something deep within him cracked wide open. She'd just said she loved him, and it fed his dragon's soul. "Say it again."

She quirked a blonde brow. "Which part?"

"You know."

"I do. I love you. Not quite sure when it crept up on me, but I'm not going to fight it anymore."

He wrapped his arms around her and kissed her once. Quick. Hot. Hard. If he did much more, they'd never get out of the passageway. Or at least not for a while. The honey-sweet taste of her remained on his lips, and the softness of her body where she'd molded to him lingered as well.

He started up the ledge system but then changed his mind and summoned a teleport spell. When the air cleared, they stood in a small cave. He kindled a mage light. Gold coins, many old and valuable, were piled about. Jewelry sparkled with gems, and loose gems had been sorted according to color.

"Oh my." Breath whistled from Erin. "Wherever did all this come from?"

"Mostly shipwrecks. There have been a lot of them in this part of the world."

"I thought dragons didn't care for water."

"We don't. I gathered almost all of this from casks that washed up on shore. We've been here for a long time. Since the days of the old wooden sailing vessels. Why do you suppose we selected this particular headland? It was particularly deadly for ships. Their remains have long since rotted, but dozens sailed their last voyage and wrecked on these shoals."

"The men?"

"We helped those we could. Most died. It is not a commodious climate for humans."

Erin left his side and wandered through his treasure trove. Streamers of steam followed her, and his beast puffed steam with the enthusiasm of a runaway locomotive. From time to time, she bent and picked up a coin or a piece of jewelry. He remained quiet. She'd know when just the right item was in her hand.

It would match her energy.

"My beast wants me to drop everything and create a hoard of our own," she murmured. "Right after we roll around in all this gold."

"You will," he assured her. "It's only a matter of time. All dragons are natural-born collectors."

She'd been crouched over a pile of brooches and bracelets. If he remembered right, they'd been tucked within a cracked oaken cask toward the tail end of the 1700s. None of the men from that ship had survived. They'd looked as if they'd been half dead from malnutrition and exposure long before their ratty old tub foundered off the headland.

Erin straightened and walked toward him with a pendant dangling from one hand. The necklace was an intricate gold weave, and the ornament consisted of strands of gold and silver shaped into the body of a woman. She held a lantern suspended in one hand, and a deer stood next to her. Moonstones and smoky quartz adorned the piece.

She held it out to him. "May I have this one?" Before he could say of course, she went on. "It's a likeness of Arianrhod. I've always had an affinity for that particular goddess."

"Certainly. She's yours." He took the necklace and settled it over her head. "Why an attraction for Arianrhod?" Konstantin didn't tell Erin he'd met the goddess a time or two and found her haughty and unapproachable. But then, he'd also heard rumors her virgin status was so much tripe.

If those rumors had been true, the goddess loved dragons. The bigger and more fire-breathing, the better.

Erin's eyes glowed, reflected by his mage light. "She's a lot like me. Alone. A virgin huntress..." Erin's cheeks flushed. "Not that I'm a virgin, but Arianrhod, she ruled the moon and the tides from a special land all her own named Caer Sidi. This will sound foolish, but surgery is sometimes like that. Particularly for the long, delicate, difficult operations, I felt as if I was alone in my own little place. Just me and my instruments and the living flesh beneath them. There's a numinous aspect to life, and it's never so near as when death hovers. Watchful. Waiting. Hoping for an opportunity to swoop in and snag another victim."

She shut her eyes for a moment, long lashes brushing her cheekbones. "I don't know what got into me. That's as romanticized a version of an OR as I've ever heard, plus all the nursing staff and the other docs, like the anesthesiologists, would feel terribly slighted."

"I'll make certain they never know."

"Not much of a concern. I'll never see that life again." She fingered the pendant. "Are you certain? It's lovely, and it sang to me."

He bent and kissed her forehead. "Of course, I'm certain. You will soon be my mate. Everything that is mine is also yours."

The steam that had slowed picked up again. The cave where he kept his hoard was thick with it. He wrapped his arms around Erin, breathing her in. She hugged him back, and he settled his mouth over hers. This kiss was different. Before, he'd never been certain of her desires. He'd recognized she lusted after him, but he hadn't known if she would ever accept all of him.

She melted into his arms and teased him with her lips, teeth, and tongue. Perhaps because he was no longer frantic about the prospect of losing her, they could relax and enjoy each other. Take all the time in the world to explore every bit of one another.

His dragon pushed for the mating flight, but not too hard. His beast recognized how dangerous it would be for them to spend time alone outside the protection of this underground grotto. No point in starting the mating flight if they ended up aborting it when dragon traitors attacked.

Erin broke their kiss. She cradled his face between her hands and smoothed her thumbs over his jawline. "You're amazing. I still can't quite believe I said yes."

He leaned his forehead against hers. "Why did you?"

"Because you and I, we feel right together. I was worried when I returned from Arctowski and you weren't here. What if something had gone wrong, and I wasn't there to save you?" A sheepish smile tugged at her lips. "I know it doesn't make sense. You're immortal, and what could I do with my set of Western medical skills, anyway, in the face of magical wounding?"

"Ssht. I love it that you want to take care of me."

"That's part of Arianrhod, too. In some myths, she was the goddess protector of the forest animals."

"Have you always been drawn to mythology?"

She nodded. "I needed a place to drown my difficult childhood."

Protectiveness ran through him like quicksilver, and he gathered her closer. "Are those who hurt you still alive?"

"No. It was a long time ago, and—"

"If they were alive, I would make them hurt the same way they hurt you. And I would ensure they understood that no one—"

She waved him to silence. "My father died in prison. I'm certain his last years were horrible. Can we talk about the future, not the past? I spent a long time putting it behind me."

Konstantin stroked her hair. It flowed, soft and silky, beneath his fingertips. "We can talk about whatever you desire, my love. Or nothing at all."

He didn't understand why he wasn't in more of a hurry to bed her. Before, it had been all he could think about. He desired her, ached for her, but their bodies would come together soon enough.

"We should join the others," she said, "but I don't want to leave your cavern. My beast is still urging me to roll around in the piles of gold."

"I don't want to leave, either, but I brought a hundred shifters here. It isn't right to steal time for myself—no matter how much I want to. You've made me a very happy man."

"I hope you're still singing that song a year from now. I'm not the easiest person to get along with. When I was a surgeon, people expected me to be a bitch. It gave me an excuse. Vindicated my short temper."

"No more excuses, eh?"

"Guess not." She rolled her eyes. "I'm still a surgeon, but no one gives a shit. Johan's the only one who has a glimmer of a clue what our life used to look like. I'm thinking it's a good thing. A chance to start over and figure out who I want to be."

"So long as the starting over includes me, we're golden. And dragons can be plenty bitchy."

Erin laughed; the silvery peals warmed him. "We are, indeed, dragons. Aren't all of us golden? Even the ones who are black and red?"

He laughed along with her, and together they ducked under the low lintel of his cave. He sealed its location with obfuscation from long habit, and they walked down a tunnel and out along a path next to the second lake down from his home.

Dinosaurs grazed, but a male wolf shifter ran to them. Red hair streamed down his back, and his leathers smelled faintly of sea serpent. "Glad I found you, Kon. We're hungry. Those of us who can't eat grass. We were thinking about leaving long enough to hunt down food elsewhere on this world."

"You don't need my permission," he replied, "but I appreciate you letting me know."

"We'll return as soon as we've fed," the wolf said.

"Who all is going?" Erin asked.

"Everyone but the herbivores. So some of the dinosaurs, all the wolves, and all the birds. Which reminds me, Gustaf said to tell you they rescued the missing raven." He stopped and looked at Konstantin as if something had just occurred to him. "What are you eating?"

"Not much," Kon said. "Katya and I had some very limited food stocks in our home, but they're mostly depleted. Soon, we shall face the same problem."

"Do you think the Daoine Sidhe will return? We've been kicking that one around, and I said I'd ask. Assuming I located you."

Konstantin shrugged. "I wish I knew. Depends what the Celtic gods have to offer for advice."

"Speaking of gods," the wolf went on, "did the land say anything further?"

"Not this time. She didn't talk with me at all."

"Damn it." The wolf thinned his mouth into a tense line. "I'll be sure to let the others know. We'll be back quite soon. Perhaps we'll teleport back here with whatever we find to eat."

"Herds of antelope are plentiful in Argentina." At the wolf's confused expression, Konstantin went on. "Nearest landmass to the north of us."

"Everything is north," the wolf mumbled and took off at a lope.

Kon tucked Erin's hand into his and started walking up the valley toward his lair. He hoped to find Johan and Katya. Magic flashed behind him. When he twisted his neck in that direction, he saw Ylon trotting toward him. The dinosaur had switched to his human form, probably so he could converse without resorting to magic.

"My guess is they will not return," Ylon rumbled when he caught up. "The dinosaurs will, but not the others."

"I'd considered the same." Konstantin nodded. "You and

your warriors are free to leave as well," he went on. "This never was your fight."

"We choose to remain, and I disagree. It's everyone's fight." Ylon's rugged face split into a smile. "Besides, I haven't had this much fun in years."

Konstantin did a quick mental tally. Thirty dinosaurs. Roughly half that number of dragons. If they were wily, cunning, struck fast and hard and withdrew before striking again, it might be enough.

"Brother! Where are you?" Katya's voice reverberated through his chest.

"Close to home. Why?"

"Meet us in the library. We found...something."

"Even I heard that," Erin said. "Let's find out what it is."

"I shall sit in," Ylon announced.

Konstantin muffled an urge to tell the dinosaur to wait elsewhere. But either they were allies. Or not. You didn't bar your partners from key bits of information from the source. He walked faster.

What the hell had his sister unearthed? Whatever it was, he'd bet his last farthing—if he still had a use for coins—his bondmate already knew what it was. The beast had been uncharacteristically quiet, hovering on the edge of not being there at all.

Clearly, he wanted an escape hatch in case Kon peppered him with questions he didn't want to answer.

DRAGON TIME

Hello again! Konstantin's dragon here. I won't take up much of your time, but we have a MATE! I can't believe it. In truth, I won't believe it until the deed is actually done, but Erin is a woman of her word.

She said she would be ours, and I believe her.

I feel a little bit bad—not much, mind you, since dragons rarely retreat or apologize—for all the times I told my bondmate he was a bloody coward for not picking a partner for us.

I paraded any number of potential dragons in front of him through the years. Naturally, they were females who appealed to me. I may even have sampled the wares a time or two. Just a wee bit of dabbling, mind you, nothing that would have committed Konstantin and me. None of the females were paired with humans yet, but that's the easy part. Or it used to be. I still haven't quite gotten over how difficult Erin's transition to dragon shifter was. I've made a couple of trips back to my world since then and spoken with others.

Dragons older even than me. They listened carefully as I described the events surrounding both Erin and Johan's transformations, asking for clarification several times.

The consensus was that magic has been dying out of all the worlds for a very long time. We didn't notice because the shift was gradual. And because the idea of magic vanishing was so farfetched, we discarded it out of hand. Hindsight is a great leveler, though, and all of us feel really stupid. Not that we could have done much to stem the tide, even if we had been paying closer attention.

Or perhaps we could have at least slowed the loss down. It's one of those things where after you pass a certain point, all you can do is stand back and watch and hope to hell it's not as bad as you fear.

I've considered talking with Konstantin, but he has a lot on his mind. He already recognizes worlds are dying at an unprecedented pace, but I don't believe he's connected the dots. By that I mean, he hasn't assigned a lack of magic as the primary reason worlds have been giving up.

He's a smart man. Eventually, he'll see the connection. I haven't pushed it because, as I said, there's not much we can do to alter the downhill slide.

Not that dragons will vanish. At least I hope we don't. Before, I'd always assumed we'd retreat to some other world. One where magic was fresher. We could still do that, but it will only stave off the inevitable.

And now, I'm being uncharacteristically pessimistic. I

don't know what the future holds, not with any greater degree of clarity than any other dragon. Katya's beast is a seer, much like her. I've done a bit of subtle digging, feeding her the odd question here and there. Just to see if she knows more than me.

Either she's been purposefully obtuse, or there's nothing to tell.

Like everything else, magic ebbs and flows. We might simply be at one of the lower points, and things will turn around. After one of our recent discussions back home on our world, a trio of dragons approached Y Ddraigh Goch. They had to track him down on a distant borderworld, and he wasn't pleased to be disturbed. Turns out it was the place he'd sequestered his children who were maimed by sea serpents. Anyway, he left off doctoring his spawn long enough to tell our contingent to leave.

If our god knows anything—and it's difficult to believe he doesn't understand more than we do—he's not in a sharing mood. I'm certain he blames himself for the havoc the serpents are causing. And he must be beside himself that dragons—a few, not many—have joined ranks with the exiled monsters.

Interesting I felt the need to put that caveat in. The one about only a few dragons signing on with our sorcerous kinsmen. It makes me feel better, but even a single dragon defector would stick in our god's craw like a cancer.

Mine too.

When the group of dragons I was chewing the fat with back on our world got through being annoyed our god was so closemouthed, we spoke of other things. And came up with a few facts I'm pretty sure are true. Remember what I said about magic growing weaker? Well, we believe it's why the serpents have lost their immortality in their human bodies.

Konstantin thought someone was angry and had punished the serpents, but it's probably not as much of a reprisal as he believes. After Y Ddraigh Goch stripped our cousins of their wings, he also diluted their magic. Because of that, they're more susceptible to a generalized decrease in the magic flowing through all worlds. Less juice to tap into means their depleted power would be even weaker.

It's also why Faery is fading. Oberon is convinced the land is holding out on him, doling out power in dribs and drabs, but she may not have any more to give than what he's tapping into. Since all of Faery is rooted in the *Dreaming*, and it's encased in Earth's force field, everything is woven together. I hope the Celtic gods understand what's happening. They hold an enormous amount of power. If they could get it pointed in the same direction, they might make a difference...

But I digress. This is about dragons, something I know a lot about. Not about the faeries, where the sum total of my knowledge is conjecture.

The other problem my small group of dragons tackled was why the hell any dragon in his—or her—right mind would have anything to do with our slimy, deceitful, erstwhile kin. That question was a whole lot harder than why serpents had lost their immortality.

We came up with a few possibilities. The leading candidate was that there's a synergistic aspect to blending magics. Such has always been true. The dragons who linked their magical reservoirs to serpent power would have become stronger. I can see where stronger would have an appeal.

I can't be the only dragon to have a sneaky hunch about our future not being as bright as the past. Maybe those traitors are hedging their bets. They might not view the serpents as anything beyond added fuel to line their tanks.

The other reason we came up with was resentment. Dragons are masters at nurturing antipathy. Over eons it turns to bitterness. And anger. Many of my kin believed Y Ddraigh Goch overreacted when he stripped the sea-serpents of their wings and exiled them. While they would have supported banishment for the group who'd actually tortured the god's children, assigning the sins of a few to the many was seen as Draconian and overkill. As our god taking the crime far too personally. Because of Konstantin's close association with Y Ddraigh Goch, he was painted with the same brush.

When he led a flight to Earth, it lacked the cohesion needed to flourish. I probably should have spoken up, shared my observations with my bondmate, but I kept hoping I was wrong. We'd gotten a new start on a new world. Surely, the malcontents would put their ill will behind them.

Never happened.

Always strained, interactions among the flight grew gradually worse. I was relieved when the other dragons left because I assumed we'd be right behind them. I've always hated Earth. Eh, perhaps hate is too strong a term. Dragons need a spot we can fly free without creating havoc. Earth was never an optimal choice for us, but it worsened over time. During the era when we arrived, men were wonderfully superstitious and still clung to their belief in magic.

When a lot of humans hold magic dear, it strengthens us.

You know what happened. Magic faded from the minds of men, replaced by one scientific theory after another. Science and magic are incompatible. As I think on it, perhaps humankind's headlong leap into science is responsible for magic's decline.

It's hard to tell which came first with these things. Nor does it matter. We have about as much chance of force-feeding humans magic as we have of winning the sea-serpent war without outside help.

There. I said it. It's the last item I want to touch on, and then I'll turn this back over to Konstantin and the others. They're far more capable of sharing their story than I am.

We won our first real battle because the Sidhe fought next to us. Conjoined magics are strongest, and between dragon and faery power, we killed serpents. A lot of them. Without the necessity of luring them into their human forms. The battle cost the Sidhe dearly. Oberon was doing his damnedest to save face, but he and his warriors didn't have another skirmish in them. Not without a good long time sucking tit in the *Dreaming* to replenish themselves. Which circles back to a big unknown: does the *Dreaming* contain enough magic to restore all those Sidhe?

My off-the-talon guess is it doesn't. Earth would need to cooperate, and from what I've seen of the land lately, she's like a sulky bitch in heat who discovered having sex won't soothe the ache in her soul.

The Sidhe are gone. I have no idea if they'll return. A good big bunch of the shifters left too, under the guise of needing to hunt. I believe they're hungry, but I have no idea if they'll show back up here. Konstantin gave them an out. And it's an honest one. This isn't their war. Not on the surface. If you scratch down a bit, though, it's everyone's war. If we have to abandon Earth, the serpents will set up shop here.

They'll strengthen themselves on human carnage and engineer a plan to capture what magic is left in the net binding all worlds together. They could live for a long time if they kept all the magic for themselves.

A very long time. While the rest of us gradually—or not so gradually—died out.

So there it is. We must find a way to win. For that, we will require divine aid. Our god. Other shifter gods. The Celts. Historically, none of them have lifted wing, finger, claw, or tail to intervene in what they consider mortal affairs. And by that, I don't mean human. To our gods, we're the mortals in their equations.

The bright spot, of course, is Konstantin and I finally have a mate. But if we can't get on top of our other problems, we won't have untold millennia to fly with her. Usually, I spare him my thoughts and opinions. It's how our bond is constructed. I know everything in his mind but am careful about what I share of my own thoughts.

No more.

Particularly after the land made a ham-handed bid to harm Erin, I owe my bondmate honesty. I shall talk with him and hold nothing back. Perhaps something I say will help as he decides what to do next.

You'll see me once more at the very end. As I've said before, we dragons like to have the last word. Let us hope I bear better news then. For all our sakes.

ERIN

The spot where the pendant hung against my breastbone throbbed warmly, almost as if the likeness of Arianrhod were alive. And she approved of my choice. Anything was possible. The necklace had been part of Konstantin's hoard for a long while. Perhaps his magic had imbued all his treasures with dragon enchantment.

I still couldn't quite believe I'd said I'd become his mate. But the unsettled place that had dogged me ever since his initial request had quieted. I wouldn't exactly say anything as schmaltzy as a sense of peace descended, but the internal push-and-pull about what I was going to do was gone.

I chalk my reticence up to my lifelong avoidance of commitments. I never wanted a husband. Or children. I had such a crap childhood, I didn't want to chance screwing up the next generation with my nonexistent parenting skills. You learn those things by example, right?

Well, I never had any. Scratch that. I had a shit ton of parenting examples, all of them bad.

It's kind of tough to shelve a twenty-year history of pushing men who wanted to get closer aside. Konstantin was persistent. I guess I assumed once we were having more-or-less-regular sex—minus intercourse—he'd back off. Sex is what men want, and sex without strings seems to satisfy a whole lot of them. Not him, though.

I figured the moment I said I'd marry him—mate with him, whatever—he'd be all over me. I was ready. Oral sex and digital penetration only go so far. I'd had some pretty graphic fantasies about that lovely appendage of his sunk inside me. Instead, he treated me like a precious jewel and took me to his hoard.

If my beast hadn't told me, I'd never have known how unusual that is. Even for mates, dragons often draw the line at hoard sharing. Perhaps once I've begun collecting my own stash, I'll understand more. But my bondmate made it abundantly clear Konstantin had offered us an almost unprecedented honor.

I'd selected a gorgeous piece of jewelry—or maybe it selected me. Once it was securely around my neck, I was looking forward to screwing Konstantin's brains out. Best laid plans, and all that.

Despite drowning in unslaked lust, I admit to curiosity about whatever Katya and Johan had unearthed. Maybe it will be something that will actually help us put the serpent hassles behind us.

I'm used to human wars. The ones with bombs and planes and people dying on all sides. Usually, there are clear-cut winners, but not always. I was certain we'd won a definitive victory saving all those people on that cruise ship. Until I discovered one was infected with hemorrhagic fever, a disease that will likely wipe out all of them with even more efficiency than the serpents would have.

For a scant moment, I wondered if the serpents would have fallen ill if we hadn't intervened when they were busily chomping through passengers. We probably wouldn't have gotten that lucky. Part of immortal must be immunity from lethal disease. Off on a medical tangent, I thought about vaccines and whether incubating deadly viruses and bacteria with dragon shifter blood could create something that would protect humans from illnesses that had no cure.

We'd reached the double stone doors leading inside. Ylon and Konstantin had been deep in conversation while my mind wandered. Within me, my beast basked contentedly. The way she viewed the world, we now had our first piece for our very own hoard. She assumed I'd prioritize adding to it. Once I staked out a private location.

I let her savor her fantasies and stifled a grin. I dreamed of hot sex. She dreamed of gold. We both hated serpents. Perhaps she and I did, indeed, have the stuff to go the distance.

The doors swung open. No one touched them, so I assume Kon gave them a magical shove. I hadn't yet gotten to the point where my use of magic was second nature. Especially for simple things like opening doors, my fallback position was to do it the old-fashioned way.

We clattered down several sets of stairs, our bare feet slapping the stone steps as we went. When we got to the great room, I saw that the illusory wall hiding the library was down. Johan and Katya sat next to one another, heads bent over a large book with a cracked and peeling leather binding that had once been a deep brown.

My sensitive dragon nose caught a whiff of fresh sex. I was jealous. Johan and Katya had made time for a quickie. All Kon and I would have needed was an extra half hour or so. Not that it would have been nearly long enough, but it would have been a starting point. We'd done enough necking and petting, we knew each other's bodies fairly well.

"There you are." Katya moved the book carefully into Johan's lap and got to her feet.

I dragged my lust-saturated brain out of the gutter and took a closer look at the book. I could see why she'd been so careful. The pages were cracked vellum. And they looked so fragile, a stray breath might be all it would take to lose half a page of the spidery script penned in faded reddish ink.

Christ! Had the book been scribed in blood? Nostrils flaring, I scented the air for something other than pheromones and didn't find much. If whoever wrote the book had used his own blood, it happened too long ago to verify.

Katya brushed dirt out of her twin's hair and turned to rake her sharp gaze over me. "Why do both of you have muck in your hair?"

"It's a long story, Sister. Let's just say the land is throwing a brass balls fit. My guess is the Celts did something to enable the faery court to move the *Dreaming*."

"How is that your fault?" Katya arched one copper brow.

"I didn't say Earth's reaction was logical. Not all worlds

are like Mu. She trusted me, probably because Mu was the dragon shifters' home world. She knew us, had watched us for countless generations. Earth reminds me of a woman who's had one too many men take advantage of her. Rather than evaluating each new suitor on his merits, she's lumping us all together as bastards out to exploit her."

"Mmph. At least you are unharmed. Not buried beneath tons of dirt." Johan had laid the book aside and scrambled to his feet as well.

"Yes, that is the most important part," Ylon chimed in.

"I take it your most recent discussion with Earth did not go well?" Johan asked.

"You mean our non-discussion," Konstantin corrected him. "No. She refused to talk with me."

"And then Kon was pretty blunt," I said.

"Good." Ylon narrowed his silver eyes. "She needs to hear the truth. Probably many times, but today will be a start."

Konstantin knelt next to the book Johan and Katya had been pouring over. "Wherever did you find this?" he asked.

"It was the oddest thing"—Katya crouched next to him —"I was looking for source materials on the beginnings of magic through all the worlds, and the book just showed up."

I did a double take. "What? As in floated through the air, and—?"

Katya shook her head. "I'd been looking through the far bank of shelves along with Johan. When I grew discouraged, I turned around, and the book was sitting on the desk. As if had been there all along, except I knew differently."

"It was fairly glowing," Johan jumped in excitedly. "I could feel magic pulsing from it halfway across the room."

"At first it made me nervous," Katya admitted.

"Wise of you," Ylon muttered. He, too, had walked to where the book lay and was examining it without touching it. "Have you ever seen it before?" he asked Konstantin. "Because I have not."

Kon looked up, a puzzled expression marring his perfect features. "Yes. If it's the same tome, I remember it from Mu." He lifted a page or two, taking exquisite care as he laid them to the other side. "Give me a few moments. I want to be certain before I pronounce it the exact same book."

He settled into a cross-legged sit and gently placed the book across his lap. His fingers glowed with magic as he riffled through pages. I caught the scents of poorly tanned leather from the binding and goat from the vellum pages. Interesting I could sort those smells, but not the blood I assumed had been used for ink. I supposed the author could have used any number of dyes to achieve that red shade, but why not write in black and have done with things?

"I thought those of us who left emptied out Mu's library," Katya said, "which is why I was so distrustful when I turned around and the book was just there."

"You two are talking in riddles," Johan said. "If the book is what you believe it to be, was it part of the library in your home world?"

"Yes," Katya replied. "A very unusual part. The books and scrolls that dealt with the most sensitive—and private—magical topics were kept in a special vault. It was temperature-and-humidity controlled to preserve the ancient documents."

"I believe this is genuine," Konstantin said. "Which means it was penned by Y Ddraigh Goch and the First Dragon. It covers the origins of our magic, and why our power is different from that of other magic wielders."

"Fascinating," Ylon murmured. "We have—or had—a similar book. It is long since lost to the vagaries of time, distance, and our nomadic lifestyle."

"But you've been on the first world in the Fleisher system for a long time," Konstantin said.

"Yes, but far from forever," Ylon replied. "What does the book say about your origins?"

"I don't know," Konstantin said. "I have never read it. Katya?"

"Johan and I were working our way through it," Katya replied. "He's a faster reader than me, but we didn't get very far."

"Should we gather the other dragons?" I asked. Ylon cleared his throat, and I added, "And dinosaurs."

"Not yet," Kon answered. Magic still played around his fingertips, lending them an incandescence as he turned pages.

I was half expecting the dragon god to show up. If the book was the real deal, who else could have plopped it into our hands? But there wasn't any sign of him. I rebuked myself. I was looking for someone to bail us out, when the reality was we had to save ourselves. I'd done the "hunting for a savior" thing a time or two as a young surgeon when I'd gotten in over my head.

Most surgeons are men. They'd rather die than admit they might have bitten off more than they could chew. I suffer from the same malady, but I didn't have it as bad as they did. Even though I knew I'd catch crap for it, I asked for assistance in time. Before the combination of my ineptitude and hubris killed the unconscious human lying on my table.

My mind was wandering. Badly. I moved close enough to Konstantin to read over his shoulder. He must have been absorbing material magically because I'd only work my way through a sentence or two before he moved to the next page. Not that the book was arranged in sentences in any alphabet I'd ever seen before. These were runes, but I understood them well enough.

Time passed. I have no idea how much. The book had its own draw. After a time, I couldn't have looked away if I wanted to. If it held danger, my bondmate would have pulled me back, or maybe she was as mesmerized as I was.

The swirl of turning pages stopped long enough for me to finish an entire page. This one dealt with fire and dragons' use of it.

"It's definitely the same book," Konstantin said. "Though how it got here is anyone's guess."

"Y Ddraigh Goch?" Johan asked. His question mirrored my earlier hypothesis.

"No. He would have showed up with it, told us which parts he wanted us to pay attention to, and left us with a list of instructions."

"If not him, then who?" Johan persisted.

"I have no idea. It doesn't have any serpent taint at all, so—"

"Give me some credit." Katya blew out an exasperated breath. "Do you think I'd have let Johan touch it unless I was certain it wasn't a velvet-coated snare?"

"Lower your hackles, Sister." Konstantin placed the book on the floor next to him. It continued to glow, and it drew my attention whether I wished it or not.

"What magic is it imbued with?" I caught Kon's eye.

"The dragon god's and the First Dragon's. Because he was first, Y Ddraigh Goch wasn't certain exactly how to construct his ability."

"If he was anything like the First Dinosaur, he was strong as sin," Ylon said.

"Exactly," Konstantin concurred.

"What is it about the book that feels like the Pied Piper of Hamelin is playing his flute?" I asked.

"Huh?" Konstantin stared at me.

"What she means," Johan said, "is the book is shedding power, almost as if it is calling her. And me. When I am near the book, it is difficult to think of anything else."

"It was written in the First Dragon's blood," Konstantin murmured. "Sometimes I can still catch a whiff, but it's faint. He was unbelievably powerful. The attraction you feel comes from remnants of his magic."

"What happened to him?" I asked.

"He was too strong for his own good. Y Ddraigh Goch sequestered him on a borderworld somewhere," Katya replied. "And then killed him."

"Seems kind of like a one-trick pony," I mumbled. "Anything goes wrong, he sends the problem to a borderworld. Good thing there are lots of them."

"What do humans do to deal with problems?" Kon glanced my way.

"We have an entire legal system. Judges. Juries. Prisons. Parole. Probation."

"How does that work?" Kon was still looking at me.

I shrugged. "Hit and miss."

"I always favored sending those who misbehave to an intergalactic prison colony and letting them duke it out for who was going to run things." Johan chuckled. "Of course, such things only exist in fiction."

A rush of intense magic, complete with the sunbaked clay and herb scents of dragon shifter power rolled through the room. Pages crackled as they turned of their own accord. Konstantin straightened and watched the book, still ensconced in his lap, until it quieted.

My eyes had widened at the spectacle. Magical books that pointed out precisely which part was meant for you were hard to accept. I could see where they'd save a whole lot of time. If this book was anything like the other magical tomes and scrolls in the library, it wasn't indexed.

I'd asked Kon how the hell you found anything. His response had been that the books ensured you had access to the knowledge you required. At the time, his answer had seemed so absurd, I'd discounted it. I could have used books like that in med school. Ones where I didn't waste precious time hunting stuff down.

Konstantin held up a hand. "I have a feeling this is important. Perhaps why the book ended up in our possession in the first place."

"Read the passage out loud," Katya told him.

He cast a beleaguered look her way. "I'll summarize it once I'm done." Magic pulsed from the crumbling pages, casting his face in an ever-changing wash of blues and greens.

"Maybe I'll read over your shoulder," Katya said.

"Not a good idea." Kon bent his head over the book. His forehead was creased in thought, and one hand hovered over the page in front of him.

Katya started toward her twin, but the colors changed to red and the power spilling from the tome developed a threatening note.

I have no idea how I knew enough to interpret any of the book's antics. I could be way off base, except the magic spoke to me at a bone-deep level, one that bypassed filtering mechanisms in my brain.

Katya stopped in her tracks. "I don't get it. The book didn't protest when I was looking through it."

Johan wrapped a protective arm around her shoulders. "Perhaps the tome tolerated us because we were the only game in town, eh?"

"It's possible," Katya mumbled.

"But how could an inanimate object know who's touching it?" I asked.

"That one does," Ylon replied. "Look. The colors have shaded back to blues and greens."

Something with long, sharp claws crawled down my spine. I didn't trust what I couldn't understand. If the book was powerful enough to identify who touched it, what else was it capable of?

"I'm not sure we want to find out," my bondmate said

quietly. Clearly, she'd been observing from her vantage point within me.

"What do you mean?" I tried for private telepathy. No one gave me the stink-eye, so perhaps I succeeded.

"Any item created by our god and the First Dragon"—she named her ancestor with reverence—*"holds enough magic to blow up worlds. Or save them."*

A numinous shrouding had formed around Kon as he read. Protectiveness surged. I couldn't let anything hurt him. What if that shiny tent-thing spirited him away, and I never saw him again?

I edged nearer, watching the lightshow very carefully. At the first hint of any alteration in it, I'd stop and wait for it to settle down. I'd moved about a foot when the misty veil turned to glowing streamers that dissipated.

Konstantin shut the book and set it aside before getting to his feet. I tried to read the expression on his face, but it contained so many elements—wonder, worry, delight, despair—I gave it up for a lost cause.

"Well?" Katya had even less patience than I did.

"I'm gathering my thoughts," her twin replied. "Right now, they're shooting in so many directions, I don't quite know where to begin."

"Take a stab at it, anyway," she urged.

I wanted to go to him and gather him close, but he didn't require comfort.

Breath tinged with smoke rattled through Konstantin's teeth. "Don't ask me how because I do not know, but the book has a full account of Y Ddraigh Goch banishing the serpents. And of their eventual escape from exile. If the book is correct, and I see no reason to doubt it, the sea-serpents only settled two places: Earth and the Fleisher borderworlds."

"That's a relief," Katya sputtered. "Someone needs to tell Y Ddraigh Goch."

"What makes you think he does not already know?" Johan asked.

"Let me finish, and then we shall talk about what this might mean," Konstantin said.

Katya nodded. "Sorry. I'll shut up."

Kon drew his index finger downward and then in a crosswise motion. Spreading two fingers, he continued a downward trajectory another foot or so. "The runes split into two distinct timelines," Konstantin went on. "In one, we battle the serpents for months. Earth sometimes assists but mostly sabotages our efforts. In the end, we leave Earth to the serpents with disastrous results. I didn't read all the way to the endgame because I had a clear enough picture, but, once we depart, the sea-serpents will be well positioned to make a grab for enough magic to cripple the rest of us."

"If that's true, why did we leave?" I blurted, followed by, "Sorry. You said not to ask questions."

"We left because we were losing." Kon turned grim eyes my way.

"What is the other path?" Ylon asked. "Before you answer that, though, where do you suppose the last batch of hybrids came from? Those bee things. We wiped out the breeding farms."

"I was wondering the same thing," Johan said.

Konstantin's nostrils flared, and ashy smoke streamed

from his mouth. “I must have missed a location when I was destroying the warren of nests sprinkled through the Fleisher worlds. I was in a hurry.”

“Unless an army of hybrids materializes,” Katya said, “I’m not too worried about them. They die easily.”

“They must require an infusion of magic,” Johan broke in. “If we keep the serpents busy enough, I would think the hybrids would wither.”

“Moving on”—Konstantin glanced at Ylon—“I am not at all certain we have enough magic to manage the second option, particularly given we were losing against the serpents. The book suggested the gods would have to help.”

“Which ones?” Ylon raised his shaggy brows in question marks.

“That was the interesting part. All of them. Including the Celts.”

Katya whistled, long and low.

“That unusual, eh?” Johan murmured.

“Very,” she told him. “Go on,” she urged her twin. “What exactly is this second option?”

“We cast the mother of all spells,” he said. “One that will swath Earth in magic-imbued ice so thick it will immobilize the serpents. They will be trapped where they swim, unable to move or to cast spells to free themselves.”

“But that will kill off a whole lot of humans,” I muttered.

“Can’t be helped,” Ylon told me. “Besides, it’s better than all of them being eaten by serpents. Where would we be during this mini Ice Age?”

“Dragon shifters could wait it out here, beneath

Antarctica," Konstantin told him. "You and your dinosaurs would be welcome to join us."

"For how long?"

"That's just it," Kon answered. "It might be as much as five annums, but probably not quite so long as that. While the serpents are frozen in ice and time, the gods will finish what Y Ddraigh Goch should have done eons ago. Once they are done and the serpents are dead, the ice will gradually melt."

"We did a fair job clearing serpents out of the Fleisher borderworlds." Ylon spoke slowly. "Food will be a problem here. It might be better for us to return home."

"I'm grateful for as much or as little assistance as you are willing to offer," Konstantin said.

"What would happen to the sea life?" Johan asked.

"Assuming the land cooperates, she would hold them in a state of suspended animation, and they would rejuvenate once the ice retreated," Konstantin said. "Another option would be to freeze localized sections of ocean—the places serpents have congregated, but it's risky. What if we miss one or two?"

"If even a few gods are involved, that shouldn't be an issue," Katya said. "They have ways of locating evil." She exhaled slowly. "I like that version better because we could move other ocean-dwellers to safety and not have to rely on the land to keep them alive."

"It would be easier on the humans too," I mumbled. I shouldn't still care as much as I did, but I couldn't argue my way out of it.

Konstantin rolled his shoulders back. "Ylon is correct

about food being a problem. The lakes down here hold fish, but not enough to feed all the dragon shifters for years."

"I've seen places where you used to grow crops," I said.

"Used to being the operative term," Katya cut in. "What we brought from Mu failed."

"Immediately?" Johan looked at his mate.

"No. It took a few years." A slow smile illuminated her face. "A few years is all we need. We could find seeds and try again."

"The Polish base supports an extensive greenhouse system," Johan said. "It has the relative advantage of being close, and we could transport their growing beds." He stopped. "Um, can you use magic to move inanimate objects?"

"Of course," Katya told him.

"We're getting ahead of things," Konstantin said. "First off, there are many unknowns. Absent assistance from the gods, none of this will happen."

"We can't worry about that," his twin said. "Not until it's apparent it's not going to materialize."

"What are our next steps?" I asked. After all my shillyshallying around about mating Konstantin, I longed for some time alone. We had other tasks facing us, though.

"Locating Y Ddraigh Goch should be first," Kon replied. "He's our god, so it makes sense to begin there. If we run the primal ice plan by him, and he laughs in our faces, we'll know it will never work."

"I would like to talk with my dinosaurs," Ylon said.

"Please let them know everything," Konstantin told him. "The other shifters too, if any of them have returned."

"They may not." Ylon bit off the words. "You and I covered that ground."

"Yes. I know, but I gave them permission to leave." Kon nodded brusquely. "I have a feeling if some of their gods join the party—Anubis. Thoth. Various Celts—they'll change their minds quick enough. All who wish to lend magic to this cause will be welcome. It's an enormous undertaking."

I couldn't even begin to wrap my head around what it would take to bring on the next ice age, particularly in the midst of a climate that had been swinging the other way for at least the last century.

But what did I know?

"We'll be back in a bit." Katya leaned into Johan.

"Where are you going?" Kon asked.

"To Arctowski. Johan's idea about, erm, borrowing their planter beds was most excellent. May as well get to them before they die from lack of attention."

"Bring back seeds as well," Konstantin said.

"We will," Johan replied and looked at me. "Want to come along?"

"Do you need a third person?" I didn't particularly want to plop into the middle of a spate of the dead and dying. Not when I couldn't do anything to ease their misery shy of killing them outright.

"Not really," Katya said.

I tried not to look too relieved. If I've learned anything through the years of my life, it's to carry my own weight.

The air around Ylon developed a liquid aspect just before he vanished. Katya and Johan left next. Konstantin walked to me and wrapped me in his arms. "I'm selfishly glad Katya didn't take you with her."

I tried to wriggle out of his embrace. "You need to spend more time with that book."

"Yes. I do. But there's not much point until I can confer with Y Ddraigh Goch. I've done what I can to reach him. Meanwhile"—his eyes glittered with tenderness and heat —"we have other priorities."

I tried to resist—surely, with everything that faced us, making love was frivolous—but I didn't try very hard. Being smushed up against him turned my brains to pablum and the rest of me to a flood of lust. When his mouth crashed down on mine, I kissed him back and dug my nails into his shoulders, hanging on for dear life.

No more stopping shy of "the deed." No more making adjustments because fucking would cement our commitment. Between our bodies, Arianrhod's pendant warmed and pulsed approvingly as if she were blessing our union.

The last of my resolve to focus all our energy on defeating the sea-serpents shattered. Reaching between us, I wrapped my fingers around his cock. My world narrowed to the man I'd fallen in love with.

KONSTANTIN

The scents that were uniquely Erin when she was aroused floated around Konstantin. Cinnamon, vanilla, and musk. Damn! He could live on those smells. He'd planned to return to the book, but his beast had been giving him nine kinds of hell to complete the mating bond. The dragon had launched argument after argument, many of them impossible to dispute.

He was here. Erin was here. Who knew when they'd have another opportunity?

Erin would be far stronger mated to him than she was in her current limbo state.

The being stronger reason was what had finally swayed him. As his mate, not just his betrothed, Erin would be able to tap into his magic. And she'd be much stronger. If she were kidnapped, he'd be able to find her with a thought. No complicated spells to cast. The dragon had other suggestions as well.

Some were a bit on the self-serving side, but just as irrefutable as everything else rolling out of the beast's mouth.

Nestled in his arms, Erin molded her body to his. The globes of her breasts were flattened against his chest, highlighting her pebbled nipples. Her hips wriggled as she pushed as close as she could get. His tongue was sunk into her mouth, and she teased it with teeth and lips. Dropping his hands lower, he gripped her high, tight ass.

No woman had any right to such a fine ass. Watching her walk gave him an erection every single time. He withdrew his tongue and swiped it along her cheek to the sensitive spot beneath her ear, and thence down to the hollow between her neck and shoulder.

She made a sound that reminded him of a hungry dragon on the prowl, low and throaty. Steam surrounded them, courtesy of both their beasts.

His cock was distended. His balls ached. It took all his willpower not to turn her around and plumb her from behind. The thought of her ass snugged against his thighs was enticing as hell.

But his dragon wasn't having it. Not yet, anyway.

He lifted his mouth from her sweet flesh. "Shift, darling." His throat was so constricted with lust he could barely get the words out.

She focused her beautiful eyes, whirling since her dragon was near the surface, on him. "But I thought—"

"And we will. In both our forms."

Momentary confusion clouded her features. "Where? There isn't room to fly."

"Outside, there is."

"The other dragons will see us."

He nodded. "They will, and they'll rejoice. I am their prince, and I am unmated. They will approve of our union and interpret it as a good omen."

Erin grinned. "I've never been into public sex, but my dragon is enthusiastic as hell. Look." She levered the hand that she'd had curled around his cock out from between them and showed him talons where fingers should have been. "Hussy dragon. She wanted to cop a feel too."

"Hussy dragon, indeed." He chuckled softly.

Erin dragged her tongue over lips swollen from their kiss. "It's good when she and I want the same thing. Saves a lot of haranguing."

Kon let go of her and very reluctantly stepped back a pace. "Come on. Hurry. I want to get outside before my beast breaks through and I have to teleport because I won't fit through the door."

"Bet you can't beat me!" Erin sprinted around him and took off across the great room for the stairs.

He ran after her, surprised he didn't actually catch up until she'd dragged the stone entry doors open. Her red beast formed faster than he'd imagined possible for such a young dragon shifter. He opened his mouth and half bugled, half roared his approval.

She bugled back as his beast broke through. He'd just spread his wings when she took to the skies. His dragon wrested control of their shared form and leapt skyward. Steam billowed from him.

Erin ducked and swooped, leading him a merry chase.

Steam puffed from her mouth too. Dragon sex was simple. What their beasts were doing was a mating dance. It stoked the lust sheeting from them both. Other dragons had heard their bugling and were pouring into the clearing around the first lake.

No modesty in dragondom. He'd understood full well that his mating dance would be cause for celebration. He'd been watching Erin's flight pattern, and it had grown predictable. She wanted him to catch her.

Her next swoop past him, he twisted midair and settled across her back. Gripping her shoulders with his forelegs, he jammed his cock into her in one quick, hard movement. He'd never had sex with another dragon. If he had, she'd be his mate and not Erin. His only comparison was sex with a human, and so he wasn't prepared for the extraordinary heat that encircled his beast's cock. Like nothing he'd ever experienced before, it was so intense he nearly came on the spot.

He hadn't known he could be this hot. This high. And not come all over everything. His entire scaled body vibrated with unslaked lust. Tilting his head, he bit her shoulder. The mating bite. It more than anything told him the ritual was nearly complete.

Erin's body tightened, surrounding him with prickles of love and lust. He let go of her shoulder. Protectiveness raced through him, so ferocious that fire streamed from his mouth, joining the clouds of steam.

More compelling than anything he'd encountered watching over his hoard, possessiveness bolted to the forefront of his mind. Erin was his. HIS. For now and forever more. His dragon was ecstatic. Apparently unconcerned with anything beyond driving them to unparalleled sexual heights, his bondmate plunged his cock into Erin's willing beast.

She mewled and roared and bugled. He felt it when her vault shuddered around him. Unlike a human climax, it just kept on rolling. "Now!" his bondmate shrieked. "Yes. Now!"

A tsunami of an orgasm blasted through him. Hot. Intense. Lasting forever. Semen pumped in white-hot jets of delight. They settled to earth with his cock still buried in her and still coming.

Around them, cheers and whistles and bugles and cries wishing them good fortune rang out, but the dragons who'd witnessed their mating had the wisdom to leave quickly. When his appendage finally deflated enough for him to detach from Erin's body, they were alone next to the lake.

He wanted to hold her, stroke her hair, tell her how much he loved her. She understood without words, and the air around her grew liquid with shift magic as she sought her human body. They stood, still breathing hard. He drank in her tumbled blonde mane. Her hard nipples. Splotches of color marking her breasts and face.

A small wound on her shoulder—the spot he'd bitten her while they were mating—changed into the likeness of a red-and black dragon. He held out his arms, and she fell into them.

"That was so amazing, I don't have words for it," she murmured against his shoulder.

"We don't require words," he told her and submerged a hand in the silk of her hair. Scooping her into his arms, he carried her back to his home—their home now—down steps, and into one of the sleeping rooms.

His cock was still hard, jutting from his body, as he set her down on a pallet and settled next to her, gathering her close. "Are you all right?"

"More than all right. My dragon is purring."

"Let's make your human half purr too."

"Yes, let's." She rolled them so she was on top. Sitting, she straddled him and took him back inside her body. She moved slowly, letting herself stretch to accommodate his girth. Arching her back, she cupped both breasts and rubbed her nipples to even stiffer peaks.

Watching her touch herself was an incredible aphrodisiac. Not that he needed anything extra. The vista of her body sitting over him, hair falling to waist level, was alluring. Her form was perfect with its combination of muscles stretching over bones, flared hips, long legs, and tempting, curvy breasts.

"You're so lovely," he said.

"I was just thinking the same thing. You're glowing with magic." Leaning forward, she planted her hands on his shoulders and rotated her hips in a sideways movement that also drew her up. The next twist brought her down until he bottomed out inside her. The combination of twist and thrust made him ache for her with a singlemindedness only another dragon could understand.

Today was a day for firsts. The sex he and Erin had had before this paled in comparison.

Maybe because they'd already mated as dragons, lovemaking with her this way was almost as mind-rattling as their earlier coupling had been. He let her set the pace, willing to go wherever she led. He was aware of orgasms ratcheting through her, and just as aware she wasn't done with him.

He cheated and leveraged magic to hold himself on a fine edge. Almost there, but not quite. When she growled, "Come, goddammit," he was more than ready to oblige.

Balls tight against his body, he gripped her hips and upped the tempo, stroking quick and sure. After half a dozen thrusts, he spilled his seed within her. She held his shoulders tight enough to draw blood with her nails. Steam poured from her. Panting and puffing, she cried. "Mine. You are MINE."

He laughed. Whether the proclamation had come from Erin or her dragon didn't matter. He was delighted. "Yes, darling. We belong to each other." He drew her down until she lay on top of him and held her close.

A whispery wisp of magic caught his attention. When he glanced toward it, more curious than alarmed, he wasn't surprised to see the outline of Y Ddraigh Goch's dragon.

"Erin. We have company."

"What the hell? I had no idea dragons were such a bunch of voyeurs." She pulled herself off his half-hard cock and rolled to a sit. "Oops. Sorry. I recognize that dragon. I didn't mean him."

Konstantin laughed again. "He's not exactly here, but he will be very soon."

"I suppose we should thank him for not interrupting us." She finger-combed the mass of tangles cascading around her body but didn't make much progress.

He sat too. "What we did was critical. It was long past time for me to select a mate. Having an unmated liege doesn't bode well for the future of our kind. Our god understands that very well. It was why he allowed us to complete the mating ritual."

"It was my reasoning, indeed." In human form, Y Ddraigh Goch shimmered into being in the doorway. Konstantin hadn't seen him that way often. The dragon god was an imposing man. Tall and broad shouldered, his long hair was golden with thick silver streaks running through it. He had a high, noble forehead and a square jaw peppered with golden stubble. Long, curved red talons tipped his fingers and toes. But his eyes were the most intriguing aspect of him. Much the same as when he was in his dragon body, they held an ever-changing collage recounting the history of dragon shifters since the beginnings of time.

Leather trousers hung low on his hips, and a colorful tunic swathed the upper part of his body. Like everything about the god, his clothes were probably either magical—or illusion.

Konstantin got to his feet and bowed. "You honor me with your presence."

Erin stood next to him and bowed her head as well.

"Congratulations on your mating," the dragon god rumbled in his deep, musical voice. "Leave it to you, Konstantin, to wait until the world hovers on the brink of destruction to finally do what you should have done years ago."

"But then, I would never have found Erin," Konstantin

said. "She is my fated one. The woman I am meant to travel my life's road with."

Y Ddraigh Goch turned his gaze to Erin. "Perhaps you are right, after all," he murmured after staring at her for long moments.

"Forgive me for speaking out of turn," Erin said, "but did you deliver the magical book to us?"

A corner of his mouth twisted downward. "It it's the book I believe it to be, it found its own way here."

Konstantin whistled. "It's that powerful?"

"I would not have said so if it weren't," the god retorted.

"Of course not. No offense meant." Kon murmured.

"You have need of me," Y Ddraigh Goch went on. "I would have been here sooner, but I couldn't resist doing away with a pod of serpents who thought to bar my path."

"They must not have recognized you," Konstantin said, "or they would have teleported out of harm's way."

"Oh, they recognized me well enough, but they're drunk on their own power. I may have wiped a few dragon minds along the way."

"How many of the dragon traitors dare to lurk near my lair?" Konstantin growled.

"Fewer than before."

It wasn't an answer, but it was all he was going to get. Questioning Y Ddraigh Goch generally didn't yield much.

"What happens to a dragon after you've cleared out their memories?" Erin asked.

The dragon god smiled with zero warmth and a whole lot of teeth. Double rows of ivory were part of his human presentation as well as his dragon one. "They start over.

Dragon and human get to know one another again. Unless I break the bond. Then the dragon is banished, and the human's life may be forfeit as well. Depends on the level of their transgressions."

Konstantin cleared his throat. All the steam and ash and fire had left a few raw spots. "For the ones who begin anew, will they possess our standard knowledge base? The one where they view serpents as enemies?"

"Of course. Otherwise, why bother to do anything?"

"Again, forgive me if this is a stupid question," Erin said, "but why would dragons join with sea-serpents? What's the allure? They feel scuzzy to me. Like I dipped my brain in slime."

Y Ddraigh Goch blew out a breath, and a tongue of fire danced across the room. "Not all my children believe in me any longer. Many were angry at the way I handled Mu's ending—and other things as well. They've been plotting ever since. An alliance with sea-serpents offered them the perfect mechanism to challenge my sovereignty."

Konstantin debated whether he should mention the debacle with the serpents that had preceded their exile. In his opinion, that was when some dragons had begun to doubt their god. He shuttered his thoughts. The serpents' downfall was bound up with Y Ddraigh Goch's children being tortured. Not a pleasant topic, nor one he wished to thrust into the limelight.

"Beyond that," the god continued, "blended magics have more power. Dragons would benefit far more from an alliance with serpents in that respect. The serpents' power has continued to fade. It is why they lost their immortality in their human bodies."

Konstantin angled his head to one side. "It sounds as if you planned things that way."

"I did. If I'd created that level of chaos when I sent them away, they'd have panicked. Fought against my edict. As it was, I smoothed things over. Planted seeds they'd be independent one day, and then I dropped them in a few locations where they'd have to work very hard to create problems."

"Did you know they'd escape?" Erin asked.

"No. If I had, I'd have done a better job defanging them before I sent them away from Mu. Enough questions." The air shimmered around him. When it cleared, the book from downstairs sat on the floor at his feet. The god crouched in front of it and ran his taloned fingers reverently over its cracked binding.

"I never thought I would see this again." Fire billowed from his mouth and surrounded the book. The ancient tome took on an eerie red-gold glow. Runes on its cover came into view.

Erin lurched forward, but Konstantin caught her arm. *"It will be all right,"* he reassured her. Y Ddraigh Goch had loved the First Dragon in the same way all parents dote on their firstborns. Konstantin hadn't been alive when the dragon god was forced to destroy his creation, but he'd heard enough to understand the decision had torn the god in two.

By then, there'd been other dragon shifters. The First Dragon was jealous, so resentful he undermined their magic. After he nearly killed one of his brothers, Y Ddraigh Goch was forced to choose.

His firstborn. Or all the others who would come later.

The book was all that was left of the First Dragon's magic. Y Ddraigh Goch would smite anyone who harmed it. Fire continued to paint the book's cover. As it cleared, the tome lost its dogeared appearance and looked fresh and new. As if it had just been created.

"Better," the god murmured. He rocked back on his heels. "I would give much to know where this book has been. I looked for it before Mu exploded and couldn't find it."

"Someone must have taken it," Erin said and slipped a hand into Konstantin's.

Y Ddraigh Goch shook his head. "Not necessarily. Articles imbued with strong magic have ways of protecting themselves. It is possible the book moved itself to safety, a spot it remained until it felt its knowledge was needed."

"Someone must have been keeping it up," Konstantin said. "I read about the serpents' exile and our current war with them."

The god cocked his head to one side. The collage of images moved faster across his multicolored eyes. "The book writes itself. This"—he tapped the cover, now a shiny brown leather—"tome was special in that way. It knows the future. And the past. And it alters what is written within it as events unfold."

Breath steamed through Erin's teeth. "Seems impossible. Not that I'm doubting you."

"It would appear inconceivable for someone raised as a mortal." The god flipped the book's cover open and waited while the pages riffled knowingly. Once they quieted, he focused on the runes. The book was scribed in dragonspeak, but it had been a long while since Konstantin had seen their language in that form. Over the years, it had become mostly a spoken tongue rather than a written one.

Y Ddraigh Goch raised his gold-and-silver eyebrows and flipped through a few pages, absorbing rather than reading rune by rune. He looked at Konstantin. "Did you read this, son?"

"If it's the part about either losing the war to the serpents or teaming up with a cadre of gods to create an ice age that will finally finish the serpents off, then yes, I did read it."

Konstantin waited. Was this when the god rolled his eyes or shook his head or burst out laughing? Deities never worked with anyone beyond their own pantheons. To expect it would happen now was akin to wishing on stardust or bringing unicorns back from the borderworld they'd retreated to to escape humans murdering them for their horns.

Y Ddraigh Goch didn't do any of those things. He remained crouched on the floor looking thoughtful. Finally, he asked, "What are your thoughts?"

The question was so unlike the god, it caught Konstantin by surprise. "I am in favor of the primal ice solution, but a modified version where we freeze the seas where the serpents are. Earth has many oceans. Surely, serpents haven't poisoned them all."

"That option is much more difficult," Y Ddraigh Goch replied. "Why do you prefer it?"

"It spares innocent creatures also living in the sea," Erin said.

"But the land would protect them, hold them in stasis."

"Maybe," Konstantin cut in. "I have had limited success dealing with her. Our last go-round, she tried to kill Erin."

"Pffft." The god did shake his head then. "Earth understands you're immortal. Perhaps she was being playful."

"No. She was out for blood," Erin said and shrugged. "Maybe she's jealous and wanted Kon all to herself. I don't know."

"You must try harder to establish détente with her," Y Ddraigh Goch warned sternly. "She will be a key element in our plans."

"I understand," Konstantin replied. "And I will."

The god flowed to his feet. "Our first task is for me to see if the other gods will even talk with me." He paused long enough to take a measured breath. "I believe I shall invite them here. It's a logical location. Dragon shifters are here, as are dinosaurs and other shifter varieties. The Sidhe were here recently if my nose doesn't deceive me."

"They were," Konstantin concurred. "I believe it was Oberon's intent to meet with the Celtic gods to see if there was some way to move the seat of their power, the *Dreaming*, to a borderworld."

"Something they should have done long ago," Y Ddraigh Goch muttered, adding, "At least the Celts won't be surprised when I approach them. They already know trouble is brewing."

"Wouldn't they have realized that long before Oberon's visit?" Erin asked.

"Young woman," the god addressed her, "if I'd known how many questions you were going to ask, I'd have left you human."

"Sorry," she mumbled.

"I will answer that one, though," he went on. "The Celts are amazingly insular. More so even than dragonkind. And they are masters at ignoring what doesn't directly concern them. If the question is have they noticed Earth going downhill? The answer is probably yes, but if the question is do they care? Then the answer is a definite no."

"Can you make them care?" Konstantin asked.

"I do not know. Lead me to your workspace here. I must ensure it's an acceptable spot for our guests. Assuming any show up."

With Erin's hand still clasped in his, Kon led the way downstairs to the great room. He'd never looked at it with a critical eye before. It fit his dragon needs perfectly. He had no idea whether a Celtic god could bide here and not deem the location beneath his dignity.

Y Ddraigh Goch turned in a circle regarding the high-ceilinged chamber with its visible veins of precious minerals in the walls. "This will do fine. While the two of you get some refreshments together, I'll issue a call to others like me."

"One last thing," Konstantin said.

The god angled an annoyed glance his way. "What?"

"You requested food. For that, we must teleport to the

surface. Did you take care of the serpents who were directly above?"

"I already said I did. Nothing would have changed between now and then. Unless Surek is beating the marsh grass hunting for me, but even he isn't quite that thickheaded." He made shooing motions. "You have your assignment. Get moving."

Konstantin sensed Erin's irritation at being treated like a servant. He hustled her out of the room before she said something ill-advised. They stopped in the kitchen long enough for him to take stock of what provisions remained.

"How can you tolerate being treated like a—?" Erin began.

Konstantin shook his head. "He only looks like a man. Y Ddraigh Goch is our deity. What it means is we respect him and do his bidding. Can you cook?"

Erin snorted. "You're joking, right? I used to live on takeout and hospital food. They feed doctors for free."

"We'll figure something out. Katya's pretty decent in the kitchen. I get by. Maybe she'll teach us whatever magic she employs. Let's get moving."

"Where are we going?"

"To tell Ylon and any other shifters we find what's in the works. After that, we're going hunting."

Erin smiled. "My dragon likes hunting."

"Of course, she does. And if we only serve platters of roasted meat, the other gods will chalk us up as a bunch of savages, but they'll eat whatever is in front of them."

"No vegans in the group?" She arched a blonde brow.

"What's that?" Konstantin asked.

"Kind of like vegetarians raised to the nth degree. I was joking. Let's get this show on the road."

He crossed the room to where she stood and closed his arms around her. "I love you. Thank you for honoring me by becoming my mate."

Erin hugged him back. "My, so formal. Like I said, wait a year or two. If you're still thanking me then, we'll have an excellent chance of not killing one another."

"I'm not worried." He chuckled and let her go. "You feel too good in my arms. If we don't get moving—"

"We may not leave?" Grinning, she swiped her mouth over his, turned, and ran lightly out the door.

KATYA

"There," Katya called to Johan. "That's the last of them. I had no idea there'd be so many." She surveyed rows upon rows of planting beds they'd moved to the C level of their complex because it still had a functioning drip system for its fields.

"Good thing we went when we did," Johan said.

"That was because of your quick thinking." She sent a fond smile winging his way.

"Polar climates are hard on everything that lives in them," he replied. "I assumed with everyone at Arctowski either dead or dying from hemorrhagic fever, no one would be paying any attention to the crops."

"Why would they?" She shrugged pragmatically. "Dead men don't eat."

"I am grateful we did not bring Erin. All those bodies would have made her sad."

"I sensed a few still alive, but you're right. She would have wanted to see if she could help the survivors, and it wasn't why we were there."

Johan twisted spigots and rearranged tubing. "'Where did you get all this stuff? Definitely human manufacture."

She rolled her eyes. "We may have borrowed an item or two. In the dead of night. From shops in Buenos Aires. We started in Ushuaia but couldn't find what we needed."

"What I meant was where did you get the idea to set up this watering system in the first place?"

Katya walked to where he was working and spread out a few of the hard-sided clear tubes. "What? Do you think humans are the only ones who've ever grown crops? Of course, we could achieve the same thing with magic, but why squander power when we can set up a mechanical system that accomplishes the same thing?"

He angled his head and blew her a kiss. "Makes sense. We ran through a lot of magic moving all of these."

"And it will take time to fully recover. At least we bypassed the headland—and the serpents."

"Wonder how that is going," he murmured. "The fires should be out. Do you suppose Bennet is still skulking about?"

Katya straightened. Something about Johan's question caught her attention. "Did he bother you? I mean, he's a total jackass, but are you worried about him?"

Johan hesitated, perhaps collecting his thoughts. "The part that irritated me was his assumption he could snap you up whenever he wanted."

"Pffft. Yeah, well, let him try. My dragon would take his on for almost any reason. She always was a stronger warrior."

He dusted dirt off his hands and turned to face her. "So much of this is new. I understand—sort of—how being in love feels. What I had not counted on is this...ferocity. A need to possess all of you, body, mind, and soul."

"It's the dragon way—and the magic of the mate bond. I feel the same about you. We belong to each other. Had Bennet been female and made a play for you, I'd probably have scratched her eyes out."

He smiled, and it made him so knockout gorgeous, she wanted to take him right there. They still hadn't managed a mating flight, something her beast reminded her of regularly.

"Oops. Damn it!"

"What?" she asked, still contemplating racy sex in the middle of the planter beds.

"The seeds. We had them tucked into the beds, but they are not here."

Katya scanned the field that sat next to the third lake. No seeds. They'd ferried the raised beds with magic. Seed bags would be easier. "Once more," she said and held out both hands.

He clasped them and chanted with her. They'd recited this incantation so many times, they no longer stumbled over any of the sections. Their first attempts had been from the Arctowski end. A quick trip back beneath the Antarctic ice sheet had shown them it wasn't the most efficient use of power.

Despite employing directional vectors, only one of the first three raised beds had made it to where they wanted. They'd had to hunt down the other two. After that, they'd returned to the Polish base and earmarked the remainder of the beds with magical vectors. They'd done the same with about twenty bags of seeds, and then they'd placed the seed bags in various planter beds.

The beds had responded to their magic, but not the seed bags. One by one, they plopped down around them. This time, their drawing spell worked. Perhaps they'd asked too much of it before.

"Is this all of them?" Johan asked.

"I think so. Let's get them inside to protect them from moisture." Short of breath from using so much power, she picked up four of the sacks and headed for the C Level dwelling.

"I will get a few too." Johan sounded as trashed as she felt. It took a ridiculous amount of magic to move inanimate objects. Much easier to move yourself. He followed her inside. "It smells like you in here."

"Is that a complaint?"

"Not at all. I love your scent. I was wondering why."

She led the way two levels down to the kitchen. All the dwellings had been constructed similarly on purpose. No reason to do otherwise. After clearing dust out of a cupboard, she plopped the seed bags on a shelf. Johan did the same.

"I sometimes use this lodging for my seer magic, and I was here rather recently."

"I would like to know more about how that type of enchantment works, but we should retrieve the remainder of the seeds."

Katya tested her magic and decided walking back and forth a couple of times was a better bet than running the last of her power down to bedrock teleporting the bags. Two more trips did the trick.

"Have a seat." Katya patted one of the chairs that lined both sides of a long, wooden table.

"I should make certain all the water lines are functioning."

"We can do that later. We deserve a break."

Johan had asked about her seer ability. It seemed like ages had passed since she'd consulted her glass, and Konstantin had broken the mirror to stop her vision. The memory of that episode chilled her and was a harsh reminder not to involve Johan in any of her scrying attempts. It had taken her twin many tries to shatter the glass and sever her connection to sorcerous magic.

"We did good work today," she said to open a fresh topic.

"Maybe, but I could sleep for a few hours. There must be a way to strengthen my magic."

"Being mated to me will help. Beyond that, use and time." She closed a hand over his and squeezed gently.

"Are you back yet?" Kon's voice rattled through her head.

"Oh-oh." Johan screwed his mouth into a frown. "I know that tone from your brother. He wants something."

"He does, indeed," Katya agreed.

"We're on C level," she replied. *"Getting the planters set up."*

"Is anything edible available right now?"

It was an odd question, coming from a dragon who could hunt to feed himself. *"Sure. Why?"*

"We're about to have, erm, company. We need to prepare food for them."

Johan was clearly following the conversation because he spun his hands in circles. She wanted more information too, but they could figure out what was going on when they got to where Konstantin was.

"How many guests?" she asked. If they were going to bring something to prepare, it would help if she knew if she was cooking for ten or fifty.

"Not sure. You might plan for twenty or so."

"Got it. See you soon."

Johan was already on his feet. "Do you suppose the Sidhe are returning?"

She shrugged. "Anybody's guess, but they're the most likely. Who else would we host?"

"Do we have baskets or bags? Something we can carry things in?"

Katya scooped some cloth sacks from a lower shelf, and they returned to the neat rows of planter beds. Spinach, kale, onions, zucchini, and cucumbers looked promising. She sprinkled magic on every cut to encourage the plant to grow another leaf or vegetable to take the place of the ones they culled.

"I would prefer to walk back," Johan said, "unless it is much farther than I think."

"Walking works for me," she said.

Half an hour later, the lake nearest their home came into

view. They'd chatted of this and that, but both of them were tired. From long habit, she scented the air except this time she hoped for a clue who their guests might be. Her eyes widened. "Y Ddraigh Goch is here."

"Good. We need him."

Katya sniffed some more and grinned.

"What? I wish I had your nose."

"They did it!" Katya squealed and walked faster, intent on congratulating her twin and Erin.

"Who did what?" Johan hustled after her.

She turned toward him. "Kon and Erin. They're mated. From the way things smell, they managed to have sex in both forms."

Steam puffed from her mouth, joining clouds from Johan. Their dragons clearly adored the idea. Talons popped through where she clutched the bags of produce.

"No!" She kept her voice stern.

"Why not?" her beast bugled.

"There you are!" Konstantin ran toward them.

Katya didn't bother negotiating with her bondmate. Konstantin's presence was all the answer necessary.

"Here we are," she agreed. "I'd hug you, but my hands are full. Congratulations to you and Erin!"

"Thank you." His stern expression was replaced by a warm smile.

"Where's your brand-new mate?" Katya asked.

"In the kitchen looking like she wants to kill me. We brought back fish to prepare, and I found a goat at one of the research stations."

"You stole a goat?" Johan asked, followed by, "Congratulations. I am happy for you both."

"It isn't as if they were using the goat for anything other than study purposes," Konstantin said. "We needed it worse than they did."

"What do we need it for?" Katya asked. Her bondmate was still raising hell. Everyone had had sex except her, and she was feeling left out of the fun.

"Y Ddraigh Goch is here—" Kon began.

"I already figured that part out," Katya cut in. "What does him being here have to do with us cooking for twenty?"

"He's doing his damnedest to gather a conclave of gods. He read the book, and—"

"What book? The same one we found in the library?" Johan asked.

Konstantin nodded. "As I suspected, it was written by the First Dragon and Y Ddraigh Goch. He is doing what he can to awaken the first part of the book's prophecy. The one requiring various deities to cooperate."

"And we're cooking for gods and goddesses who may not come because—?" Katya asked.

"Y Ddraigh Goch asked us to."

"Sounds positively medieval," Johan said, "but naturally we will help."

A plaintive bleat was followed by a galloping goat with Erin close behind it. "Come back here, you little fucker," she screeched.

A white goat with brown markings ran right to Katya and buried its head in her side, bleating piteously. She dropped the sacks of produce to cradle its head. "Don't worry," she crooned. "No one will hurt you."

Erin skidded to a halt, panting. "I'm no good at all at this. All my meat came from restaurants or the store. Besides, he's cute. I hesitated instead of killing him, and he was smart enough to skedaddle."

Katya knelt next to the goat and held it, infusing soothing magic until it quit trembling.

"Guess it picked the right person as its savior." Konstantin grinned and shook his head. "Come on," he told Johan. "We're going to need to get more fish. No one would ever take pity on them. Besides, we'd just be in the way in the kitchen." Power shimmered around him and Johan before her twin's teleport spell snapped them up.

The goat had shifted from bleating to baaing. It edged to a thick patch of marsh grass and bent its head to graze. Erin grabbed the sacks Johan had left. "I'll move these inside." She glanced at the goat. "It's a relief he's okay. My dragon is laughing her head off, but I didn't really want the goat's death on my conscience."

Katya picked up the rest of the fresh produce and walked back toward the house with Erin. "Congratulations, Sister! Welcome to our family. I'm happy for you."

Erin's eyes sparkled with merriment. "I'm surprisingly happy myself. I've avoided commitments forever, but Kon and I feel right together."

Katya passed through the open door and started down the stairs. "It's because you are right together. My brother has needed someone like you for years."

"What exactly did you mean by that?" Erin asked.

Katya picked her words carefully. There'd been a prickly note in Erin's question. "You're not like us. Not yet. You'll become more dragon shifterish given time, but your human qualities are what drew him. You're bright and incisive and compassionate. You think for yourself and aren't afraid to disagree with him."

She set the vegetables down on the long ledge spanning the length of the kitchen and looked at stacks of fish, some small and some weighing as much as two stone.

"Thank you," Erin said. "You're being kind. I can be bitchy as fuck."

"We all can. Dragon shifters aren't known for their kindheartedness and gentle ways. Did you have any ideas for the fish?"

Erin snorted. "You're kidding, right? I was wondering if I needed to skin and bone them before or after I cooked them. Johan is better at this than me. He at least cooked for himself. I tried to eat at the hospital so I wouldn't have to bother with food at home."

"Let's make a kind of casserole," Katya suggested. "We can add to it as we go."

KATYA HAD A CREDIBLE MIXTURE SIMMERING. Threads of dragonfire wrapped around two large urns created a perfect temperature. If the goat had been female, she'd have used a spot of magic to encourage milk to flow. Milk would have gone well in her fish stew. The men had returned, and all of them sat around the kitchen table drinking a mildly alcoholic beverage she and her twin took turns distilling.

A wave of magic so potent it stole her breath rolled through the room. Followed by several more.

"What the hell?" Erin sputtered. "It's not serpents. I recognize them."

"Well, well. It would appear Y Ddraigh Goch's call to parley was successful," Konstantin said. "Enough time had passed, I figured the other gods were ignoring him. We've never been particularly well placed in the magical pecking order."

"Not where the Celts are concerned," Katya muttered. "They never had much use for us once we made it clear we weren't magical steeds for them to summon at will."

"Shall we join them?" Johan raised a well-formed dark brow.

"We should wait until the dragon god requests our presence," Kon replied.

"But that makes us look like scullery staff," Erin protested. "Good enough to cook for them, but not good enough to include in a discussion about a future that impacts us all."

"I would clap, but it would probably not be appreciated," Johan mumbled.

Katya got to her feet slowly. She was still considering what she wanted to do, but this might be her one chance to lay eyes on anyone from the Celtic pantheon. It was too enticing a prospect to walk away from. "I'm going downstairs," she said. "Y Ddraigh Goch can chase me out of there if he doesn't want me to remain."

"Bad idea, Sister," Konstantin said.

She tipped her chin in his direction. "I know you believe that, but I happen to hold a different opinion." She wound a length of cloth around one of the urn's bails and hefted it. "Probably cooked enough. For all I know, the Celts prefer their repast raw. I'll be the delivery dragon."

Erin stood and grabbed the other urn. "I want to come too. Oomph. Heavier than it looks."

Smoke-tinged ash flew from Konstantin's mouth as he stood. "We will all go."

"I can carry that," Johan told Katya.

She shook her head. "No. Women do this type of work. It would make you appear weak."

"That is stupid, circular reasoning," he said and snatched the pot from her.

Before Katya had a chance to argue back, Erin cleared her throat. "Will we need silverware? Napkins? Bowls?"

"All of the above," Konstantin said. "Katya will bring them." He leveled a pointed look her way. She rustled through a cupboard, coming up with the requisite items.

"Let our mate take care of us," Katya's beast said quietly, employing their private mind speech. *"It speaks well for him and bodes well for us."*

"But I only wished him to make a good impression on the gods," Katya replied in kind.

"I understand. If they pay any attention at all to us, they will view him favorably. He was an excellent choice for us, although I admit to doubts when he had so much trouble shifting."

"Doubts? I was scared out of my mind he'd die."

"Yes, that too, except he did not. And now he is ours."

Konstantin led the way downstairs. As their prince, it was fitting for him to take the front position. Katya was holding her breath. She let it out in a whoosh that filled the stairwell with smoke.

"Sorry," she murmured.

They came out into the great room. Several people stood in proximity to Y Ddraigh Goch. The dragon god turned their way and actually smiled. Katya had rarely seen him do anything but look stern and foreboding.

"Here are some of my dragons," he boomed. "They have made a lovely repast for us. Go on, children, put everything down over there." He gestured toward a spot at the far end of the room.

Katya bristled at being referred to as a child, but it was common for their god to label them thusly. At least he hadn't ordered them out of the room. Not yet, anyway. Once Erin and Johan had set the urns down and she'd placed the napkins, bowls, and forks nearby, she waited.

And took in the men and women—gods and goddesses —trying to determine who was here. A burly man with a tumble of very blond hair and eyes the shade of a summer sky was garbed in a white robe with runic embroidery in red and blue. Leather bags hung from a black sash belted low across his hips. He gripped a fascinating staff that glowed with an inner light. Her bet was this was Gwydion, warrior magician and master enchanter. A short reddish beard followed the line of his jaw.

Next to him stood a man as dark as he was fair. Straight black hair fell to waist level. Intense dark eyes peered out of a sharp-boned, smooth-shaven face. This man wore black robes sashed in white. He was probably Arawn, god of the dead.

Katya was getting into her appraisal. Another tall blond man was less heavily built than Gwydion. He had coppery eyes, an otherworldly look about him, and wore formfitting hunting leathers that left nothing to the imagination. He could be Bran, god of prophecy, war, the sun, music, and other arts. Her heart beat double-time. If she was right, he was the Celts' seer. Maybe she could learn something from him.

A woman who looked like a Valkyrie wearing battle leathers and with her blonde hair in a Celtic warrior pattern might be Andraste. Her sharp green eyes zeroed in on Katya. "I can save ye the trouble, dragon shifter." Pointing, she said, "Meet my kin. Gwydion. Bran. Arawn. Ceridwen. Arianrhod. I am Andraste, goddess of war. Over there are Thoth and Anubis. Other shifter deities are on their way."

"Thank you," Katya murmured. "Forgive me if I was rude to stare, but I grew up steeped in stories of Celtic glory."

"We are humbled in your presence." Konstantin bowed low.

"Stop that!" Gwydion clapped his hands smartly together. "None of us has land-linked magic. Stand tall, dragon prince. I knew Inmar. Ye do his legacy proud."

More deities shimmered into view. Johan moved to her side and took her hand. "It is like the old tales come to life," he whispered.

"Yes." She nodded. "Only better."

Delighted the gods weren't going to chase them away, she settled in to listen to what the outcome of their discussion would be. Just because the others had hearkened to Y Ddraigh Goch's call didn't mean they'd be willing to help. She reminded herself to keep quiet. No one wanted to hear from her.

Konstantin, maybe, but if she mouthed off to anyone, they'd send her packing, and she wanted to remain in this room, bathing in all these mixed magics, as much as she'd ever wanted anything.

JOHAN

I still couldn't believe the men and women I'd read about in mythology existed. Oh, I'd guessed the stories were patterned after true events, but I'd assumed the players were mortal. Within me, my beast was as fascinated as I was, but likely for different reasons. Magical creatures probably didn't waste even a second worrying about whether they were real. They'd have been affronted had anyone suggested otherwise.

Given his reaction, I assumed my bondmate had never met any of the Celts before. For the umpteenth time, I wished I knew more about him. I'd done my best to be respectful of our bond, so I hadn't asked any questions, but I wanted to. Since he could read all my thoughts, he must know how curious I was about him, yet he'd chosen to remain silent about who he'd been and what he'd done before linking his fortunes to mine.

I'd been casting surreptitious glances around the large

room. We hosted quite an august gathering. On the Celtic side, Ceridwen, Andraste, Bran, Arawn, Gwydion, and Arianrhod were present. On the shifter side of the house were our god, Anubis, Thoth, and Bast. Not surprisingly, Oberon and Titania had shown up. More closely bound to Earth than any of the rest of us, they had a stake in the outcome of this war council.

Katya labelled it a discussion, but I disagreed. Before we disbanded, we would know who would fight alongside us. So far, there's been a lot of mudslinging. Ceridwen and Bran are seers. She has her cauldron. God only knows what he uses. Anyway, both of them saw nothing but trouble on the heels of Y Ddraigh Goch's clemency toward the sea-serpents.

The dragon god held onto his temper—for a while. "What is the purpose to this?" he asked at last. "If you had knowledge, you didn't share it with me."

"Surely, ye have your own seers." Ceridwen scanned the room. Her gaze landed on Katya. "Like her, for example."

Next to me, Katya stiffened. Rather than lashing out, she inclined her head. "Thank you for recognizing my poor ability. It is nothing compared to yours." She stopped on the prudent side of saying anything further. Her opinions about the serpents' fortunes wouldn't have mattered once Y Ddraigh Goch made up his mind.

With a shock, I noticed Ceridwen and Y Ddraigh Goch had the same eyes. By that I mean, a string of images marched across them. Sometimes faster, sometimes slower, but I felt certain if I stared long enough, the pictures would tell a story. Were the two related? Not the kind of question I could ask. Ceridwen and her cauldron dated to the beginnings of the world, but perhaps the dragon god did as well.

I dragged my attention back to the conversation, which had finally moved past blaming Y Ddraigh Goch for the present problems. I hadn't caught all of what he'd said, but it had been something like if he had it to do over again, he'd destroy every single serpent and have done with it.

Bast had taken her cat form and was washing her front feet. Titania sat next to her. So far, no one had bothered sampling the fish concoction. I was hungry, but it would be rude to help myself first.

The air around Y Ddraigh Goch brightened until I shielded my eyes with a hand. When the glare quieted, the book that had caused all the havoc was clasped in his hands. "May I read you something?" he asked.

"What lore is that?" Gwydion marched to his side and peered at the tome. It looked a whole lot newer than it had when it first showed up in the library.

Konstantin brought a hand downward and the illusion hiding the library fell away revealing all the overflowing shelves. "The book came to us," he said.

"It was scribed by me," Y Ddraigh Goch added, "and the First Dragon."

"What happened to him again?" Thoth tilted his head in a very avian gesture. Tufts of dark hair stuck out from his head at odd angles, and his amber eyes gleamed with keen intelligence. He looked like an absentminded professor, complete with his angular body stuffed into corduroy pants and a linen shirt.

"He killed him." Ceridwen extended an index finger

toward Y Ddraigh Goch. “Like he should have killed the serpents.”

“Are you quite done?” Y Ddraigh Goch looked pointedly at Ceridwen before adding, “Sister.”

Aha! So they were related. Intriguing. Who had their parents been? But I was interpreting events with my human brain. For all I knew, they’d risen from mold or sunshine or interplanetary dust.

“Perhaps,” she replied.

“We didn’t come to rehash the past,” Gwydion reminded her.

“Back to the book,” the dragon god said. “May I read you a passage? It won’t take long.”

No one objected, and I listened as the dragon god outlined the two paths related to our current situation.

“Mmph,” Gwydion tapped his staff, glowing brighter than ever, on the stone floor. “How do we know there are no other options?”

“There may be,” Y Ddraigh Goch agreed. “It’s why we are all here in the same room. To discuss how to proceed.”

“Before we do,” Oberon spoke up, “know that leaving Earth is not possible for the Sidhe. We are bound here because of the *Dreaming*.”

“That is changing.” Ceridwen nailed him with her eerie eyes.

“Aye, but not fast enough. It might take a hundred annums afore the *Dreaming* rises anew on a borderworld.”

“Not quite that long,” she retorted. “Have a wee bit of faith, Faery King.”

Gwydion made a chopping motion. “As I understand the

prophecy, if we leave this world to the serpents, they will make a grab for enough magic to disrupt the rest of us. How likely are they to succeed?"

"Very," Y Ddraigh Goch said. "Earth holds a wealth of resources. With no one standing in the sea-serpents' path, they will become far more powerful than they are today. It pains me to admit this, but a few dragons have aligned themselves with the serpents. It compounds our problem."

Gwydion raised bushy blond brows. "Dragons? Do ye not have better control of your subjects than that?"

"Apparently not," the dragon god growled.

"A problem for a different day." Andraste blew out an annoyed-sounding breath. "We must select one problem and see it through to its conclusion afore we look at aught else."

"List the ingredients in the ice-spell," Anubis woofed. It surprised me to hear speech roll from his mouth since he'd taken the form of a horse-sized black dog.

Y Ddraigh Goch rattled off a complex casting requiring many elements I could only guess at. At Ceridwen's request, he repeated them twice more. She moved her hands in a complex pattern, and a large iron pot materialized in front of her.

I'd thought I'd moved beyond being surprised by much of anything, but I wasn't expecting the Mother Goddess of the World to summon her cauldron. Magic sheeted from its bubbling contents, reminding me of the witches in Macbeth.

A bit of blackened charcoal appeared in her hand, and she knelt and scribbled the list of spell components on the floor. She had her own method because she grouped the items into five columns. “Is this all of them?” she looked up at Y Ddraigh Goch.

He peered at her hieroglyphics since she’d used runes rather than letters. “Not quite. Add the North Wind to the third group, and we’ll need a sea god to mix the elements in the fifth group.”

Konstantin had walked near enough to peer over Ceridwen’s shoulder. “Where does the land come into play?”

The goddess rocked back on her heels. “Och, we need her to blend everything together and ensure it remains so long enough to snare the serpents in magic.”

“What if she doesn’t cooperate?”

Gwydion trotted closer. “Do ye have reason to believe she may not?”

“Perhaps.”

“Say more.” Y Ddraigh Goch skewered Konstantin with his command.

Kon shrugged. “This is entirely conjecture, but she is weary and feels she’s been sorely used. That part is true. I did my best to direct her to look forward rather than being mired in past slights, but my last go-round with her didn’t go well.”

“I instructed you to try again,” the dragon god said.

“I know. I haven’t had time.”

“We can invite her into our midst,” Ceridwen suggested silkily and turned to Oberon. “She likes you. Perhaps the summons—er, invitation—should come from you.”

“She knows we are trying to unshackle the *Dreaming* from her purview.” Oberon spread his hands in front of him.

"She is furious and has appeared in my dreams threatening to crush Faery."

"I like the idea of requesting her presence among us," Konstantin said. "If I'm reading her correctly—and I may not be—she feels everyone is plotting behind her back and is out to get her. It wouldn't surprise me if she were close by, listening to us talk. She is ancient, deserving of our respect and consideration."

"If mankind had respected her," I blurted, "we would not be in this predicament. We were the first to treat her with contempt, and it has hardened her heart, embittered her toward everyone."

"And ye are?" Bran focused his hazel gaze on me so intensely it made my skin crawl with his magic. He frowned. "Aye. A dragon shifter, but a brand-new one. How has this come to be? I believed ye were born with the bondmate already in place."

Konstantin inclined his head. "Generally, that is true. By the grace of our god, we have two new dragon shifters. Johan and Erin. The transition was fraught with peril. Both nearly perished bonding with their dragons."

"Are we in agreement about inviting the land to our gathering?" Y Ddraigh Goch broke in. I was grateful he'd refocused the discussion before it truly slithered off onto a tangent. And I wasn't interested in revisiting the agony of my first shift.

Amid a chorus of ayes and yesses, the dragon god told Konstantin. "Do what you have to. Make outrageous promises but bring Earth to us."

Konstantin nodded and turned to leave. He was halfway

to the stairs when a glowing portal formed near him. Power reminiscent of earthquakes and floods and cyclones burst through the gateway. When the clouds of incandescent light cleared, a tall woman with regal bearing stood regarding us. Her hair was made of leaves and twigs and vines. Green, brown, and gold, it wound around her head and fell around her in a cascade nearly to the floor.

Her eyes were gray-blue like the sky on an overcast day or the restless sea. In place of limbs, sheaves of pliable grain grew, and her gnarled, long-nailed hands reminded me of flesh-colored twigs. She wasn't exactly dressed, but neither was she naked. Diaphanous streamers of pink and gray wound around her body, covering her from chest level to her bare feet. Reddish-brown streaked the streamers, thicker in spots, thinner in others. Was it her blood?

"I am saving you the trouble of hunting for me."

Her voice, low, rich, and lyrical fed right into my mind. It took me a moment to determine the language was an archaic form of Gaelic. The thick scent of new-mown hay filled the air. Laced into it was the smell of damp earth just after a rainstorm. I couldn't stop staring. Earth was beautiful, but beyond that something about the apparition glowing before me sang to my soul.

"Thank you for gifting us with your presence." Konstantin bowed so low his forehead nearly touched the floor.

I stole a glance at Erin. Earth had tried to smother her, and she'd have every right not to trust the shimmering form who'd entered the room. Rather than appearing angry, she looked just as astonished as I was.

"We appreciate that ye're here." Gwydion turned to face her.

"Aye, I may be here, but 'tisn't without reservations."

"Will ye aid us or no?" Ceridwen raised dark brows. Black hair splashed with thick chunks of silver fell about her, and she wore a long, leather skirt covered with a cream-colored linen tunic. I hadn't realized until that moment how tall she was. Perhaps two meters, she towered over me.

Earth glided nearer Konstantin, who murmured, "My lady. You're wounded. Healers stand amongst us. Let them aid you."

The crimson stains I'd noticed deepened, as if his words had opened her hurt places. Rather than the copper smell of blood, the scents of resin and sap thickened around me. Ignoring Konstantin's offer, she said, *"What is required of me? I am depleted and have very little to give."*

Before anyone answered her, she turned reproachful eyes on Oberon and Titania. *"I believed you loyal, yet you would strip me in the same way men have. They are ignorant. You cannot claim that excuse."*

I wanted to scream that the men who'd raped and pillaged her bounty had been far from ignorant. They hadn't given a fuck, so long as they made money.

"Not a good idea," Katya breathed into my mind and tightened her grip on my hand.

"We are sorry," Titania said in a clear, ringing voice.

"Aye, if ye will promise to stand and fight, we shall not move the *Dreaming*," Oberon said.

"The only reason we considered such a move—"

"Not considered." Earth's voice was implacable as she cut Titania off. *"Already put into motion."*

"The only reason we considered such a move," Titania began anew, "is because we sensed ye were on the verge of giving up. Had ye done so, we would have withered along with ye."

More of the red ichor flowed, pooling around Earth. Where it formed puddles, small green shoots started upward.

"What is required of me?" Earth asked once again.

Konstantin repositioned himself so he faced Earth, or how the land had chosen to present herself. I was certain she wasn't corporeal in the same way we were. "Two paths have been shown to us," he began. "In one, we battle the serpents for a long while. They wear us down, and we leave."

Earth's regal face crumpled. Red tears welled in her eyes, staining her cheeks as they flowed. *"You do not need me to assist unless it would be to hasten my destruction."* She paused, gathering herself, and shook a twiglike finger at Konstantin. *"You gave me your word, you would aid me. As you aided Mu."*

My heart hurt for her. She was within an angstrom of giving up. It must have stretched her diminished resources to show herself to us, yet she'd understood we were about to search for her. Perhaps it was simpler for her to be here than to hide herself from a phalanx of gods.

"Hear me out," Konstantin said. "The second path involves coating this world in ice. Magical ice that will immobilize the serpents. While they are unable to escape, the gods and goddesses who stand before you will kill them one by one." He made a face. "While they're about it, they will do away with treacherous dragons who have joined with the serpents."

"I have tried to leverage ice myself, but it costs me dear. This ice of yours. How long would it last?" Earth sounded hopeful for the first time since she'd arrived in our midst.

"As long as is required to do away with the serpents," Kon replied.

"Would it be pervasive enough to get rid of the men who have tormented me?"

"Some of them. Your task," Kon went on, "would be to ensure all the other creatures that live in the sea remain alive. You would also need to hold the various elements of our enchantment together. Oversee things."

"I could do that." Earth spoke slowly. *"Particularly if men are occupied doing something other than drilling new holes in my hide."*

"And now we must decide." Gwydion let his very blue eyes rest on one god after another.

"Decide what?" Earth looked confused. She held a fragility that smote me and filled me with guilt. I may not have been the one crafting drilling plans, but I'd held plenty of drills. Been thrilled at discovering promising veins of ore and as eager as the next bastard to drag mineral wealth out of the ground. Once we'd emptied out one shaft, we excavated another.

Y Ddraigh Goch had been silent through the exchange. He walked to where Konstantin stood facing Earth. "I am humbled to meet you, my lady." The dragon god bowed low. "I am—"

"I know who you are." Her odd eyes, more green than blue

now, scanned the room. *"I know who all of you are. You did not answer my question. Decide what?"*

"I was getting there," Y Ddraigh Goch said. "A very old lore book found us. It delineated the two possible avenues Konstantin described. Working alone, dragon shifters lack sufficient magic to manage the second option. We required assistance for such an ambitious undertaking, so I asked the other gods to heed my request. It's why they are here. The first step—their presence—has been accomplished, but they have yet to declare themselves on one side or another."

Earth nodded as understanding filled her. *"Which shall it be?"* she asked in a somewhat stronger voice. *"Will you aid me or cast me asunder?"*

"Before you answer..." Y Ddraigh Goch returned his attention to the Celts and assorted shifter gods. Bast was on her feet, ears pricked forward. Anubis too. "Know that if you walk away, the serpents will eventually commandeer sufficient magic to create serious problems for every other magic wielder throughout every world. It's not simply a matter of relocating to a distant borderworld. Eventually, there will be nowhere left to go. Magic is finite. If the serpents appropriate too much for too long, we shall fade into oblivion."

"This is your fault," Gwydion leveled his gaze at the dragon god.

"I take full responsibility, yet even I cannot turn the hands of time backward. Where do we go from here, Master Enchanter?"

"I have seen this in my glass," Bran said.

"As have I in my cauldron," Ceridwen muttered. "It could go very badly."

"It could," Bran agreed, "yet I doona see where we have a choice."

"I shall aid you," Anubis woofed.

"As shall I," Bast said in a melodic purr.

"My birds will be your allies." Thoth bobbed his head on his stalk of a neck.

"I would know more about your vision." Y Ddraigh Goch stared at Bran.

The god of prophecy shook his head. "Some future-seeings never come to pass. Most of them, in fact. If I give voice to what I have seen, I will weight the probability of it happening. I doona wish to do so."

"Is it the same with you?" the dragon god asked Ceridwen.

She nodded. "Exactly. 'Tis how seer magic works for all of us with that gift."

Katya leaned into me. Something about the exchange must have verified her own prophecy-seeking because she seemed relieved.

Gwydion pounded his staff against the floor twice. "We shall aid you. We had mostly decided to do so afore we arrived, but we needed to lay eyes on our allies afore making a firm commitment."

"Thank you. I shall keep my end of our bargain." Earth's voice was fading, and her along with it. I blinked at the spot she'd stood, not surprised to find it empty.

"Wait. Come back!" Ceridwen called. I'm sure she tried to sound inviting, but her tone was peremptory enough, I'd have had second thoughts about responding to it. She reminded me of my mother calling me in for dinner—the third time—in a you'd-better-show-up-now-or-else voice.

"She was exhausted," Konstantin said. "I felt her power ebbing long before she left. Projections aren't easy. I know where to find her to impart information, but it may not be necessary."

"I can still feel her presence," Erin said. "Don't ask me how, but I know she's still here and listening to us."

Arianrhod ran forward. "Where did ye get that?" She pointed at a pendant hanging from Erin's neck.

Erin edged closer to Kon. "My mate gave it to me."

"Fine. Where did he get it?" Arianrhod rolled her eyes. Odd eyes were the name of the game here. One of hers was gold, the other silver. Blonde hair streaked with silver had been braided out of the way, but it fell to her knees. She wore dark brown leather trousers, a matching jacket, and carried an ornate bow over one shoulder. A quiver of arrows was lashed across her back.

Konstantin blew out an ash-and-smoke-tinged breath. "Let me see. I believe that piece came from a shipwreck in the early 1700s." He shook his head. "Nope. Late 1700s. It was in one of the chests that washed ashore. Why?"

Arianrhod stalked forward. "I gifted it to a special mortal."

"If he was aboard that ship, he died in a hurricane," Konstantin said.

"Which would explain why I never heard aught from him," she muttered and held out a hand. "'Tis mine. Give it to me."

Erin just stared at her. "You're kidding, right? My husband gave me this. I'm sorry you lost it, but—"

"Give it to me." Arianrhod shrieked and launched herself at Erin.

Kon stepped between them. "This is my fault. If you wish to be angry at someone, be angry with me. I have many other gems from that ship. You'd be welcome to any of them."

Ceridwen had materialized out of thin air and hooked a hand beneath Arianrhod's arm. "'Tis a compliment she chose you, dearie. Not cause to start a war. These are our new *allies*." She stressed the word.

"Mmph. I suppose ye're right." As quickly as Arianrhod's temper had flared, it cooled.

Erin, however, was still furious. She'd been ready to go to the mat for her bit of jewelry. Kon must have said something to her privately because she uncurled her fisted hands and said very stiffly, "It is a pleasure to meet the goddess whose necklace I wear."

Arianrhod hooded her eyes. "Save your words, dragon, until they are not forced. Andraste!"

The goddess of war bolted forward. "Yes, dearie?"

"We have a war to plan."

"Ye're singing my song."

Arianrhod blew out a tight breath. "I ken well enough. Ye and Gwydion, do your thing. The rest of us will figure out where we fit in."

"First off, we must rustle up Poseidon and the North Wind." Andraste clacked her teeth together.

"I shall deal with that part of things," Ceridwen said. "They're more likely to heed my summons than yours."

Andraste rolled her green eyes. "As ye will."

I wanted to talk with Katya, ask her how she thought our fragile alliance would hold up, but there was no way I could do so without someone laughing their socks off at my pathetic telepathy attempt. Or taking offense at my doubts.

"Have something to eat," Kon invited.

Gwydion strode to the food. "Good call, mate. I think better when my belly is full."

"Enjoy," Y Ddraigh Goch said. "I shall return shortly."

"Where are ye going?" Ceridwen asked. Damn but her voice reminded me of nails on a chalkboard.

"To rustle up Ylon, head of the dinosaur shifters, and apprise him of the outcome of this meeting. I shall let the other dragons know as well."

"I remember Ylon," Arawn boomed. "Stellar fellow. Invite him to join us, why don't you."

The dragon god bolted up the stairs. Katya nudged me. *"Good excuse for him to escape for a while. He's never done well with anyone ordering him about."*

"None of us do." I didn't bother with mind speech. No reason for it since my comment could mean anything. "Shall we grab a bite?"

She nodded. "Who knows when we'll eat next. I suspect this will unfold quickly. The Celts never were inclined to let grass grow under their feet."

Gwydion must have heard her because he said, "Why wait? Sooner we get this behind us, the sooner I can return to the lissome lassie waiting in my chamber in Inverlochy Castle."

Andraste slapped him across the back. "That slut? Ye're still fucking her?"

"Ye've no right to judge. Why, the last mortal ye took to rut with was..."

Katya dragged me toward the food. Rightly so. I didn't need to hear about the Celts' bedroom habits. I'd have liked it a whole lot better if they were more ethereal. Less human.

My dragon burst out laughing, and clouds of smoke billowed from my mouth.

"What's so funny?" Katya handed me a bowl.

I shrugged. "Nothing. Not really." I didn't want to get tangled up in telling her what an idealistic fool I was.

KONSTANTIN

Konstantin had been deeply relieved and touched Earth had taken both the time and a big chunk of her failing energy to create a projection and join them. He'd felt how much it cost her but hadn't wished to embarrass her by pointing out her weakness. Her presence had made it almost impossible for the Celts to withhold their aid.

They might be insular, but only a coldhearted bastard could refuse a maiden in obvious distress. Whether Earth had picked that guise on purpose was anyone's guess, but he believed she'd chosen and chosen well.

The great room was crowded. All the dragons and dinosaurs had returned on Y Ddraigh Goch's heels. Kon wasn't surprised. They'd want to hear how their next steps would unfold firsthand. Even though everyone was in their human form, there wasn't any extra space.

The kettles were long since empty. He'd debated asking

Katya to whip up more, but once all the shifters began pouring in, he decided against it. The fish stew had been a good faith offering to the gods. One that had apparently helped loosen their historical aversion to aiding anyone.

Shifters were an enterprising bunch. More than capable of feeding themselves. Or asking if any food was available.

"'Tis close in here," Gwydion said.

"We should move outside," Anubis woofed. "My shifters are returning from foraging."

"As are mine, and outside would be an improvement," Bast said in a purr-laced flurry of words.

The North Wind, who'd appeared as a squat fellow with long, white hair vanished in the shadow of an icy squall that blew through the room. Poseidon, garbed in long blue robes with seaweed woven into his mounds of gray hair, left next. His staff was pink coral seeded with hundreds of pearls. Kon would have liked to have gotten a closer look.

Rather than everyone else crowding into the stairwell, most opted to use magic. The air thickened with the mixed scents of rain-washed beaches, damp greenery, sunbaked sand, and fresh flowers. When it cleared, he, his twin, and their mates were the only ones left in the great room.

"Come on." He snatched up an empty urn and started up the stairs.

"Do you need to make certain Earth is part of what happens next?" Erin asked.

"The land is close. She has been ever since she appeared to us." He plonked the urn just inside the kitchen door. Katya placed the other one next to it.

"No more trips down the mineshaft?" Erin tilted her head to one side.

"Not right now." Konstantin turned so he faced Erin, Katya, and Johan. "Before we join the others, I want to make certain you know we will be in this subterranean world beneath a world for a long while."

"We understand," Johan said. "Depending on how many others remain with us, our food stocks may not last."

"I assumed we would be able to teleport away from here." Katya frowned.

"Not while the magic is at its zenith. If I understand the casting correctly, it will form an impenetrable barrier that will immobilize anyone trying to move through it. We would end up just as trapped as the serpents."

"Can we wait this out on a borderworld?" Erin asked.

"The rest of you can, but I must remain here," Konstantin answered his mate. "Someone must support Earth. She will not take it well if all of us leave."

"That's settled then." Katya nodded brusquely. "The four of us shall remain."

"Food will not be a problem with so few," Johan murmured.

Konstantin focused intently on his mate and raised one brow in an unspoken question. He wanted her to stay with him... Wanted was a vast understatement. He would have moved worlds to coax her to stay, but if she wished to wait for him on a borderworld, he would respect her choice.

"If you're here," Erin said to Konstantin, "then I will be too. Plenty of reading material in the library. By the time we're out of quarantine, my magic should be in tiptop shape."

Johan nudged her. "Quarantine?"

"Eh, slip of the tongue. It's how we medical types view enforced isolation."

"Thank you," Kon told her. The words didn't do his thoughts justice. He was delighted and vastly relieved she didn't want to be apart from him.

"I never was into long-distance relationships." Erin paused. "Or relationships at all. You've accomplished the impossible, Sir Dragon. I'd think you'd want to keep me as close as you could."

"Oh, I do. Believe me."

Before they got sidetracked cooing endearments, Konstantin bolted up the next three sets of risers and out into the open area between the entrance to his home and the nearest lake. His eyes widened. Hundreds of shifters had gathered. Presumably, Anubis, Bast, and Thoth had put out the call to their people.

Ylon trotted over. Keeping his voice low, he said, "Nice to have all this help, but we scarcely need them to cast the spell Y Ddraigh Goch outlined."

"Maybe we do." Kon mouthed the words. Shifters had exceptionally keen hearing, and it wouldn't do to offend anyone. He scanned the assemblage and located Y Ddraigh Goch. The dragon god stood with the other deities. Heads together, they were clearly deep in discussion.

Katya grabbed his upper arm. "What's that?" she hissed. Nostrils flaring widely, she tipped her head this way and that, scenting the air.

He started to tell her it was simply the blend of so many magics that had caught her attention, but Earth shrieked into his mind. *"We are under attack. Under attack, I tell you. I cannot keep them out."*

"Who?"

"I do not know," she wailed.

"What's going on?" Erin shook herself as talons shot through where her fingers had been. "My beast wants out."

Kon's dragon made a strong bid for ascendency too. *"You need me,"* he bugled.

Ever so faint, the reek of rotting flesh threaded through the other smells surrounding him. "Serpents?" He stared at Ylon, incredulous. How had the unholy bastards found this place?

"Smells like it," the dinosaur growled.

Konstantin trumpeted to get everyone's attention. "We are under attack," he shouted. "Look to your strongest magic. The serpents are mortal as humans."

"Hell, Dragon, we can kill anything," Gwydion whooped. His glowing staff turned into a battle axe, and he swung it in a circle above his head. A lance and a long blade whistled through the air to where Andraste stood. She caught both handily. Poseidon hefted his staff, and it turned into a deadly trident.

Beside him, Katya's golden dragon took shape. Erin's red beast and Johan's green one were almost fully formed. His bondmate uttered a string of blistering rebukes and dragged control into his talons. In record time, black scales and wings took shape, and he was swooping through the air. Riotous air fed by the North Wind.

Other dragons, the ones from the Fleisher borderworlds, joined him, along with Katya, Johan, and Erin.

"We should send our mate inside," his beast said, its protectiveness in full bloom.

"She wouldn't go," Konstantin countered. He scanned nooks, crannies, and shadows but didn't see a single serpent. Why could he smell them? Where were they coming from?

"Beneath your wings," Earth answered his unspoken questions. At least it proved she'd joined with him. Mu had done much the same. Kon craned his neck, peering beneath him, but saw nothing. The serpents' stench had intensified, though.

Wherever they were, they were nearer than they'd been.

Ceridwen and Y Ddraigh Goch were gathering a company of mixed shifters. The other gods were doing much the same. No one tagged the five of them, so Kon formed his own troop. Yle joined them, rounding it out to six. All of them were airborne except for Ylon. His dinosaur bulk spread next to the first lake, and power fanned around him.

At least Erin flew near him. It was as much of a concession as he was likely to get to keep her safe.

A deep, malevolent booming throbbed around him. The rocky wall forming a border to the right of the lake fell in. Serpents swarmed through the break. Dragons flew above them, bugling commands.

Kon swallowed his horror and antipathy at what appeared to be a mass defection by his own kind. "Keep an eye on each dragon," he roared in dragonspeak. "Make certain you tag them for destruction."

Ceridwen and Y Ddraigh Goch raced toward one side of

the pulsing hole that was disgorging evil. Gwydion and his troop took the other side. A bow materialized in Ceridwen's hands. Gwydion tossed his war axe. It cleaved through a dragon's neck and returned to him, much like a boomerang might have. The headless dragon pinwheeled out of the air, blood geysering everywhere.

For each dragon or serpent that fell, two more barged through. Konstantin stopped counting at fifty. While his attention had been diverted, serpents flowed in a thick tide of destruction. They headed for the lake, and he heard the land moaning piteously. A quick glance through her eyes showed black cancerous sores forming all along her body.

Unlike the projection she'd hidden behind, the land had parts of herself spread throughout all layers and levels of her world. The sores filled with orangish pus that burst and scarred everything the liquid came into contact with.

"Do something," she begged.

"You heard the spell along with the rest of us," he told her. *"Once they're all in the lake, freeze them in place."* Konstantin waited, but the land didn't answer.

Katya had organized Johan, Erin, Ylon, and Yle into a one-two punch. She and Johan dragged the human out of the serpent. Erin and Ylon stomped it into oblivion with Yle's help. It wasn't efficient, but they'd killed three. The dirt beneath them ran red with blood.

A large copper dragon shot fire along Konstantin's back. He roared his outrage and turned to face his enemy. Of course, he knew the dragon, but he had to shelve that part deep. Whoever these dragons had been once upon a time, they'd renounced everything it meant to be a dragon shifter when they'd embraced sorcerous power.

Fire streamed from the copper dragon's open mouth. Kon blasted him with flames of his own. It was stupid. Neither of them would win this battle. All it would do was drain power Kon could better employ elsewhere. Feinting to the side, he rolled out on top of the copper and flattened his body atop the other dragon, driving him downward.

He'd employed this move on a borderworld, and it worked so long as he held the element of surprise. By the time the copper dragon recovered and tried to fight his way out from beneath Kon's bulk, he was nearly to Ylon's waiting clutches. Yle swooped in from the side and impaled the dragon's eyes with his sharp beak.

The copper bellowed in pain and outrage. He could regrow his lost sight with magic, but he'd be dead long before then. Ylon and Yle had things under control. Konstantin flapped hard to gain altitude and hunted for his next victim. Three dragons later, he was panting, but what they were doing wasn't making much of a dent.

In anything.

While he'd been focused on dragons, enough serpents had filed through to fill the lake with their dull-colored scales. The same shades as dragons, their coloration was muted, muddy. He took a deep breath to clear his mind and wished he hadn't.

Not much was left of the clean, fresh scents of shifter magic or Celtic enchantment. The sickish-sweet rot of serpents left its slimy trail all over everything they touched.

Y Ddraigh Goch bugled at a dragon who'd taken him on.

Below him, every square meter of dirt contained hardscrabble fighting. When magic wasn't doing the trick, shifters were grappling with sea-serpents, trying to bite through their thick hides.

"Do not let them drag you into the water," Kon trumpeted. The Earth moaned again deep in his mind. He wanted to say something comforting, but comfort was a lie. This part of her domain would never be the same, or not for a very long time.

Y Ddraigh Goch's adversary had closed on the dragon god and had his talons dug into the god's shoulders. Konstantin flew close and shouted, "Kill him!"

The dragon god glanced past the red dragon and met Kon's gaze. His spinning eyes were filled with anguish. He could kill the dragon, but the beast was his child. His creation. He wanted to do something less destructive but recognized he had no time for elegant solutions like wiping his mind.

Y Ddraigh Goch spoke a power word that hurt Kon's dragon's soul. The red shrieked once and exploded into a million motes of matter that floated downward. Konstantin started to say something but shut his jaws with a harsh clack.

What could he say? Congratulating the dragon god for moving past his personal demons was inappropriate.

"I know who is behind this," Y Ddraigh Goch spoke into his mind.

"Let's find them and fix this," Konstantin urged.

"Would that it were so easy."

They hovered next to one another, treading air. Kon

waited, but the dragon god didn't add to his enigmatic comment. *"What does that mean?"* he finally asked.

"It's the First Dragon."

Kon's beast bellowed with rage before Kon got him under better control. *"But you killed him."*

The gold-and-silver dragon shook his huge head sadly. *"Not exactly. I was weak, and now all of us are paying the price."*

"I don't understand. Where has he been all these millennia?"

"I barricaded him into the molten core of a distant world where he would burn and regenerate in perpetuity. I didn't believe he could escape."

Konstantin digested the information. Maybe Y Ddraigh Goch was wrong, but what he'd revealed was very much in concert with what Kon knew about him. He might bluster and roar, but he was ruled by compassion. It was a trait that made dragons special among their shifter kin. They were capable of great destruction but also understood full well the negative impact of the full use of their power.

This wasn't the time for how-could-you-have recriminations.

"Use the power word," he urged in dragonspeak. "End this."

"Not so easy," the god sputtered. "It must be matched to a dragon's particular energy."

"Fine. Pick them off one by one. I'll get everyone else focused on the serpents." He hesitated. *"Do it. Think about it later, my liege. It is either us or them. You no longer have a choice."*

He had no more words. Y Ddraigh Goch would rise to their need. Kon was certain of it. Sticking to his liege's side like a starving tick wouldn't accomplish anything. All it would do is convince the dragon god that Kon didn't trust him.

He flew to where Katya, Johan, and Erin were methodically killing serpents. The pile had grown, and he added his magic to forcing the wyrms back into their human shapes. Below them, Ylon and Yle took care of killing them once they were no longer immortal.

Earth had been busy. The piles of bodies were vanishing as she sucked them into holes that she filled in. She hadn't done much with the lake yet, but a thin layer of ice had formed across one end. It was a start.

Yle flew back from somewhere, cawing outrage. *"We have sustained losses."*

It didn't surprise Konstantin. How could they engage in a battle as extensive as this one and come out unscathed? The serpents' poison was deadly if you weren't careful and inhaled it. Or got it on your skin. *"How many?"*

"At least a dozen. Wolves. Birds. One dinosaur. One dragon."

Kon wanted to ask which dragon had fallen, but he'd find out eventually. He could question his beast. The dragons always knew who was missing, but he couldn't value his kinsman over any other shifter. "I am so sorry. For all our fallen companions," he told Yle.

Should he tell them about Y Ddraigh Goch's confession? He dithered back and forth. His bondmate hadn't blurted the truth, so perhaps he'd decided protecting their god was more important than absolute honesty.

Shrieks and cries had turned into background noise. He paid them little heed. *"How are you doing?"* he asked the land

and turned his focus inward. At least her pitiful moans and squawks had quieted.

"We are holding our own," she informed him. *"I am feeling stronger. Poseidon promised to flood all the low-lying lands. It should displace enough men and create sufficient havoc they will leave off their destructive habits."*

Konstantin had expected a tirade blaming Y Ddraigh Goch. It didn't come. Earth was apparently moving past her wounded/blaming stage, which had to bode well. The sea god's help was timely, indeed. Earth had enormous cities that would vanish if the seas rose even a meter. Feeling relieved for the land, he took to the skies again, staring through smoke and murk as he assessed how the various groups were doing. Unbelievably, the portal still disgorged serpents and dragons. Where the fuck were all of them coming from?

If the First Dragon was still alive and well, he must have spent a long time amassing such an impressive army. Gwydion's war axe cleaved through another dragon neck. This time, the beast vanished in a poof of fiery air.

The Warrior Magician bellowed, "Illusion. That one was illusion." He barked a string of power words. Different from the one uttered by Y Ddraigh Goch, they still hurt Konstantin's ears. Each separate clump of syllables hit him like a roundhouse punch to the gut.

The flood of serpents and dragons halted abruptly. At least fifty serpents and ten dragons flamed out, much as the one that had alerted Gwydion had done. Too bad they couldn't rid themselves of the rest of these bastards so easily.

Arrows flew from Arianrhod's bow. Ceridwen's as well.

Poseidon's trident crashed into serpent after serpent. Whatever the gods hit screamed and fell, blood shooting from every orifice. Around them, the wind howled merrily, shoving serpents and dragons to their doom. Konstantin stared at the gateway, not trusting it to remain empty.

"Can you get rid of it?" he asked the land.

"Nay. Do you not think I haven't tried? 'Tis rooted in a distant place. One I cannot find, let alone have any control over."

On a hunt for anything, that might help him destroy the blasted portal, Konstantin sent seeking magic through its ragged opening. Something impossibly strong got a grip on his magic. He couldn't withdraw it, so he cut the flow. What was beyond the breach? His beast headed right for the opening, intent on flying through and engaging whatever lurked there in battle.

Kon held him back. *"Bad idea."*

"But we know something's in there. Something powerful. We must kill it?"

"What makes you think we can?" Kon countered. *"Hell, I couldn't even retrieve my magic."*

A wave of dragon shifter magic so potent it nearly knocked him out of the air rolled from the gateway. *"Whatever it is,"* he told his beast, *"it's coming out."*

Y Ddraigh Goch flew past him and landed, planting himself in front of the portal. "Come out," he bellowed. "I command you."

Konstantin considered landing, but he had better leverage from the air. Katya, Erin, and Johan flew near, joining him. "What's going on?" Katya asked.

"I don't know," he hedged. He had a pretty good idea

what was on the far side of the gateway. Only another dragon would have been strong enough to hang onto his magic. Or a god. And from what he could see, all the gods were ranged below him, sucking the life out of serpent after serpent.

The ground in front of the gateway cracked in protest. One huge, scaled taloned foreleg poked through, followed by a dragon half again the size of Y Ddraigh Goch. Gold and silver like his maker, the First Dragon's hide bore more scars than scales. Buckled from burns, skin showed through gaps in his scales. Misshapen, warped, he looked like a caricature of a dragon.

No wonder he was furious at the dragon god. Kon lacked details, but he would have bet his last gold doubloon the First Dragon had been plotting revenge ever since Y Ddraigh Goch locked him away.

The Celts ranged themselves on both sides of Y Ddraigh Goch. Ceridwen, Arawn, Poseidon, and Bran on one side. Gwydion, Arianrhod, and Andraste on the other. "Apparently, ye dinna have the stomach to kill him," Ceridwen said dryly. "We shall deal with that issue later."

Kon looked for Anubis, Bast, and Thoth, but they were still at the head of their groups dealing with serpents.

"What makes you think you have a later?" the First Dragon inquired. For such a huge monster, his words were deceptively soft, mild even.

Before Ceridwen could answer, he went on. "I have no problems with any of the rest of you. This argument is between him"—he pointed at Y Ddraigh Goch with a taloned foreleg—"and me."

Konstantin flew nearer. "You would have encouraged the serpents to take over Earth."

The First Dragon shrugged. Scales that should have rattled tapped dully on the scar tissue crisscrossing his bulk. "Merely a ploy. I knew if I was outrageous enough, dear old Dad would show up."

Y Ddraigh Goch growled. Smoke and fire flew from his jaws.

"You're going to have to do better than that," the First Dragon chortled. "I know all your tricks. And all your magic."

Ceridwen hummed a note. Gwydion picked up a harmonizing one. Konstantin recognized the beginnings of a spell, but it wasn't familiar to him.

"This problem is of my making," Y Ddraigh Goch screeched. "I shall be who deals with it."

Nodding at one another, the Celts backed off a few paces, offering the dragon god space. Magic sheeted from him as he launched himself at his spawn, shouting a string of power words.

KATYA

Katya felt like she should do something. Her beast was pushing hard against the end of her tether. She wanted to take a stand next to Y Ddraigh Goch. She didn't care the god had lied. He was in trouble, and she aimed to protect him. The power words made her ears ache, but that pain was nothing compared with the agony that dug deep into her soul.

Dragons didn't destroy other dragons. They did everything possible to salvage them. She expected Y Ddraigh Goch's power word to flatten the First Dragon, but he didn't even sway on his feet.

Where had he been? What had happened to him that resulted in all those burns? Most of his hide was covered in scars that had formed on top of other scars. She almost felt sorry for him. He'd suffered terribly.

"Don't waste your energy," her beast said sternly. *"He was given more chances than he deserved."*

The second power word might have had a slight impact. Maybe. The dragon god gripped the First Dragon with his talons. Because the First Dragon's scales didn't do much of a job protecting the flesh beneath, Y Ddraigh Goch was able to dig his claws in deep enough to draw blood. Rather than red, it spurted black and thick, smelling much like the serpents' poison.

She remembered how the sea-serpent venom had burned when it landed on her skin, how much damage it had done, and how much power it had taken to neutralize it. She still had a scar from the suppurating hole with blackened edges that had formed almost instantly.

Bellowing, trumpeting, and blowing smoke and fire into one another's faces, the dragon god and his first son ripped into each other. The third power word was so harsh it made her bones ache. The First Dragon shook his head and kept on slugging.

Behind her, the noise of ice scraping against itself seemed odd and out of place. On the surface near the headlands perhaps, but not down here. A quick glance told her the lake was well on its way to being frozen. Serpents were scrambling to leave the rapidly expanding ice, but Gwydion and Ceridwen barked spells of their own. Using a combination of power words and more standard incantations, they held the serpents in place while the lake froze from end to end.

Phantoms took shape at the far end of the body of congealing ice. Oberon on one side, Titania on the other, and Earth in the middle. The land wore the same guise she had earlier, but the reddish streaks cutting through her garments were fainter. The king and queen of Faery each had an arm around Earth. The trio seemed to have moved past the bad blood that had marred their interdependency.

Katya puffed smoke and ash in approval as more serpents were herded into the icy slurry the lake had become. Primal ice was in play, but in a far more localized manner than their original plans. Would any serpents remain once this was over? They'd have to wait and see.

An agonized howl brought her back around in time to see Y Ddraigh Goch clutch a spot where his shoulder had caught fire. How was it possible? Dragon scales were impervious to flames.

"This is what you condemned me to," the First Dragon shouted. "To burn and burn and burn, and then to burn some more. Did you have any idea what you were doing? Why didn't you just kill me?"

Y Ddraigh Goch didn't answer. Fury streamed from him, adding a reddish tinge to the air. The fire that had been consuming his shoulder winked out abruptly. Below Katya's extended wings, the shifters and their gods were herding the remaining serpents into the slushy lake. A series of notes trilled up and down the scale, repeating themselves. The song was compelling, so much so she might have followed the serpents into the lake were it not for her beast who fanned its wings away from the hypnotic music.

"It reminds me of a children's tale," Johan told her.

"Children followed a flautist to their doom?" Katya asked.

"Not precisely. A town in Medieval Germany hired a piper with a magic flute to lure rats out of their town. When the townspeople refused to pay him, the piper turned the same magic that had lured the rats on the town's children. They cheerfully followed him out of town and into a cave and were never seen again."

"Not a happy story," Katya said.

"Not happy at all. I believe three children were spared. One was lame and unable to walk fast enough. One was deaf and could not hear the piping. The third was blind. According to legend, they told the townspeople what happened."

He angled a wingtip toward Y Ddraigh Goch, locked in what was clearly mortal combat with the First Dragon. "Should we help?"

"I don't know," Katya replied. "He was clear at the beginning this was his problem."

"*Ja*, well, it is also all of ours if"—Johan hesitated before continuing—"things do not go well."

Fire licked down one of Y Ddraigh Goch's flanks. He ignored it and ripped another chunk of bloody flesh from the thing that had been his proudest creation. "I taught you everything," he screamed.

"And now you shall regret those lessons," the First Dragon countered. Jaws spread, he showered the dragon god with fire that caught wherever it landed.

Katya flew nearer Konstantin. *"We have to do something."*

"What do you have in mind?"

"I don't know. Divert the First Dragon? Why is his fire burning holes in our god?"

Kon turned his whirling gaze on her. *"Same question I've been asking myself."*

Y Ddraigh Goch let go, backed up a few steps, and hurled himself at the First Dragon again. Where the burning parts of him contacted the First Dragon, he too caught fire.

Another power word burst from him. This one had an effect. The First Dragon cringed before spewing more fire. Y Ddraigh Goch batted the flames aside and splayed one forefoot across the First Dragon's misshapen face.

"Die. This is what pity bought me. I shall never make that mistake again."

"I may perish, old man, but you will burn forever. This fire had no antidote."

"We shall see." Y Ddraigh Goch barked more power words. One after the next until Katya clapped her forelegs over her ears. The words were everything harsh and wicked and evil. They were the stuff of endless nightmares. Of spells that blew up in your face. Of vampires sucking the marrow from your bones and resurrecting you to do it again and again.

Kind of like the fire.

Gwydion and Ceridwen spewed their own power words. The First Dragon fell to his knees, wings spread to both sides of him. They had huge rents in them, holes so big she was certain he hadn't flown for a long time.

Immersed in fire, Y Ddraigh Goch threw himself across the First Dragon's back. The two Celtic gods changed up the words and pitch of their incantation. Katya blinked in surprise as the fire left the dragon god and sank into the First Dragon beneath him.

Konstantin flew low and wrapped his forelegs around Y Ddraigh Goch, dragging him off the prostrate form beneath him. A low whooshing began deep in the earth just before the First Dragon's body turned into a pyre. He raised his head and howled, "Finish it this time. I am done burning."

The compassion Katya had battled before swept through her. Y Ddraigh Goch had been selfish. A clean kill was always preferable to leaving your victim to suffer. Tears flooded her eyes, clattering to earth as a fortune in precious gemstones.

"Stop!" her bondmate adjured. *"We have no idea why he did what he did. He is our god, and deserving of our respect."*

Katya did her best to clear her thoughts. Kon and Y Ddraigh Goch had disappeared. *"Should we follow them?"* she asked her beast.

"No. We will land and add our magic to purging the serpents."

Katya joined Erin and Johan on the ground. Stragglers were still being herded into the partially frozen lake. Between the Celts and the shifter gods, they scarcely required her magic. She didn't want the nasty, stinking serpents polluting her lake, but she was being petty. Water could be cleansed. Besides, nothing would hold her and Johan here once this was done.

Except Kon's link to the land.

She raised her mind voice and addressed her twin. *"Where are you?"*

"Third lake. Our liege required water."

She wanted to protest that dragons didn't like water. Instead, she asked, *"Do you need help?"*

"Nay, Sister. We shall return presently."

The last of the serpents stumbled into the lake, moving like sleepwalkers. She was fairly certain the Celts had ensorcelled them, but the absence of the First Dragon's magic probably weakened his minions. Had they done away with the other dragon traitors? The ones who'd offered their allegiance to the First Dragon?

She understood better how events must have unfolded. Dragons would never have tendered zip squat to a serpent, but the First Dragon was another story, entirely. Second only to Y Ddraigh Goch in myth, he'd been known for his honor and bravery before arrogance got the better of him.

She swallowed a bitter smile. The First Dragon had been a delight as an only child, but sharing the limelight with siblings hadn't been on his menu. He didn't see why the dragon world required any occupants beyond himself and his maker, and he'd acted accordingly.

Had Y Ddraigh Goch tried to reason with him? She'd never know, and it probably didn't matter.

The Celts were mowing through the serpents, killing one after the other. The North Wind batted foot-draggers their way. Better the Celts than her. She'd lost her heart for mindless slaughter. Even if the victims deserved killing.

"You are a dragon," her beast reminded her.

"Does that mean I have no heart?" she countered.

Her bondmate had no reply, and she was grateful not to be drawn into an argument with her. The pyre that had been the First Dragon was winding down. Still burning, but not as high as it had been. The king and queen of Faery had joined the Celts. Earth was nowhere to be seen.

Katya wasn't sure what dew her attention back to the portal. It should have been destroyed after the First Dragon surged through, yet no one had viewed it as a priority. She started toward it but stopped as Surek slithered through.

"Kill him!" she shouted, her earlier thoughts about compassion vanishing in the space between two breaths. Andraste and Arianrhod notched arrows aimed at the serpent's head.

Surek raised his gray, scaled form off the dirt until about a meter of him stood tall. He tossed his head back. "I request clemency. If you release my serpents, you have my word, we shall never bother this world or any others again."

"Ha!" Gwydion sneered. "Where will ye bide? The space between worlds?"

"We would return to the world where Y Ddraigh Goch put us. And there we shall remain. The only reason we left was because the First Dragon lured us with promises of freedom and glory. Of gaining retribution for being banished." His forked tongue flicked from his mouth as he took a breath. "We deserved exile. What we did to our god's children was inexcusable."

"He is only saying that because he knows he is beaten," Andraste cried.

"I'm not so sure." Katya projected her voice. "He did not have to enter our midst. He was safely away from this place." She twisted to face Surek. "Are other serpents on the surface?"

He nodded. "Aye, perhaps fifty of us. They would leave as well."

"It pains me to say aught on his behalf, but he speaks true," Ceridwen said.

Surek barked something that might have been a laugh.

"Spouting lies in the midst of gods and goddesses would be pointless. And stupid." He bowed his head. "May I leave with my serpents? A few in the lake are not yet dead."

Katya started to say yes, but it wasn't her decision to make. She looked from one Celt to the next, and then to Anubis, Bast, and Thoth.

"Ye have caused much trouble," Anubis woofed. "Several of my shifters died this day."

"For that, I am truly sorry," Surek said. "My losses exceed yours, but I accept them. We were the aggressors because we were stupid and misled."

"'Tisn't an excuse," Ceridwen told him tartly.

"No, it's not, but it is the best I can offer." Surek shook his gray triangular head. "That one"—he jerked his chin at what was left of the First Dragon—"was very hard to say no to. He shared his blood with me. And his madness. I am thankful he is dead."

Katya clacked her double rows of teeth together. It explained why the First Dragon's blood had been black. He'd dabbled in the worst kind of sorcery, the type where you bent others to your will.

Arawn, god of the dead, tossed his dark hair over his shoulders. "I would impose a condition on ye leaving."

"Anything," Surek said.

"Ye will transport your dead to my halls where I will keep them from further ill deeds. No one will be able to reanimate them. Once that task is done, ye will tell me where ye will reside. If at any time ye leave that spot without first letting one of us know, ye will be fair game for us to finish what we began today."

"Agreed." Surek didn't even hesitate.

Katya was glad he and his people had been offered a second chance. Somehow it made the carnage more bearable.

Konstantin and Y Ddraigh Goch flew into their midst and touched down near Surek. "I heard some of that," the dragon god said.

Surek lowered his body until he lay in the dirt. "Forgive me, my liege. I shall do better."

"I believe you will. Katya asked if serpents bided above. She did not ask about dragons. Are there more who were corrupted by…" Y Ddraigh Goch's voice faltered, but not for long. "By the First Dragon?"

"I do not believe so, but I am not certain."

"We will check," Konstantin said.

"I will do that," the dragon god said. He looked haggard. Fire had stripped divots across both flanks. Katya remembered the First Dragon's prediction and wondered if Y Ddraigh Goch would bear permanent scars.

The ice cracked and cracked again. A few sea-serpents slithered out of the lake and hurried to Surek's side. "We have a task," he told them. "We must move our dead to Arawn's halls."

The god of the dead made a sweeping motion with one hand. A black-and-gold edged gateway took shape. "Through there," he said. "My realm has infinite entry points."

Surek and the serpents started with the nearest corpse. A combination of magic and brute force moved the carcasses

—some human, some serpent—through Arawn's portal. Waves formed in the lake, washing bodies onto the shore.

Katya figured it was Earth's doing, and she was happy for the land. After a rough beginning with Konstantin, Earth was beginning to believe in her nascent power again.

Johan lumbered next to her and shifted back to his human form. She did the same. No reason to be dragons, and it would be easier to talk. "I am glad we did not kill the rest of them after Surek asked for mercy," he said quietly.

"Me too. This had a better outcome than I expected."

"I wonder." Johan looked toward Y Ddraigh Goch. The dragon god was helping move serpent bodies through Arawn's gateway. "Do you suppose he will ever forgive himself?"

"Probably." She blew out a long, jagged breath. "When you live forever, it's impossible not to do things you're eventually very sorry for. You find ways to keep going."

The corners of Johan's mouth twitched. "Doesn't appear to bother the Celts."

"They play by different rules."

"How so?" he asked.

She shrugged. "I'm talking out of my ass. I've obviously never been a Celtic god, so I have no idea how they view the world or how they deal with decisions that backfired on them."

"How about you?" Johan speared her with his dark eyes.

"How about me, what?" Katya hedged, understanding his meaning well enough.

"Do you have things you're sorry for?"

A corner of her mouth quirked into an enigmatic smile. “Of course, but leave a gal her secrets.”

Johan tipped his head and smiled softly. “I love you. No matter what you’ve done. Or not done.”

“Same.” She smiled back.

The shifters were clearing out. Ylon and Yle, back in their human bodies, walked close to her and Johan. “We are returning to our borderworld,” Ylon said.

“Hold a moment,” Katya told him. “Let me grab Kon. I’m certain he’ll want to thank you.”

“Brother!” She employed their private mind speech.

Konstantin trudged to her with Erin next to him. He shook off his dragon form. When shifter magic stopped glowing around him, he was human again. Erin took longer to shift, and he waited until his mate was done with her transformation before he nodded solemnly to all of them.

“We did a good day’s work.”

“Many days,” Yle said. “We cleared serpent contamination from our worlds as well.”

“Who would have thought the First Dragon was behind all of this?” Erin rolled her eyes. “I mean, I’ve heard of outrageous offspring, but cripes. He would have laid waste to every world he touched.”

“Feeling wronged has deep roots,” Konstantin said. “I’m just glad this is over.”

Katya wondered if he was right or engaging in wishful thinking. Surely, one or two serpents and dragons would escape their net.

Thoth, Bast, and Anubis joined them. “We will be on our way.” Thoth bobbed his head.

Konstantin bowed low. When he straightened, he said, "Thank you so much for heeding Y Ddraigh Goch's call. And for offering your shifters to fight by our side."

"Ye would do the same for us," Anubis woofed.

"Yes," Kon said, "we would indeed. I am forever in your debt and am as near as telepathy should you ever have need of me or my dragons."

Power surged around the three. When it cleared, they were gone along with their assorted shifters. Oberon and Titania trooped to Konstantin's side. "We are returning to Faery," Oberon said.

"Aye. Please join us in our realm. Now that our misunderstanding with Earth is cleared up, the *Dreaming* holds sufficient magic to power Faery forever," Titania said.

Konstantin bowed again. "Thank you for lending your warriors to our cause."

Oberon cocked his head to one side. "Never thank a Sidhe. We have ways of holding your feet to the fire to repay us."

Konstantin shrugged. "The deed is done. I am yours should you have need of me."

Amid Titania's rippling, silvery laughter, the royal couple took their leave, vanishing in a cloud of golden fairy dust. Katya brushed it off her shoulders and shook it out of her hair.

She snorted. "I need to figure out how to make grand exits and entrances like that."

Ylon tapped Kon's shoulder. "We, too, are leaving. Please feel free to visit us on our borderworld."

Yle let his gaze fall on Katya. "I am particularly interested in you visiting, Madame Seer. We could learn from one another."

"Thank you so much," Katya said. "I shall take you up on your offer." A glance over one shoulder told her Arawn's gateway was shut. The Celts were gone. So much for tapping into Bran's or Ceridwen's knowledge of prophecies. But then, she hadn't expected much on that front.

With a noise like a brisk wind in trees that didn't grow in their underground world, the dinosaurs trooped through a portal that Ylon first created and then held open with his magic. He jumped through before it winked out, leaving residual power pulsing around where it had been.

All the serpents were gone but Surek. He and Y Ddraigh Goch had their heads together. While she watched, the dragon god wrapped his arms around Surek's thick neck and kissed his scaled forehead. Power bubbled around them, bright with dragon colors and scented with the baked clay smell of dragon magic.

When it cleared, they were gone.

Konstantin blew out a tired breath. "They have gone to round up the remaining serpents on the headlands. And any dragons who may have escaped our net."

"What will happen to them? The dragons, I mean?" Johan asked.

"Y Draigh Goch will destroy them," Kon answered. "And Surek will kill any serpents who are not fully cooperative with returning to their borderworld."

"Will they need help?" Erin sounded worried.

"If they do, they know where to find us," Konstantin said.

Katya glanced at the lake. "Somehow, I'd expected the water to still be red and black and filled with crud," she said.

"The land is cleansing it." Kon smiled softly. "She is pleased to have such tasks."

Questions rolled through Katya's mind. Where would they go? Would they still live here? Even if they wished to leave, would Kon's link to the land bind them to Earth? Speaking of Earth, how about her gradual decline at the hands of mankind? Would Poseidon's intervention be enough to reverse things?

Or was worrying about such things even her job?

She shook her head.

"Are you all right?" Johan wrapped an arm around her.

"Yes. My thoughts were getting ahead of themselves."

"We should enjoy our victory," Konstantin said. "For it is, indeed, a victory. And one I didn't anticipate."

Johan laughed. "My dragon is incorrigible."

"They all are," Katya said. "What does that beast of yours want now?"

He turned her until she faced him and placed his hands on her shoulders. "What do you think? He wishes us to complete our mating ritual. We never did the dragon portion of it."

"Yes!" Katya's bondmate shrieked so loud she was certain everyone heard her.

Erin and Konstantin burst out laughing. "The dragons have spoken," Konstantin said when he could talk.

Erin slid a hand beneath his arm. "Shall we go inside and offer them a spot of privacy?"

"Good idea, my love." He walked slowly by her side.

Before they'd gotten too far away, he twisted and called, "We'll try to have something put together for you to eat. Mating is hungry business."

Katya bugled her thanks. Her dragon was so eager, she was already half-formed. Johan's green beast breathed clouds of steam to hurry her along. She felt torn. It seemed wrong to jump back into a life that had nearly been snatched away from them, but it seemed right too.

The best thing they could do for dragonkind was to go on living, and living as fully as they could. Steam puffed from her until she and Johan were swathed in puffy, white clouds of it.

"I love you," she said in dragonspeak.

"I love you too. My heart, my life," he replied and leapt skyward.

She followed him. Suddenly, she couldn't wait. Heat and need and love roared through her in an irresistible mélange. When her beast made a bid for freedom, she gave it willingly. Her bondmate had been patient. She deserved all the joy she could harvest from this moment.

Johan's dragon bugled. She bugled back. They dipped and swooped and swerved toward and away from one another until the magical moment when the weight of Johan's dragon settled across her back. He gripped her shoulders with his talons and closed his jaws over her neck.

His cock slid into her body in a single powerful thrust. Joined with the man she loved, she let the air currents take her as they completed the mating ritual. Beyond the exquisite sensuality of making love as a dragon, something she'd never done before, she felt whole in a way she hadn't believed possible.

Tomorrow didn't matter. Only today. Only now.

All the rest would fall into place. She waited for her beast to offer up an I-told-you-so, but the dragon was lost in pleasure. Heat crested, retreated, and crested once more. They settled to the ground still joined. Johan wrapped his wings around them and laid his snout across her shoulder, breathing steam and love.

She leaned her head against his, basking in their shared delight while his cock deflated enough to untangle their bodies. *"We will do that every day,"* her beast announced.

Johan bugled laughter and began to shift.

Katya did the same. Before her fingers were quite done forming, she threw herself into Johan's arms and held on tight. He threaded his arms around her and buried his face in her tangled hair. "No matter what happens next," he said, "we are bonded."

"Forever," she murmured.

"I like the sound of that, Liebchen."

"Do you want to go inside?" she asked.

"Not yet." He smoothed curls out of her face. "What we just shared, it felt magical to me. Sacred. I want to savor it before we fall back into the real world."

She tightened her hold on him. "It was magical, because we are, but savor it we shall."

They were still holding one another when Kon and Erin came looking for them.

DRAGON TIME

Greetings, readers! It's Konstantin's dragon again. I promised you I'd stop in at the end of the book, and here we are. Once everyone had left, I didn't see why Erin's dragon and I couldn't have joined Katya and Johan in the mating flight, but Konstantin said we'd already done that.

As if once was all I was going to get. I started to give him hell, but he shut me up by telling me that while it had been acceptable for him and Erin to have a public mating dance, Katya and Johan deserved privacy. I understood, sort of. Konstantin is the dragon prince, and different rules apply.

I'm convinced one of the reasons we won the field today was because I insisted on completing the mating ritual. Having an unmated dragon lord tempts fate. And not in good ways. Not that we had to deal with any of the amoral, immortal hussies like succubae today, but we could have.

The mating bond is the best protection there is against wraiths that exert control starting with your manhood.

I'm getting sidetracked. We had plenty of problems without wraiths or succubae. We won, but we cannot rest on our laurels. No. We must dissect how we ended up in a predicament where we fought our own kind. It's almost unheard of for dragons to challenge other dragons, and we must never forget how and why such a dreadful outcome came to be.

I was shocked by what had become of the First Dragon. I remember him from before our god supposedly knocked him aside. He was always arrogant, full of himself, but the dragon I remember was sane. The one who showed up today had given up all pretense of sanity. He was sunk so deep into madness, it hurt my dragon's heart to breathe the same air.

He was a disgrace to dragonkind. I tried to reach the dragon part of things—and was soundly rebuffed. It was as if he'd renounced being a dragon. Wonder what the hell he thought he was?

I understand Y Ddraigh Goch well. At least I thought I did. Knowing he'd hedged about what became of the First Dragon shook my confidence in him a little bit. If the First Dragon had accepted he'd done wrong, our liege would have allowed him to return and take his rightful place by his side. Maybe. Explaining to the rest of us that the First Dragon wasn't exactly dead would have required a deft hand.

But Y Ddraigh Goch could have pulled it off. We all love him. Love forgives a whole lot.

Beyond what is now looking like a lie of omission, I'd always assumed exile would allow plenty of time to think, to revisit just how and why you ended up all by yourself—an unnatural situation for dragons. Rather than developing a fuller understanding of his sins, it appears the First Dragon nurtured bitterness.

A grudge that grew over time, eating away at what remained of his mind.

As I've said, none of us realized he was still alive. Y Ddraigh Goch didn't come out and say he'd done away with the First Dragon, but he inferred it. I've been trying to reconstruct precisely what he said, but I can't. Regardless, all of us were convinced the First Dragon was dead.

Until a little while ago when he sashayed through a portal and it turned out all the grief we'd gone through was because he ensorcelled the serpents—and other dragons—to be partners in his shared madness.

I admit, it's a relief about the other dragons. I'd have been horribly disappointed in my kinsmen if they'd been seduced by sea-serpents. But it's not much better that they didn't recognize how far removed from reality the First Dragon was.

Maybe he'd looked better than he did before he showed up here today. Yes. That must have been it. I'm not going to name them—doing so would remind me of who they once were—but some of the dragons who defected used to be my friends.

Fallout from the First Dragon's treachery will be with us for many a long year. Perhaps forever.

Katya and Johan have completed the mating ritual. I'm happy for them. And ever so grateful for my own mate. We'll rest and regroup, but our troubles are far from over. Worlds are still dying, and there may be someone much more powerful than the First Dragon pulling strings behind the scenes.

For all I know he—or she—could have been the force behind the First Dragon's rebellion. I know how those things go. Find a weak link and exploit it to do your bidding. When things fall apart—as they so often do—you've remained invisible. Your front man took the fall for you, and your true identity stays hidden.

And now, I'm rambling. Many thanks for sharing our journey. I will do my best to take care of my bondmate, and Erin too. Our god would never acknowledge this, but he could use some nurturing. Finally consigning the First Dragon to the flames cost him. I saw it in his face and in the set of every single scale.

He was devastated, but tougher too. No more shying away from the inevitable. No more allowing compassion to get in the way of necessity. None of us are exempt from life lessons. Speaking of Y Ddraigh Goch, I'm going to go pester Konstantin about heading to the surface to look in on him. We can be subtle about it. So stealthy, he won't even know we're there.

Unless he needs us, and then our presence will be a very good thing.

I shall bid you farewell. You never know, we may meet again. If you want more Ice Dragon books, drop the author a line. She loves to hear from someone other than her characters. We nag the poor woman half to death.

It's so hard to stop talking. May wind race beneath your wings and dragon steam surround you. Now and always.

~

You've reached the end of *Primal Ice*, and the end of the Ice Dragon Trilogy. I do hope you've enjoyed these books. Please leave a review for *Primal Ice*. Doesn't have to be fancy. A sentence or two will do it. Reviews help other readers discover books you've loved.

~

The end of this book makes me think of an old Buffy Sainte-Marie song, "Sometimes When I Get To Thinking About You"

Let me leave you with the last three verses:

...Think of the years before we were a pair,
Years lived apart we spent learning to farm.
Sowing, growing and learning to care
For ourselves, and preparing for each other's arms.

Love is a flower, blooms when we're too young;
Pluck it, it's gone, tended it grows.
We've been tending since the first sprout was sprung -
To the most patient farmer, the best harvest goes.

Sometimes I recall what others have said:
Love is for lovers in love and full grown,
Life's for the living and death's for the dead,
And the depth of a heart is a fathom unknown.

If you adore dragon books, keep reading for a sample from my Dragon Lore series. Five unforgettable books that will plop you into the heart of the Scottish Highlands.

ABOUT THE AUTHOR

Ann Gimpel is a USA Today bestselling author. A lifelong aficionado of the unusual, she began writing speculative fiction a few years ago. Since then her short fiction has appeared in many webzines and anthologies. Her longer books run the gamut from urban fantasy to paranormal romance. Once upon a time, she nurtured clients. Now she nurtures dark, gritty fantasy stories that push hard against reality. When she's not writing, she's in the backcountry getting down and dirty with her camera. She's published over 75 books to date, with several more planned for 2019 and beyond. A husband, grown children, grandchildren, and wolf hybrids round out her family.

Keep up with her at www.anngimpel.com or http://anngimpel.blogspot.com

If you enjoyed what you read, get in line for special offers and pre-release special reads. Newsletter Signup!

BOOK DESCRIPTION: HIGHLAND SECRETS

Furious and weary, Angus Shea wants out, but he can't stop the magic powering his visions. The Celts kidnapped him when he wasn't much more than a boy. He's sick of them and their endless assignments, but they wiped his memories, and he has no idea where he came from.

Arianrhod prefers to work alone and guards her privacy for the best of reasons. She's not exactly a virgin, and she'd be laughed out of the Pantheon if the truth surfaced. Despite the complications of leading a double life, she's never found a lover who tempted her to walk away from the Celtic gods.

Dragon shifters are disappearing from the Scottish Highlands. The Celtic Council sends Angus and Arianrhod to Fire Mountain, the dragons' home world. Attraction ignites, so urgent Arianrhod's carefully balanced life teeters on the brink of discovery.

Can they risk everything?

Will they?

If they do, can they live with the consequences?

HIGHLAND SECRETS, CHAPTER ONE

Angus Shea stroked beneath icy waters off the northern tip of Ireland, blending his energy with a pod of Selkies. The sea creatures cut through choppy waves in front, behind, and above him. He'd rather dive and play in the deeps with them—and if it were any other day, he would have—but he needed to keep an eye on the skies, so he edged toward the surface, pushing his head free.

Celene, a coal black Selkie he'd done more than swim with, drew close enough her lush pelt stroked his skin. He draped an arm around her, and she nuzzled his neck with her snout.

"*Where have you been?*" She spoke deep into his mind. Accommodating vocal chords were part of her human form, not her seal, and he'd never learned the Selkies' lyrical language.

"I spent a little time at my home in Scotland, but mostly I've ranged far from the Irish Sea."

"That doesn't tell me anything." She nipped playfully at his shoulder with her squared-off teeth.

"Prying ears are everywhere." He leaned into her warmth, enjoying a respite from the cold water.

"We could go where no one would hear."

He was tempted, so tempted he toyed with saying yes and taking a break from watching for the dragon he expected. Dragons interpreted time in their own way, and the damned thing might not show up today or tomorrow or even this week. If it showed at all.

How much could he tell the Selkie?

An answer crowded on the heels of his question.

Nothing.

Angus shuttered his mind, so the creature swimming by his side couldn't read it. Much as he yearned to talk with someone, anyone, about the impossibilities the gods tasked him with, prudence won out. Not that this assignment was worse than any of the others, but he'd finally figured out they'd never end.

I could say no. Tell them I'm done.

He cut off the bitter laugh that wanted out. Whoever had the balls to refuse the Celts risked swift and certain punishment. He could hear Gwydion, master enchanter, or Ceridwen, goddess of the world, laughing their heads off—before they cut out his tongue or killed him on the spot.

"You don't have to say a word." Celene went on, almost as if she'd peeked into his thoughts before he took care to protect them. Selkie laughter buffeted him, spraying him with a warm, rich melody mixed with salty water. *"I'm curious, but I miss your body."*

He missed hers too. She'd been his only break from solitude for more years than he wanted to admit. He cast another glance skyward. Though he tried to be subtle, he heard a smug murmur near his ear and knew he hadn't fooled the Selkie.

"You wait for an Ancient One." The tenor of her mind speech shifted as she shielded it from anyone who might be close. Without stopping for him to corroborate, she forged ahead. *"We can take up the banner and watch for you. My kin will let us know."*

Angus picked his way carefully, as if he walked through a field of unexploded ordnance. "I appreciate the thought, but no one can know of my comings or goings, lass."

"We know more than you think." Celene batted him with a flipper. *"In truth, very little escapes us, but here isn't the place to share what I heard about your latest mission."*

Concern rippled through him. If the Selkies knew, who else might? Hell, he didn't know much beyond his assigned meeting place with the dragon, and they'd be heading into danger.

What else was new? Danger was so second nature, his adrenaline pumps barely flinched at anything these days.

"Come with me." Either Celene was oblivious to the turmoil rumbling through him, or she ignored it. She swam from beneath his arm and herded him toward shore. *"There's a secluded glade deep in marsh grass. No one will find us, and my kin will keep watch for the dragon. I already asked."*

The Selkies would do their best—and maybe today it would be enough—but they were no match for evil that had sunk its roots deep into the fabric of the Old Country and the rest of this world. It was why the gods stooped to using him—half-mortal, half-divine, or whatever the hell he was—to do their dirty work. Arawn, god of the dead, revenge, and terror, caught him skulking in the time-travel tunnels when he wasn't much more than a boy and trapped him, cutting off any possibility of return. To make certain Angus remained, the god altered his memories, so he had no idea where he came from.

Now almost twenty-five years later, Arawn and the others still came up with enough for him to do that a life to call his own was out of the question. The carrot they dangled was the truth about his birth, but they never came close to divulging it. The stick was his fear of what they'd do, if he told them he was done.

Over time, he'd stopped asking about his origins. He cared, but it wasn't worth the energy to run up against their stony faces and cunningly crafted half-truths that revealed exactly nothing. Despite his reservations about a quick dalliance with Celene—and maybe missing his rendezvous with the dragon—he was sick of his self-imposed isolation.

She chivied him into shallow water. Once she was certain he'd follow, she drew ahead easily. As if the other Selkies understood, the pod dispersed. When he peered through gray-green water for their multi-colored pelts, they weren't there.

By the time he clambered onto the rocky shore, Celene had shucked her skin. In human form, she opened her arms to welcome him. Long black hair shrouded her almost to her feet. Violet eyes gleamed in welcome. Her generous breasts peeked through the curtain of hair, their copper-colored nipples already pebbled with wanting him.

Angus had tucked his clothes beneath a rock before joining the Selkie pod. Because he swam nude, nothing was in the way as he plunged into Celene's offered embrace. God, how he'd missed the touch of another against him, skin to skin. Celene's body felt warm against his chilled one. She closed her arms around him and ran her hands down his back, lingering over the curve of his butt.

He hugged her in return. The scent of her, salt and mint, flooded his mind with images of their lovemaking, and his cock hardened between their bodies. He trailed his fingertips down her smooth skin, marveling at how different she felt from a human woman. Velvety and charged with electricity. Some Selkies walked among humans, even took permanent partners. Angus didn't understand how they eluded discovery.

Celene closed her mouth over the junction between his neck and shoulder, licking, sucking, biting. He moved a hand from her back to cup the side of her face and lowered his lips over hers. Desire engulfed him. Hot, urgent, desperate, he sank his tongue into her waiting mouth.

She grappled with his ass, pulling his body hard against hers as her hips writhed and breath hitched in her throat. Tearing her mouth from his, she gasped. "Too long. It's been too long."

Liquid heat trailed the path of her mouth as she licked her way down his chest, stopping to tease his nipples. He kissed the top of her head and wove his fingers into her long hair. Every nerve came alive with wanting her, but it ran deeper than that.

Touch was such a basic need, and he'd denied that essential part of his humanity—along with every other comfort.

For what?

No matter how much he gave the Celts, they took every shred—and him—for granted. He wanted to get a job, blend in with humans. Something mundane like driving a cab, or flipping burgers in a grill, but his requests were denied. The Celts provided for him. So long as they housed and fed him, why would he need to clutter his time with anything as humdrum as earning a living? What if they needed him, and he was in the middle of washing dishes in some nameless restaurant? He could almost hear Gwydion's voice. See the master enchanter with a long-suffering look on his face—

He wiped his Celtic masters from his mind. This time was for him and Celene. No one else belonged in his head. Just because he'd chosen a semimonastic existence was no reason he couldn't give her everything she needed. Months had passed since they'd last been together, maybe as much as a year. He moved back enough to fill his hands with her breasts, rubbing her erect nipples before he bent to suck on them, remembering the little biting motions she loved.

A low, guttural moan escaped her, and she threaded her fingers through his hair. Holding him against her breasts, she began to sing as he loved her. A series of low, sweet notes rose in cadence and intensity as she lost herself in his touch. He'd asked her about the music once, and she told him it was how sea people vocalized their joy. The music filled him with unbearable hunger—poignant, mind-bending need for another person's touch.

Although he'd never done it before, he raised his voice and joined her song. The change was instantaneous. In that moment, he sensed her loneliness and isolation, twin to his own and recognized that both of them needed more kisses, more touches—even more than they needed sex.

"Lay on your belly." His voice rasped with wanting her. He tore tufts of marsh grass and arranged them to make her a bed on a sandy stretch between rocks.

She lay down, continuing to sing. Angus sang too, as he straddled her and ran his hands down her back rubbing tension from her muscles. He followed his hands with his mouth and strung kisses across her shoulder blades and down the line of vertebrae from her neck to the curves of her ass. Between their song, the feel of her skin beneath his fingertips, and his cock getting stiffer by the moment, waiting became almost painful, yet he held back, not quite sure why.

The rhythm and cadence of her song shifted as he alternated his mouth and hands across the sculpted planes of her back. The intense pressure in his balls receded almost as if he'd reached a peak, though he hadn't come. Maybe she sensed his need for warmth, contact, much as he'd sensed hers.

"Move off me so I can look at you." Celene flipped over to face him, kneeling above her. Rose and gold splotched her pale skin, and a broad smile split her exotic, high-cheekboned face. "Today was different. You sang with me. You've never done that before."

He shrugged, suddenly self-conscious. "It felt right. Even

though I wasn't inside you, what happened between us felt right."

She cocked her head to one side and trained her gaze on him. "Are you sure you don't have sea blood?"

A flicker of annoyance at the Celts' staunch refusal to disclose anything about his birth narrowed his eyes. "I have no idea what I am." He ticked what he did know off on his fingers. "I'm not immortal, but I'll live well beyond human lifespans. My magic is closer to seer and witch than anything else, yet I'm neither of those. The covens acknowledge me as one of theirs, but only because the local witches are too kind to tell me to go away. The time-travel portals accept me." He shrugged again. "I don't suppose knowing more would make a hell of a lot of difference."

"You're not from Scotland, even though you live there." She stated it baldly, as fact.

He frowned. "Why would you say that?"

"Your speech. There's something about the lilt of Scotland that's impossible to rid yourself of. You don't sound Irish or British, either, at least not from the time we live in." Her nostrils flared. "Maybe that's it."

"Maybe what's it?"

"You could be from the past, and not just a few years back, perhaps hundreds—or even more. I'm not old enough to recall what human speech sounded like then, but some Selkies are."

"Fine." Frustration tightened his chest, like it always did when the mystery of his origins became a point of discussion. "My first memories are when the god of the dead dragged me out of a time-travel portal when I was fifteen."

"I'm sorry." She draped a hand over his hip, cradling it. "I've upset you."

He started to protest, but she silenced him with a look. "Don't insult me with a lie, Angus, but you don't have to talk about it, either. Such a pretty man." She stroked hair back from his face. "With your deep brown hair and amber eyes. Did you know they shade to dark gold when you're angry?"

She was trying to divert him with flattery, but he wasn't buying it. "You have no idea what it's like not knowing—" He shook his head, and the rest of his words died unspoken. It didn't matter what she knew or didn't know about him. She'd never be more than an occasional lover, and both of them knew it.

"It could be more," she said softly, obviously having been in his mind.

Angus took her hands in his and gazed at her. "You get more of me than anyone, and you see how pathetically little that is. There's nothing more to give."

"There could be," she persisted. "You could refuse next time they send you on—"

He bent toward her and laid a hand over her mouth. "I'm not free. Not now. Not ever."

"I don't understand." She pushed his hand away and closed very white teeth over her full lower lip.

He smiled crookedly. "Not sure I do, either. Every man has a life's work. No matter how I feel about it, this appears to be mine."

Even though it wasn't wise, he started to ask what she knew about his current assignment, but a flash of unusual energy drew his gaze skyward. He leapt to his feet. A copper-colored dragon circled to land not far from him. Maybe the Ancient One had seen him with Celene and decided to be considerate.

Not very fucking likely. Dragons were a force unto themselves.

"I have to go," he said. "Let me walk you to your skin, so I know you're safely on your way home."

A sad expression crossed her face, creasing the skin around her eyes into a network of fine lines. "It's right here." She scrambled to her feet and gripped both his upper arms, forcing him to look at her. "Thank you."

"For what?"

"Being you." She brushed her lips over his and moved to a marsh grass thicket. In moments, she'd dragged her pelt over her human body. Transformed into a seal, she waded into the surf.

Before it engulfed her, she turned to gaze at him. *"Be careful, and think on what I said."*

He didn't answer, just watched her head bob in the waves before turning toward his clothing. It wasn't far from the place Celene had led them. His body felt vibrant, alive, and he still tingled from her touch. He longed for a woman of his own, children, a home, before he stuffed the impossible so deep under wraps he couldn't mourn the loss.

Angus moved the large rock he'd placed over his clothes to protect them from the wind. He pulled a ragged dark blue fisherman's knit sweater over his head and stepped into thick, black woolen trousers. Settling on a log, he pulled on socks and laced up stout leather boots. Though the breeze was raw, he'd worn neither hat nor gloves.

Ready as he figured he'd ever be, he covered the fifty yards to where the dragon had settled up the beach. He didn't recognize this one, but he'd only met a bare handful of the hundreds living in Fire Mountain and on other worlds as well. When he drew near, he stopped and bowed his head respectfully, waiting for the dragon to speak first.

"I don't like this any better than you do," the dragon muttered. "Come close enough I don't have to broadcast our business to the world."

Angus walked closer. He could've suggested the dragon use telepathy since all the Ancient Ones were conversant in the technique, but he kept his mouth shut. The dragon was smaller than many he'd seen. Copper scales shaded to burnished gold on its chest, and dark eyes with golden centers whirled so fast they held a hypnotic quality. Lethal, six-inch-long red claws tipped its stubby forelegs. The dragon stood upright on hind legs tipped with the same sharp claws and kept its gaze averted, not saying anything.

What the hell? Every other dragon he'd met was proud, imperious, and quick to remind Angus of his inferiority. This one seemed young, but was it? After another long few minutes, Angus tossed respect—and caution—to the winds.

"What's your name? And what are we supposed to be doing? All Ceridwen told me was to meet you here."

The dragon opened its mouth, and a gout of flame landed scant inches from Angus's boots.

He frowned and drew his brows together. "If we're going to work together, I need to know what to call you." He sent a speculative gaze across the air between them. "If you annihilate me, they'll just assign you a new partner, and I'm a hell of a lot easier to get along with than any of the Celts."

"Tell me something I don't know," the dragon rumbled and belched smoke.

Frustration in its voice struck a note in Angus's soul, and he gestured with both hands. "You may as well tell me who you are and what we're supposed to do together." He infused his words with subtle persuasion. If the dragon didn't care for the Celts, either, they'd likely get along well enough.

"Why? What I should do is leave." The dragon sounded sulky—and scared.

"If you could, you'd already be gone." Angus was as certain of that as he was of anything. The dragon needed him for something, and whatever it was, the Ancient One wasn't particularly proud of it. "What happened? Am I some sort of punishment for you?" Tension settled like a steel bar across his shoulders, and he curled his hands into fists before he realized what he'd done.

"Oh I'd be gone, would I?"

The dragon ignored Angus's questions, and it mimicked his tone with eerie precision. It furled its wings and flapped them a time or two. Dirt swirled; small pebbles slapped Angus in the face. The creature belched steam and looked so distraught, he felt sorry for it.

"My life's not exactly a picnic, either," he ventured, on a hunt for common ground. "I'm a permanent mercenary, with no time off and no possibility of parole."

That got the dragon's attention, and it focused its whirling gaze on him. The golden centers of its eyes deepened with fiery motes that looked like little shooting stars. "Why would you want a respite from being a warrior?"

Good question.

"Because I'm tired. I'd like what most men have."

"What's that?" The dragon raised its brows, and its scales clanked against each other in a dissonant tinkling.

He shook his head. "It doesn't matter. The sooner you spit out whatever you need to say, the easier it'll be. The worst part about holding something you're ashamed of inside is it eats at you until you're nothing but a hollow shell."

Wings flapped, and those intense, whirling eyes shifted to the rocky beach. "I'm not *ashamed* of anything. I've been banished. Ceridwen said if I worked with you—and we were successful—I might be able to return."

Angus kept surprise out of his voice. "Banished from Fire Mountain?"

Steam puffed from the dragon's open mouth. "No. Idiot. I could live with that. They've banished me from the Highlands. My home."

"What happened?"

"It doesn't matter." The dragon threw his words back at him. "We have to go to Fire Mountain, where I'm to find one of the First Born. Once we have him—or her—"

"One of the six First Born dragons?" Angus broke in, scarcely believing the dragon's words. "They'll never show themselves—unless it's in their best interest."

Another wing flap and a defiant head toss. "There are actually ten. One of them was my father."

"When's the last time you saw him?" The words slipped

out before he could stop them. Dragon males frequently didn't hang about once mating was over with, but the trembling mass of scales in front of him likely didn't need to be reminded.

"Never. Mother said he was too immersed in battles on another world to return for our hatching."

Angus unclenched his fists and hunted for something soothing to say that wasn't an outright lie. Dragon energy poked past his wards and into his mind. He tried to block it, but couldn't.

"You believe locating a First Born is hopeless." The dragon sounded resigned. "I may as well throw myself into a crater at Fire Mountain. I'll never see the Highlands again—or my mate." More wing rustling and the dragon rose a few feet off the ground, clearly intent on leaving.

"Hold on." Angus loped forward until he was right beneath the dragon. "I didn't say that—or think it, either. I don't know enough to make any sort of judgment. How about if you start at the beginning? If we're going to work together, I deserve that much."

The dragon circled a few times, indecision stamped in its erratic flight pattern.

"I know what it is to be alone." He kept his voice gentle. "And to not have anyone who cares if I live or die."

Maybe it wasn't totally true. Celene might shed a tear or two, but she'd be the only one. He kept his gaze trained on the sky, relieved the dragon wasn't putting distance between them. Something about the creature's pain tugged at his heart and made it feel like a kindred spirit.

The copper dragon folded its wings and settled heavily

to earth a few feet from where Angus stood. It straightened its shoulders and tipped its chin defiantly.

"My name is Eletea," the dragon announced, revealing its gender.

"Angus Shea, though you likely know that."

"Yes, I do. I killed a mage, who fancied herself a dragon shifter." Eletea's eyes whirled faster, as if she dared Angus to say something.

He crinkled his forehead as he dredged up what he knew about dragon shifters. "Don't mages take their chances when they show up seeking a dragon to pair with?"

She nodded once, sharply. "The mage seduced one of us into believing her. I saved him by killing her, but he turned on me. Reported me to the Dragons' Council, and they roped the Celts into deciding my fate, since the one I killed had Celtic blood." Eletea's scales rippled in the dragon equivalent of a shrug. "I don't understand why they're bothering. It's not like I went after one of the gods. They're immortal. The one all the fuss is over barely qualified as a Celt."

Angus kept his expression neutral. "Celtic blood aside, I thought mages only bonded with same sex dragons."

"That was another problem," Eletea said, sounding vindicated. "No one saw it but me, though."

Sensing the worst was out on the table, Angus settled on a nearby rock and invited, "Start at the beginning. We have time."

"No, we don't," Eletea protested. "We should've been at Fire Mountain yesterday." She hung her head. "I didn't know what I wanted to do, so I flew and flew and flew. I almost didn't land this afternoon."

Angus did his best to project optimism. "Let's open a time-travel portal and be on our way to Fire Mountain." At the dragon's reluctant nod, he went on. "I understand you have your own ways of returning home, but if you travel with me, you can fill me in as we go."

What he didn't say was it probably wouldn't matter when they arrived at the dragons' home world. First Borns wouldn't give them the time of day, whether they showed up early, late, or right on time. He held many concerns, such as what would a First Born do, assuming they could locate one? But he held those cares inside for now.

He could've dreamed the future. Instead, he summoned a spell to take them to a time-traveling portal. Once the undulating gray-pink tube admitted them, he gradually paid out questions.

Reticent and quiet at first, Eletea finally began to talk.

www.ingramcontent.com/pod-product-compliance
Lightning Source LLC
Chambersburg PA
CBHW051007180726
48291CB00006B/2011

* 9 7 8 1 9 4 8 8 7 1 5 3 2 *